BRING ME BACK

AMY OLIVEIRA

First e-book edition March 2022

Book design by The Pretty Little Design Co.

Edited by Marcela Ferros

Proofreading by Blazing Butterfly

E-BOOK: 978-1-7397895-0-3

PAPERBACK: 978-1-7397895-1-0

www.amyoliveira.com

To Katleen,
The true heart behind Hallie's art.

Prologue

THIS TOWN OF OURS stretched along the coast in sinuous grace. It thrived on diligence and ostentation. But mostly gossip.

The gossip fueled Bluehaven; it fed and destroyed. To make sure not to ever be swallowed, I kept quiet. My eyes alert, my mouth shut, my opinions to myself. It was a foolproof way to remain untouched.

I floated away, cutting down my roots. But when you don't belong anywhere, *nothing belongs to you*. As I drifted, I chanted the stories of my own life. The perdurable reasons I had to keep going and never look back.

There were three of them.

When I was six years old, my mother was taken from me. It was what the adults murmured between themselves at the funeral. I hugged my favorite doll as Dad taught me how to respond to the mourners. Though it was never required of me to respond, they never cared to address me directly. Nothing was sadder than a six-year-old without a mother.

"Left a small child..." They sighed above my head.

"It's just too sad." They shivered.

"Taken so young..."

Taken.

They said it like it was deliberate, but even at six, I knew it wasn't.

Accidents were things that happened without time or reason. I knew there wasn't a reason for mom's death. She got into a car and was never coming back. It didn't matter how much Dad cried, or how scared and young I was.

I was six years old when I learned things *happen*.

The next precious thing I lost was my last name. We weren't sure how, but I knew this time Dad and I were responsible. We let it be taken.

Dad—Preston White—liked when people called me the *Delos Santos* girl. He was hellbent on holding onto anything that reminded us of mom.

My thick hair, tone of voice, my build. I looked more Filipino when I was a child, but even as my features changed and I looked more like my dad's side of the family, it was already too late.

I was only Delos Santos. I wasn't White anymore.

The last thing they took was the beach.

As a grieving man, Dad tried. He tried to like the same things I liked, but from a young age, what I liked was to make dresses and he wore the same pair of cargo shorts for the last ten years.

Preston White and Hallie Delos Santos were two strangers sitting at the same table. Time ticked by and the glue that held us together never came back from that car ride. The only thing we had was fishing.

I wasn't sure why I liked it, but I did. It was soothing and required little talking. Dad gave me a horrible fishing hat with dangling pins and an inexplicable attached net, and I wore it each time.

On Saturdays, we'd pack a few sandwiches and threw the fishing hook into the shallow waters. My pants were rolled up to my calves so I could dip my toes into the warm sand. *It was our thing.*

But the beach that once belonged to the kids and families now belonged to the pre-teens. The girls wore two-piece bikinis, and the boys joked around and threw them in the water. I was thirteen when it started.

I had nothing to fill a bikini top, and I wasn't ready to let the fishing go. I'd feared it was the last thread linking Dad and me.

By the time I was fifteen, it became unbearable. Dad didn't notice. His lungs were filled with salty air and his gaze was focused on the ocean. He liked to get lost within himself while we were fishing, but I heard every word they said.

The teasing, the scoffs, the name calling. I heard it enough at school and I managed to keep my head high, but at the beach? Their words sliced through me. It felt like they invaded my home just to mock me. They picked my clothes apart; they smirked at my every move. I couldn't fish, I couldn't *be*. My skin felt too tight, stretched over my bones. And finally, I couldn't take it anymore.

On a particular Saturday, I took the hat off when we arrived home. Without explaining myself, I told Dad I was done fishing.

The beach was theirs, and I let them have it.

I left Bluehaven as soon as I could. Dusting off the town that was never mine, I tipped my head up and promised to find a home some place else.

Five years later, I was back.

1.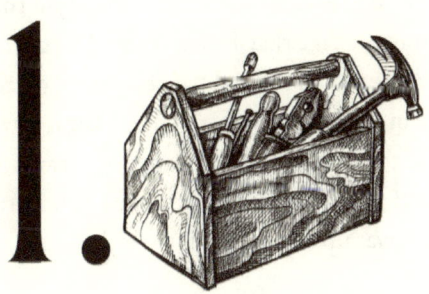

I LOOKED OVER THE stage and sighed. I'd welcome anything to keep me busy after school hours, but for the first time in my life, I thought of backing out. Helen's ideas were always too ambitious, but this one might have taken the cake. My hands closed in fists as I scanned the stage filled with last year's *Romeo & Juliet* props. I wish it was any other Shakespearian play we could've converted and adapted, but *A Midsummer Night's Dream* required more than the old Juliet's balcony had to offer.

Helen -Mrs. Carr -was a drama teacher with big aspirations. She still rocked the 80s mullet and had a quirky way with the kids. I had a soft spot for her. She was an excellent teacher who always went above and beyond to help the pupils. Plus, the drama department was grossly overlooked. Helen needed help, and I needed *a reason*.

I glanced down at the paper she gave me with a rough sketch of what was needed for this year's set. I was a woodwork teacher with time to spare. Helping her came easily to me, but now she was asking too much. I scratched my beard, cursing myself. I should've nipped this in the bud.

I knew the stage; I knew the budget. An interconnected scenery wasn't achievable in Bluehaven High.

"There must be a smart way to go about this, Daniel. Can you at least have a look if anything from last year can be converted?" It was what she said after handing me her ambitious sketch. I should've refused right there.

I searched my brain for a miracle. Juliet's old balcony stood exactly where I left it last year. It wasn't just the style that was completely different. It was the fact that Helen wanted a full Athens set as much as she wanted the woods. Wood panels, paint and time was I all could offer. I wasn't in the business of miracles. I knew it was impossible from the second she thrusted her folded paper of dreams into my hands. But now, as I turned around the stage, reminded of how small it actually was, I understood it was up to me to crush her dreams.

"Sorry?"

The feminine voice spoke behind me and took me away from my racing thoughts. Turning toward the theater's double doors, I tried to make sense of the silhouette arriving. I never bothered with the lights that far back, so I could barely make sense of the last row of chairs where she was standing by. But slowly, the newcomer walked to me, making her way to the stage.

My eyes traced from head to toe; jeans, a loose white t-shirt and thick black hair piled on top of her head. I squinted. Her face was still obscured.

"Can I help you?" I asked.

"Is Mrs. Carr around?" She took a step forward, finally coming to the light.

I gave myself a second to register her features. Heart-shaped face, deep dark irises and a fuller bottom lip. I narrowed my eyes, trying to jog my memory, but I couldn't place her anywhere. And I'd never forget a face like hers.

"Who's looking?" I tipped my head up, trying to get a name out of her. The backpack over one shoulder played with the possibility of her being a student, but she looked older than seventeen. She looked young, but not a kid.

I waited for her reply, but it never came. Her eyes scanned over my face, lips parted, but they never uttered a word. Eventually, I lost my patience. "She'll be here soon. You can wait if you like."

I didn't add that I wanted her to stay. That I wanted a name, too.

Her forehead formed a crease, and she blinked away from me. I did not know what she was thinking, and I figured I would never find out as - still in silence she turned on her heels and left.

I stared at the theater's double doors as they closed quietly behind her. She spoke two sentences and almost made me forget myself. Shaking it off, I went back to the stage and Helen's impossible dreams.

"GOING OUT THIS WEEKEND?" My brother asked from across the state, calling to annoy me as he usually did.

"Nope."

"You should."

I sighed and glanced at the ceiling. Mark had taken over the role of helicopter parent from mom since my divorce. Mom called and asked all kinds of questions, but when she didn't believe I was being truthful, Mark called to do her bidding. We lived far, but since Kelly left our home and Bluehaven, Mark started making trips over for absolutely no reason. When he wasn't here, he was calling to ask about my goddamn day. Then, of course, his wife was trying to set me up with women.

Since my divorce, I tried once, and it was enough for me to see that maybe being alone wasn't that bad. There were no fights over the remote control, no conversations about what we were going to eat.

Being single wasn't that bad, even though it was new to me. I was with Kelly since we were teenagers, when I was young and dumb enough to believe in forever. No, I was good the way I was. My half-baked attempt at a relationship six months ago taught me that. I just needed to survive in this town. I needed to find a reason to stay and wake up every day, and that reason needed to be me. Not some woman.

But my older brother was eternally in love with Abby and raising my two nieces. He couldn't begin to understand solitude.

"Why don't you move here? Set a shop or something?" Mark tried again.

"I'm good where I am, Mark," I replied quickly, before he started with his old dream for me: my own furniture shop. It almost happened, but since moving to Bluehaven...

I sighed. There was no reason to dwell in the past. Moving wasn't the answer. Furniture shop wasn't the answer. I needed more. I just had to find out what.

"How are the girls?" I tried to change topics.

"They are ok." Mark took my bait. "April is saying hi."

I smiled. April was Mark's youngest. She was eight while her older sister, Rose, was ten years old. They were the greatest and the only reason I'd ever considered moving close to Mark.

"Say hi to her. Are they ready for the school year?"

"Yes. Had to buy three hundred colorful gel pens, as I'm told they're essential material."

"She's not wrong. I'm a teacher, believe me," I said, taking a swig of the beer in my hands.

"You're a woodwork teacher, Dan. You're not shaping the minds of the youth of today."

"Thanks," I said, without paying much attention to his dig.

"Are you ready to go back to class?"

"Three hundred gel pens and all."

Mark laughed. What I did could barely count as class time. My classes were taught over the benches. It was considered an escape. A class with low expectations and rock music playing in the background. Most days, I forgot I was still inside the school grounds until the bell rang.

"School year is about to start and I know your excuses, Dan," my brother started.

"Do you?" I held my phone between my cheek and shoulder and grabbed the remote, trying to find something good to watch.

"Sure do. Every time I ask about dates and real life, you bullshit me about work and the damn theater. You hide September to June."

"Hmmm..."

"No joke, Dan. You need to put yourself out there..." and he whispered the next part. "Don't you miss being with someone?"

I chuckled, finding a good movie. I was five seconds away from hanging up on Mark.

"Is that your family man's way of asking me if I'm fucking?"

"Fuck..." he grumbled.

"Mom, daddy said a bad word!" I heard April snitching.

"Snitches get stitches, April!" Mark hissed.

I chuckled, "I'm fine, Mark. Stop listening to mom and doing her dirty work. You're almost forty. It is a little ridiculous."

"I'm not mom's errand boy."

"Sounds like it."

"I worry."

"Well, you shouldn't."

I almost heard his gulp as he asked, "Are you?"

"Worried?" I cracked my knuckles. "No."

"No..." he inhaled. "Are you..." a little pause. "Seeing someone?"

I rested my back on the couch, wondering when my big brother became a teenage girl, asking about my business over the phone.

"It was nice to talk to you, Mark. Send my love to Abby and the girls."

"Dan..."

But I didn't let him finish. I hung up and pressed play on the movie. Worried or not, I had to draw the line somewhere.

Avoiding Mark's calls for the next two weeks, I concentrated on finishing a set of new chairs for my kitchen and drawing up options for Helen's play. But now that my projects were finished, the walls of my home started to close in on me again. I was ready to be back at school full time.

When the first day back finally arrived, I parked my car at the staff's parking lot and headed straight to the theater. My first class was second period, and I wanted to catch Helen before the first day's craziness. Even with my altered plans for the set, I had a suspicion we'd need extra money.

"You can take anything you want!" Helen was at the downstage center, arms open like she was coordinating the world.

"I just want to have a look at them," a voice called off stage as I trotted down, my boots heavy on the floor. "It's ok if I make them here?"

"Of course, Hallie. Whatever you need."

The sound of my arrival finally took Helen away from the conversation, as she turned to me with a smile. "Oh Daniel, I'm glad you're here!"

"Hey, there, Helen. I just wanted to have a chat before classes start."

"Sure, sure... come up, I want you to meet someone..."

I went up the steps by the side, my eyes scanning to see if I could spot who Helen was talking with, but whoever was, it was well hidden between the curtains.

"Hallie, this is Daniel," Helen called, turning her face upstage. If I hadn't heard the voice replying to Helen, I'd have guessed we had a theater ghost on our hands.

Before I could wonder any longer, the owner of the feminine voice stepped from backstage, arms full of old costumes. I sucked in air when she came closer, blinking up at me with those intense dark eyes. I spotted the same reluctancy stamped in her expression as the first time I saw her a couple of weeks ago. I couldn't hide my satisfied smile. The silent girl was back.

"Dan is the woodwork teacher. He's helping me with my crazy ideas."

I almost missed the affectionate smile Helen threw my way. My eyes were fixed on the silent girl, hating myself for not paying enough attention when Helen said her name.

Without breaking eye contact, I extended my hand. "Daniel Miller."

She was a foot smaller, her long neck craned up to face me. A second passed and she looked down at her arms; they were full of clothes. I chuckled at my mistake, putting my hand away since she couldn't shake it.

"I'm Hallie..." a gulp, "Delos Santos."

I nodded, stuffing my hand into my pockets. I savored her name in my tongue, dying to repeat it out loud.

"Hallie is Preston White's kid," Helen interrupted my thoughts. "She's back in town and offered to help. Isn't she darling?"

I looked back at Hallie, trying to find her dad in her. Preston White was the hardware store owner, so of course I knew him. Good guy, honest businessman, and a chatterbox if I ever met one. Preston was tall, blond, and full of smiles. I couldn't think of anyone more different from the woman in front of me. And while I was sure she wasn't a student, my suspicions about her age only grew. Preston wasn't old enough to have an adult daughter. At least I didn't think so.

"Mrs. Carr told me you'll most likely to be around here building the set." Hallie's voice was only a volume up from a murmur.

I brought my hands to my waist, dipping my chin down.

"Hallie will work here too," Helen told me.

"It will make more sense than working from the shed," Hallie offered apologetically.

"The shed?"

Her mouth closed, her eyes diverted, and I knew she was done talking. I fought back a smile. Wasn't she weird?

Hallie said little, and still, I couldn't stop myself from being fascinated. Normally, I'd tell her I'll be coming and going, since a lot could be accomplished from my workshop. But suddenly my plans had changed, and I wasn't interested in working alone anymore.

"You can work here as much as you want." I told her, not asking about the shed again.

"I won't be in your way," she promised.

"No, you won't." I assured her. I wasn't trying to be rude. It was just a fact and something told me Hallie appreciated being talked to directly.

"Do you want to bring those with you?" Helen cut the silence after my statement.

Hallie looked down at the clothes she had with her. A little frown formed as she thought about it, and I wondered why everything looked like a struggle to her. Finally, she shook her head.

"No. I'll be back tomorrow with some drawings, and I'll see how much fabric we'll need."

"That's great, Hallie." Helen smiled like Hallie hung over the damn moon.

Even though she wasn't bringing the costumes with her, the silent girl held them close to her chest as she glanced up at me.

"It was great to meet you, Mr. Miller. I'll see you soon."

She disappeared through the curtains and I let out a breath.

2.

DAD FLICKERED THE COFFEEMAKER on and turned from the counter. His big arms crossed in front of his chest, and he threw me a tired smile.

"All we moved from the city were fabric rolls. Are you opening a shop, bug?"

I sat in the chair in the middle of the kitchen. The coffeemaker chimed in the background as the familiar smell invaded the house. I arrived home a week ago when Dad picked me up from my old apartment in the city and brought me back to Bluehaven. Between moving in and establishing a new routine, we were still catching up.

Dad paid little attention when we were loading his truck, but now that he was converting the shed to give me a space to sew, he noticed how much fabric I brought with me.

I licked my lips and chanced a smile. "Maybe sixty percent of all I own is fabric."

I stuffed my clothes and shoes in one suitcase, leaving the other for textbooks. In one small cardboard box, I put random things like a wine opener and some fun magnets. But everything else was fabric. Scraps from other projects I worked on, things I bought just because. Boxes and more boxes filled with random buttons, ribbons and zippers.

Since Dad barely used the shed in the back of the house, he suggested converting it to my needs so I could keep working on my projects. Volunteering for the school play wasn't necessarily what I called work, but looking for Mrs. Carr was the right thing to do. I didn't have many good memories of our small town, especially at my old school, but Mrs. Carr was a memory to cherish. I smiled just to think about her inexplicable mullet and the way she opened her arms mid-sentence, like in the middle of a monologue.

When the coffeemaker was done brewing, Dad turned and grabbed mugs for both of us. I followed as he served and felt bad about how little I had shared with him since coming home. I wasn't trying to be distant, it just happened. I sighed. I didn't even tell him about volunteering.

"I'm glad you're home, bug," he told me, placing a mug in front of me. I mouthed a thank you, but it was for much more than the coffee.

I looked through the window to catch a glimpse of the garden. Mom loved roses, so he planted rose bushes all over the garden after she died. It was a way to comfort us, even though most of the time it made me sadder. Letting my eyes drift, I saw his tools aligned by the shed's door. A clear sign he was planning to work on it.

"I don't want you doing any extra work. I can make myself at home."

"You *are* home."

My eyes found his face again, and he looked hurt. I meant making myself at home at the shed, but it was clear Dad wasn't sure what to do with me. Since I left, I only came back for the holidays. I had no friends in Bluehaven and Dad worked on the weekends. I wouldn't mind helping him at the shop, but I was too scared of bumping into people. I felt the sour taste of irony on my tongue. It couldn't be avoided anymore.

"Where are the clothes you make?" Dad changed the subject when I failed to reply.

"Sorry?"

"What happens to the clothes after you make them?"

He had a good reason to ask. The fabric I purchased was vibrant and smooth to the touch, and the clothes I wore were old looking jeans, basic t-shirts and sneakers.

"I gave them to the school close to the apartment." I lifted one shoulder. "They had a really good drama teacher. She put on the best plays."

"You donated?"

"Yeah. They struggled with budget."

That was the understatement of the year. After I finished college, I wanted to save money on rent, so I moved while keeping Dad in the dark about what kind of building I was living in. He wasn't very happy when he found out. Needless to say, the local school suffered from a lack of funding and the theater department wouldn't exist if it wasn't for the determination and creativity of Ms. Handall.

"That was very nice of you, bug."

My cheeks warmed, and I sipped my coffee. I liked to make costumes and Ms. Handall put them to good use. That was why I looked for Mrs. Carr the second I was back in town. She was a good teacher, just like Ms. Handall, and I couldn't see myself doing anything but creating.

"Are you sure you don't want me to work at the shop with you?" I changed the subject.

I needed a paying job and Dad knew it, but it felt weird not to offer to work at the shop with him. He waved me off. "Nah, the Thompson kid is coming around after school. He can handle it for now. Go get yourself a job and save money."

"So you weren't planning on paying me?" I took from his words.

"No," he deadpanned with a little smile, and I smiled back. I felt our distance the most in times like this. It reminded me we didn't share a smile very often.

"I'll walk around and see who's hiring," I told him. Even though I knew the only place I wanted to work and was planning on paying them a visit this afternoon.

"What about your... clothes?" he interrupted my thoughts.

I arched an eyebrow. "What about them?"

"I don't want you forgetting about your profession because you're here."

I nodded. "Oh yes, I visited Mrs. Carr and volunteered to help with costumes for the school play."

"You'll be going to the school?" His eyebrows soared.

I pretended not to see the surprise on his face. "Yes, I will," I defied.

He cleared his throat. "Good idea. I don't want you to give up."

"I'm not giving up." I frowned.

"Sorry, bug, I didn't mean like that."

He never told me what he meant. I knew he was biting his tongue to ask me why I was back after five years. A year ago, I'd cower from walking around town. But now, look at me. Still shaking like a leaf but I facing the storm coming my way.

"OH MY, LOOK WHAT the cat dragged in. Torres, come over here!"

I brushed a hair strand out of my face, my cheeks warming from the reception I was getting. Marian watched me with a wide grin, waiting for her husband to come in front. Since the second I decided to go back to Bluehaven, I knew Torres' was the only place I could be comfortable enough to ask for employment. At the moment, I had my fingers and toes crossed she'd say yes. Marian was mom's best friend. She was loud and crude but also protective and the best person to have in my corner. Torres was a big burly man who flipped burgers in the back and had an exceptional hearing.

Torres squeezed his big frame through the kitchen's door, and I beamed at him. Nowhere in town made me feel like I belonged. Only the Torres'.

"Shit, kid. Give us a hug," Torres ordered.

I stepped to the other side of the counter, going on my tiptoes to hug Torres. He was warm and smelled like my favorite foods. I hugged Marian too. Her bony fingers tipped my head up as we stepped apart. I was under her careful eyes, tracing my features as she searched for something.

"So no accident?"

"Huh?" She let my face go.

"No lost memory?"

I bit my lip and shook my head.

"You see, Torres?" Marian slapped her husband's stomach. "So she's alive and well."

"She sure looks so, Mar."

I winced. "I'm sorry."

I had no excuse to give for my absence. I missed Marian and Torres terribly, but I was scared for so long, I forgot how not to be.

"It wasn't about you. I'm sorry I didn't visit more often," I offered.

Marian had a tea towel over her shoulder as she shrugged off my apology. That was Marian's superpower. She could make people feel comfortable in their own skin. It was a rare gift and worked even when I felt guilty.

"We missed you." Marian pinned me in place with a look.

I spoke sincerely, "I missed you, too."

"Ok, ok, let the kid go..." Torres broke us apart. "What do you want?"

"Cheeseburger with crispy onions," Marian answered for me.

I was a creature of habit, and they knew it. My mouth watered just thinking of their cheeseburger.

"Coming right up." Torres turned around on his feet.

I gulped, gathering my courage. "I also need a job. If you have one of those."

Marian rose one eyebrow. Leaning her hip on the counter, she crossed her arms over her chest. "Did you hear it, Torres? Kid needs a job."

Torres' head poked out the door and he looked me up and down like he had never seen me before.

"I'm a hard worker," I told them. "Fast leaner, and I already know your menu by heart."

"Maybe we changed," Torres said from the door.

Marian shrugged. "Maybe we changed."

I shook my head. "The menu is the same," I tried my luck. "And I have waitress experience now. I used to work in a coffee shop close to campus and..."

Torres chuckled. "Never heard her talking so much. Give the girl an apron, Marian. She must really want it."

Marian still watched me, but I saw the twinkle in her eyes. She made a motion with her finger to get me back to my side of the counter. Torres went back to the kitchen, hopefully to make my burger, as Marian asked, "Aren't you going to help Preston with the shop?"

I sat up on a stool. "I offered. He said the Thompson kid was at it."

Marian chuckled. "Cheap bastard, he pays pennies to the kid."

"He told me he would not pay me *at all*."

We both laughed. Dad was a good man, but boy, he didn't mess around with the shop.

"Alright," she breathed.

"Really?"

"Yeah, sure. Why not? I don't want Cecilia's spirit haunting me because I didn't give her kid a chance."

I swallowed and nodded. "I will be good. You won't regret it."

She waved away my promises. "We'll see. Summer rush is done with..." She pursed her lips, looking me right in the eyes. "But school is back; there will be a lot of kids coming over."

I squirmed in my seat and got her meaning. Marian knew about my past more than Dad. It was easy to notice something was wrong when I sat alone in one booth as my classmates sat together in another. Though we never talked about it, she made clear all I ever needed to do was ask for help.

Soon I was going to be around teenagers once more. I almost winced, but held back. "I'll be fine," I guaranteed.

I wasn't sure if she believed me, but kept it to herself. Nodding, Marian passed me a royal blue apron from behind the counter. With a smile, I accepted it and stuffed it in my backpack.

I didn't ask how much they'd pay; I imagined minimum wage. Frankly, even if it was less, I would have accepted because the idea of working anywhere else sounded terrifying. Marian and Torres were a security blanket. It was probably a childish way to face the world, but everything in Bluehaven made me squeamish and I needed the training wheels for a little longer.

Eventually, Torres brought my burger out, and I held back a moan when I tried the first mouthful. They asked questions about my life in the last five years. How was college? *Fine*. Did I make any friends? *A couple*. Why was I back? *Shrug*.

When I finished polishing off the burger and drank the rest of my milkshake, Marian shook her head.

"Sometimes it takes a minute to believe you're Cecilia and Preston's daughter."

I looked up at her, frowning in question, as I wiped my mouth on a napkin.

"Don't get me wrong, you're as beautiful as your mama, Hallie. But damn..." she shook her head. "Cecilia wouldn't shut up. All day she babbled non stop. I met her at the bus stop, you know?" Marian told me again, "And she talked my ear off all the way home. I had no choice."

I heard that before. Mom was an extrovert. She talked to everyone and made friends everywhere she went. Her funeral was so full, we could barely fit the people in our house. Dad was the same. He was always saying hello to everyone when we walked around town; his voice projected across rooms.

I said nothing to Marian. I never tried to be more outgoing like my parents, but I had a suspicion I wouldn't be able to do it even if I tried really hard.

3.

FEAR WAS MY MOST loyal companion. It followed me down the streets I knew so well, and to the coffee shops I liked. It burned with me at every corner, every blond girl I saw. At least at the diner, I had Marian's watchful eyes over me. Working there gave me more human interaction than I'd ever wished for, but my fear stayed away with Marian and Torres in my corner.

The owner took my training into her hands. Her eyes followed me around, correcting every other order I took. Marian might have sounded like a brute - the smoker's voice didn't help - but I took comfort in her personality. Not only it was familiar, but I had a lifetime trying to decode people's half-words. Her brass attitude was a godsend.

"Join us among the living!" I was taken from my head as Marian poked a finger into my forehead.

I had the apology right on my tongue, but she continued talking. "You're never present. You gotta be present, baby girl, because even with a big brain like yours, you won't remember shit."

She was full of confusing advice that didn't help with the actual task at hand. With the same breath she spun her inspirational crap, she'd say, "I thought you knew the menu by heart, bubblehead."

By the time I could take a break, my feet were protesting the incessant standing and my head was dizzy from all the talking. I decided to stay in the kitchen, chatting with Torres as he fried my crispy onion burger and told me tales of people I didn't remember.

"The Bradshaw kid only lasted a couple of weeks..." Torres drawled, not worried who else could hear him over the fryer. "Too greasy, he tells me. Kid ever fried goddamn bacon? Telling you,,,"

Marian's face appeared by the open door as she knocked it twice to get our attention.

"Preston is out there. Go have your burger with your daddy."

It was a Thursday afternoon. Without the Thompson's kid to take care of the shop, Dad had to close it to come over. The uneasiness gripped me by the throat. I thought things were going well between us, but maybe I was wrong. Torres passed me my burger and fries, and even though I felt like I did something wrong, I headed to the customer area.

Turning the right corner, I could see Dad's head over everyone else. He was a tall man, but it was his smile that always drew attention. Watching him from afar, I wondered why he had never dated again. At forty-five, he was still young, but to my knowledge, he remained single all these years.

I shook my questions away and dropped my food on the table at the same time Marian approached with fresh coffee.

"How are you keeping, Preston?"

"Alright, Marian. Taking care of my girl?"

"She's ours too."

I curved my mouth in a little smile. Marian left without taking Dad's order, but if I wasn't mistaken, he wasn't planning on staying for a meal.

"Hey, Dad."

"Fried onions?" He started with a smile that did not reach his eyes.

It put me on edge. "You know me."

Dad's eyes scanned the diner. With a big inhale, he asked, "Are you doing ok here, bug?"

I parted my lips, but closed them just as quickly. It was my first week. Of course, I was struggling. Again, I failed to reply to him. I didn't mean to be silent, it simply happened. Dad rolled his shoulders back. His piercing blue eyes traced my features.

"What happened in the city, Hallie?"

I gulped and looked down. The rehearsed line fell off my lips. "I ran out of money."

I heard him sigh, but I didn't dare to look his way. "You were doing well out there. Working with that school theater…"

"I'm doing the same here," I argued.

Well, technically, I hadn't started just yet, but soon my life in Blue-haven was going to be very similar to the one I left behind. Minus the expensive housing.

"Yes, yes…" he agreed. "But I'm your dad and it's my job to worry."

I chewed on a fry, feeling like shit. I didn't want him ever to worry about me. I could handle myself. "I'm ok, dad." I looked straight into his eyes, trying to make him see.

His mouth opened, and I braced myself, but he didn't follow through. Dipping his chin, Dad sipped his coffee. "So what's your plan?"

I frowned. "This is my plan," I said, looking around the diner.

"Are you staying in Bluehaven?"

I sat back in the booth, upset for the first time. Living the rest of my life in the town that chased me away five years ago wasn't the dream, no. But I also didn't have anywhere else to go. We weren't rich. I couldn't try every city in the world and test my luck until I found a place that suited me. At least Bluehaven had Dad, Marian, and Torres…

"I'm not sending you away, bug," Dad told me, sensing my annoyance.

I glared at him, but not on purpose.

"I'm just wondering if you know what you're doing," he breathed, putting his cards on the table. "I can foot the bills if you want to go back, in a better neighborhood, bug."

My lips closed in a line. It was hard to believe a hardware shop in Bluehaven was enough to afford a better place for me in the city. I shook my head. It was neither here nor there.

The reason I came back was just mine. I was tired of my life being a string of reactions. I wanted to take action without being cornered first. This was the path I'd chosen. I was going to see it through.

"I'm good where I'm, Dad." There. Final. No room for arguments.

The man who raised me looked me dead in the eyes, searching for something, a wince or a sliver of a lie. There was no lie. I hated Bluehaven, but now I hated the city, too.

Dad watched me for a second too long as I busied myself with my fries. Finally, he nodded. "Are you going to help Mrs. Carr today?" he wanted to know.

I nodded. "I have just an hour left here."

"Ask Marian to let you off early. I'll give you a ride..."

I shook my head. Of course I would not ask that. An hour wasn't much to keep working, and I just took a half an hour break and a burger. I wasn't supposed to be more trouble than help.

"You can go, kid," Marian said from behind me. I turned to look up at her, a tray on her hip. "Just go ahead and tomorrow you can do an extra hour. What do you think?"

When I turned around, Dad was rising to his feet and leaving cash on top of the table. I sighed; I needed more time with the dresses, anyway. I still hadn't come up with a plan of how to make beautiful Greek inspired costumes with the materials we had. I knew Mrs. Carr wanted magic on the stage, but costume wise she couldn't pick something more complicated.

Sending a grateful glance toward Marian, I picked my backpack up from behind the counter and followed Dad out.

We drove in silence. The school wasn't far, and Dad parked behind the building to give me easier access to the theater. I took my bag from the back seat and smiled at him. "Thanks for the ride."

"No problem. See you at dinner?"

I nodded and swung the door open, stopping only when another car arrived.

I sucked my lip into my mouth. Daniel Miller. I watched his perfect face behind the wheel, dark eyes smoldering like he was on the cover of a romance book rather than a school parking lot. He pulled up two spaces from Dad's car and his eyes locked onto mine.

I severed the connection, glancing down to my feet and walking toward the back doors just as Dad called. "Miller!"

I gritted my teeth, but I turned to see Dad coming out of his car at the same time Daniel Miller left his. Dad gave the man a half hug like they were old friends. Maybe they were, I couldn't be sure.

"How's it going, Preston?" Mr. Miller opened a smile.

"You know my girl, Hallie?" Dad pointed at me, including me, in a conversation I had no interest in taking part.

"Helen introduced us."

"She's a good kid," Dad said, like I wasn't there.

I couldn't stop the scowl. I hated when people talked like I wasn't there, but since I was quiet, that happened a lot. Daniel's eyes flashed in my direction and caught my expression. His lip twitched, but said nothing. Soon he was back talking to Dad, but I tuned them out.

God's honest truth? The man unnerved me.

He was gorgeous, with floppy light brown hair, a shadow of a beard, and muscular build. His hands were gigantic when he brushed the hair out of his face and the corner of his eyes had wrinkles from smiling. More than being annoyingly good looking, his eyes were observant. My breath got caught just when he looked in my direction, like he was taking notes on my next move.

"I might need to add a few things to the school order. Principal made a mess with orders this year."

"Just bring it over whenever you can," Dad replied.

I cleared my throat. "I'm going in. Thanks again for the ride, Dad."

Dad shook his blond head. "Don't worry, bug. Call me if you need a ride home."

"I can give her a ride."

I caught myself before glaring at Miller because I didn't need any rides. The school was ten minutes walking distance to Dad's house. Also, it felt weird to get into the car of a stranger. And Daniel Miller was a stranger, my dad smiling at him or not.

"I'll be fine," I grumbled and turned around to escape.

I reached the metal door and got myself in. Not a second later, walking down the hall, someone fell into step with me. Cedar and pine scent announced Miller's arrival. Of course, he smelled like wood.

"I only offered to be nice. Your dad gives the school a discount."

Instead of looking at him, I faced my shoes, black Chucks with barely tied laces just an inch under my blue jeans.

"You looked like you were going to kill me out there, so I thought it was worth telling you."

"Didn't seem like neither of you needed my input."

I heard his low chuckle as we turned right, lockers on both sides. I fought the shivers as we approached the theater's door. I was trying to block them out, but there were kids everywhere. Their laughter was a trigger, but I was too proud to admit it, even to myself.

Stop, Hallie! People were just laughing, but the instinct to fold myself in a small ball was overwhelming.

A kid called Miller's attention. I almost died praying that they didn't mean to come over. I put more speed in my step; the theater was so close I could almost taste it. I soothed myself, promising never to arrive early again. I squeezed my eyes and let a slow breath out. My steps came to a halt as a student stepped back and bumped into me. I reeled back, looking down at my shoes. I edged away and willed myself not to bolt. I rushed a whispered apology that I wasn't sure if the kid heard it or not, but I was at the theater's door and I was stopping for nothing.

As my hand closed around the knob, I heard people whispering behind my back: *"Why the hell is Delos Santos back?"*

4.

DE LOS SANTOS, NOT White.

By the time I finished glaring at the kid who bumped into Hallie, she was already inside the theater. Quick as a cat, silent too. Nothing prepared me to witness the way her back stiffed once we were inside the school. Hallie's silence was defying, but now, her eyes were cast down and her back curved. That kid knew her, even though she was obviously older. Preston wasn't head of one of the rich families of Bluehaven; there was no reason for people to know her name, even in a small town.

"Delos Santos is back," that was what he said. It replayed in my mind over and over again, my curiosity piqued.

I got inside too, closing the door behind me and muffling the noise from the hall. My eyes scanned the theater's seats, trying to spot a pile of jet-black hair, but she was quick to hide. Why was I so interested in her? I couldn't explain. Though there was an almost addictive quality about her.

The door opened behind me and I glanced back, expecting to see the kid who recognized Hallie, but it wasn't him. Other kids came in, script in hands. It was the first day of casting and I almost forgot the biggest reason to stay away. I sighed when Helen came from backstage, smiling at the kids and then at me. I rubbed my face and cursed Hallie for distracting me, even if she never meant to.

"Oh great, Daniel. Staying for the casting?"

I had better things to do. Helen was using the stage, and I wasn't going to be able to work, anyway. There was no reason for me to be submitted to high school theater. Still, I nodded.

There were worse ways to die, I guessed.

I met Helen as we both took a seat in the first row. She handed me a script. "How long?"

"However long it takes to make magic happen."

I couldn't stop my chuckle. "So a long time."

She shrugged. "Usually it is."

I looked one side to the other, still waiting to find Hallie. When I couldn't spot her, I dared to ask. "So, Preston's daughter?"

It was enough to have Helen turning to me, lips closed into a crisp line as she nodded.

"She's a good girl."

"I heard that before," I said, almost just to myself. "How old is she?"

Helen turned to me with an expression I couldn't decipher. I hurried to explain. "I heard the kids recognizing her. I know she isn't a student but..."

"She just finished college," Helen said as she rested her back on the seat. "Some of the kids have older siblings so..."

I looked in front, a million questions about Hallie on the tip of my tongue.

"Let's hear first from the Demetrias," Helen called, clapping her hands.

The other kids left the stage; a few girls remained. Even though my class was open to whoever, I only got a couple of girls since I started working at the school. I barely knew their faces. I saw them around and they usually called me Mr. Miller, but I couldn't pick them out of a line-up.

"Alright, Amalia, you start," Helen said.

Amalia started with the monologue, and from the first line, I knew I had to go. *How rude would be if I simply walked away? Maybe between Amalia and the next I could find time to leave undetected?*

As the girl butchered Shakespeare's work, Helen sighed and whispered to me.

"They weren't nice to Hallie. She's a good person, Daniel. But a flight risk."

I rubbed my fingers over my mouth. I already got she was a flight risk. It wasn't hard to see. Why would a college graduate seem so scared of school kids?

"What do you mean not nice?" I asked for clarification.

Helen nodded at whatever Amalia was doing. "A little more intention, perhaps?" she asked conversationally.

"There was... bullying." She whispered back to me as Amalia started over, as painful as the first time. "The more she made herself small, the more they went for blood."

My whole body shook in the small chair. Feeling uncomfortable, I asked the next question. "What about the administration?"

"I talked to Anderson many times," she explained about the dickhead who currently sat as principal. "He wasn't worried. Kids being kids and all that."

I shook my head. "It doesn't sound much like that."

I wanted Helen to assure me they were just silly pranks, but she didn't. The silence stretched for a moment too long. I turned to see Helen's eyes scanning the stage, nodding to Amalia, her head in some place else. "She always been good, very talented." Helen cleared her throat. "She survived and left. Now she's back and I know she's stronger."

I closed my eyes and thought back to the girl who folded herself in two, walking down the halls. She didn't seem stronger there.

"Are you sure about that?"

Helen turned to me with a vague smile. "Why else would she come back willingly?"

Again, I wanted to ask more, but I stopped myself. Helen wrapped up with Amalia, going to the next girl. I shifted in my seat, and after a few minutes, movement by the back curtains caught my attention.

Excusing myself, I sneaked out. Not to my workshop like I should have, but backstage.

I lied, whispering to Helen I needed to grab a few things, but I wasn't even sure if she believed me. Up the steps, I kept forward to the backstage entrance on the right-hand side.

Hallie was sitting right on the floor, costumes all around her as she stitched something really small; her eyes were half of an inch away from the fabric. When my boots announced my arrival, she looked up from her work.

The fabric made waves around her like she was lost at sea. Her dark eyes focused on me. She gulped.

"You're quick," I said.

Hallie looked down back at the costumes, but a questioning frown in place.

"No, I mean over there. You ran in."

She glanced back up and lifted one shoulder. I chuckled. She had no problem answering direct questions from Preston or Helen. It might be my ones she didn't mind leaving unanswered.

"Are you staying for the casting?"

Shrug. Maybe? Probably meant maybe.

Alright, I liked the game. I came as close as I could without stepping over the costumes and crouched to her eye level. Hallie's eyes widened in alarm, darting from one side of the room to the other.

"Tell me, why are you so quiet?"

She stared at me.

"Come on, I'm curious. I saw you talking before."

Still, nothing.

"I don't mind; I like when people aren't just saying things to fill the silence," I told her to see if she found a friend in me.

But no, she said nothing. I stood up; her eyes followed me. We were lost in a stare down, neither of us moving. I licked my lips looking down at her; somewhere out there Shakespeare's words rang above us.

"Why are you so quiet, Hallie?" I asked again, my voice barely above a whisper.

"Because I can," she finally replied.

THE NEXT DAY, PRESTON came back with his truck full of scraps of fabric, boxes of mismatched buttons, and a white sewing machine that was set at the back. I was told Hallie wasn't afraid to part with it, as she had a nicer model at home.

For the next few days, we worked silently around the casting schedule. A simpler set was approved by Helen, even as she let me know it didn't have the dramatics she was looking for.

After a full week working side by side, I started to feel soothed by Hallie's presence. And sure, I could have worked from my workshop, but suddenly I grew tired of the boring stillness of my life. I wanted Hallie's brand of silence; the defying kind. I liked the way it felt when she was around, how she carried herself and challenged me with just a look. I barely knew her and I already couldn't understand my feelings around her. I was happy not talking, but I also ached to hear her voice.

Like a switch, things changed between us when she realized I wanted her to talk. We started playing.

I knew it was a game just by reading her reactions. An annoyed flick on her earlobe when I stared too long. A bite on her bottom lip to hold her smile when a kid tripped on their words on stage. Hallie did all she could not to show herself to me, and by doing so, I started to understand more and more of her.

The sound of scissors on fabric was the background noise to the auditions on stage, and I watched her once more. One girl trying for Helena transformed the monologue with current slang, arguing that Shakespeare needed modernizing. As we heard the words, my gaze flew to Hallie. She was sitting on the floor with such a serious expression I almost thought she didn't hear what the girl was saying out there. But then the girl's voice carried as she uttered, "My mother wants me to marry; she's a cunt."

We heard the gasp from the other kids, as well as Helen's shrieks to stop the audition. My eyes widened, and I looked at Hallie. It was impossible she didn't hear it. She lowered her head to the bunch of fabric and groaned into it. I watched, baffled, as she pressed the fabric to her face to hide her smile.

"Not even *that* deserves something?" I pressed, fascinated by our game.

Hallie raised her head a little and blinked.

"Really? Come on!" I protested, but laughed.

Still, she gave me nothing.

The next week, I talked non-stop.

"How's your day going?"

"What's your favorite color?"

"Do you want a ride home?"

She was very careful in giving me answers without giving me words. It was impressive to see. I became a specialist in her language; I could read her like a book.

"That can work, don't you think? If I raise those panels? And maybe we can work with shadow and light to create the depth of the woods."

Hallie nodded, pencil in her mouth as she thrusted a bunch of light material into my hands. I looked down. "You think it's better to do it with fabric than wood?" When she lifted a shoulder, I chuckled. "I am the woodwork teacher, Hallie."

She rolled her eyes and went back to her own work. I took the fabric between my fingers, bringing it under the light to examine it better.

"Half-wood, half-fabric?" I offered.

Hallie arched an eyebrow, and I knew it was the right answer.

Anyone who heard me that week would have thought I was insane, but I was just fascinated. The girl didn't take part in the land of the living. She was always surrounded by fabric, old and new, stitching or not; she was an island, and it made me relentless to figure out what happened when she went to Bluehaven High.

They—the adults around while she was a teenager—told me she was bullied. But her body language, on the rare occasions she roamed the halls while school was still in session, gave me hints that the bullying was worse than people were willing to accept. She had baggage; anyone could see it. It was selfish and not right, but I became obsessed with finding out Hallie's secrets.

Finally, the last day of casting arrived, and after a round of particularly terrible Pucks, our game was flying high. That afternoon, I tried to engage Hallie again. Coming close, I asked, "Isn't it better to wait until casting so you can measure them?"

I had no idea what she was doing; for all I knew, she was just sitting there fiddling with things. I knew she needed the right measurements to make costumes, but that was as far as my knowledge went.

Hallie looked up and opened her mouth. I could almost taste her words. But as soon as she saw my smirk, it closed back with a snap.

"Almost gotcha." I grinned.

She raised her chin up, twisting the needle in fabric and staring at me.

We both knew she was going to talk eventually, but it was fun to see how long she lasted. I was still smiling and almost missed when Helen came through the door, script in hands, distracted as she talked.

"They were ok, weren't they?" she asked no one in particular.

I grunted, lacking anything nice to say. Hallie pursed her lips and nodded. I didn't think she had anything nice to say, either.

"Tommy Garrison wants to be Lysander, but I think he would be a great Puck," Helen talked to herself. "I always give them the part they want..."

Silence.

"... But I think he would do great things with Puck."

The case of who played who didn't seem like something I wanted to weigh in on. It was a school play; there wasn't much to be said about it. They could do well or not; if we were lucky, we'd get one mediocre actor in the bunch. Helen was committed, though. The annual play was her baby, and she took every bit seriously.

"Maybe I should just give him Puck," she wondered. "That's what a good teacher would do. Give something that he can excel at. See the potential he doesn't see in himself. That's what a good teacher does, isn't it?"

I opened my mouth to reply, as I was the only educator present, but Hallie got there first.

"What I always liked about you is that you listen. You never decided what was good for me."

Helen blinked at her ex-student with a far-away smile. "You always knew what you wanted."

Hallie shifted on her own butt, tasting the words before they were out. "And only a few people listen. It was good that you did."

Helen considered Hallie's words, tilting her head right as she looked down at the script. Eventually, she nodded. "That's right. Tommy is Lysander then..."

She said more things about the casting, but I wasn't interested anymore. My eyes were glued on Hallie; she was nodding to Helen's words but offered nothing else. I smirked when, without taking her eyes off Helen, Hallie flicked her earlobe, demanding me to stop staring.

I shook my head just a little for her to see, and she wrinkled her nose and rubbed her thighs in reply. I liked too much that we had our own way to communicate. It was stupid as fuck, but made me feel worthy.

When Helen finally left, Hallie sliced me a look like we were in the middle of an argument.

"I'm like the Han Solo for your Chewbacca."

She did not like that.

5.

Tommy was Lysander.

He was a cute kid, younger than the rest. I knew from the minute I heard his eager voice onstage, he had something to prove. Whatever it was, I recognized it in the tone of his voice. Shyness, eagerness, fierceness. He was determined to make Lysander work for him. There was so much passion in his monologue, I almost cheered from backstage. Whatever reason he thought Lysander was for him, I wanted him to have it.

So Puck went to Scott Garcia.

I had a few minutes before the bell rang, little time until there were kids everywhere. Looking from one side of the hall to the other, I read the call sheet taped beside the theater's doors. My fingertips traced the names on the call sheet, one after the other, more from curiosity than anything else. And then I saw the last name I wanted to see.

Campbell.

Delilah Campbell, it was her name. I didn't know Delilah, but I knew her sister too well. My fingers trembled as they hovered over the printed name. I schooled my features. I had no reason to be scared. I was an adult now. I was a twenty-two-year-old woman who shouldn't fear teenagers.

I didn't want to think how much of a disappointment I was to myself. When I approached Mrs. Carr and volunteered, I felt a great deal of accomplishment. I was a grownup, ready to ignore the past. Coming to Bluehaven High was my biggest achievement. But in the weeks that followed, I didn't feel fearless, rather the opposite. I hid when the bell rang. I winced if someone talked directly to me. I used Mr. Miller's presence as a shield. I knew very little about him, but he looked like someone who wouldn't stay still in the face of cruelty.

Cruelty.

Rationally, I knew they couldn't do anything to me. Not anymore, and even if they did, I wouldn't have let them walk away like last time. I urged myself to be braver, and every time I flinched, I was defeated. Relying on Miller was a poor choice. I could have been completely wrong about him, but something told me I was not.

His calming presence always seemed to pull me back from the edge, and he definitely had a sense of humor. Daniel Miller, for some reason, decided my silence was the most amusing thing to ever happen to him.

I wasn't the chatty type, and I was taking the morning and lunch shifts at the diner to make it to the theater after school hours, so by the time he was in my presence, I was all talked out. That was an explanation.

Though it was more than that. It was our thing.

When I kept quiet, he'd ask questions to encourage me to talk. To that, I'd reply with nothing more than a shrug, or an arch of an eyebrow. I'd flash him a look. I loved that he found it funny, but I couldn't deny it was more to me than a silly game.

By the end of the week, I was fascinated he could understand full sentences when no words left my lips. I held back a smile, thinking about how silly the game was, when an icy tone brought me back to Earth.

"My sister told me about you."

I spun around to come face to face with a blond girl. The second I looked at her, I knew she was Delilah Campbell. Katie's sister. My finger was still hovering over her name, suspended on air. I retracted back and closed my hand in a fist, hiding it behind my back as I blinked at the girl.

I wasn't bothered enough to reply to Delilah. Whatever Katie said about me wasn't kind or true.

It was minutes before the bell rang, and I did not know why she wasn't in class. There were years and years of history between me and Katie, a thread that I did not want to pull.

Delilah licked her teeth with the tip of her tongue, looking at me with a sly smile. I wanted to end it. I needed to be left alone. I stepped back; I knew my knuckles must have been turning white with the force I held a fist. I hated to be cornered.

"Lost?" a voice interrupted Delilah's staring game.

The breath I locked inside my lungs escaped. A warm hand spread on my lower back and the intense scent of cedar embraced me. *Wood*. Daniel Miller.

I almost collapsed when I felt his body next to mine, and I kept my gaze from his in case he saw how much I needed his rescuing.

I was supposed to rescue myself.

Delilah blinked up at him, her expression morphing. "Sorry, Mr. Miller. I was just on my way to the bathroom and I saw my name here..." she pointed at the list with a smile. "I'm Hermia."

"Go back to class."

Just that. *Go back to class.* Even though she was smiling at him using the sweetest tone of voice and cocking her head to the side.

"Aren't you going to congratulate me?" she whined.

Steam rolled off Mr. Miller's body, and I glanced his way. He stood tall with his chin up. The man who joked around my silence was gone. He looked like every bit the authority figure I knew he was.

"Congratulations," he offered. "Now back to class before I write you up."

Delilah finally was done pushing; stepping back once, she still watched Miller with a pleasant smile in place. When her eyes flashed at me, I could only see hatred.

"Do you know her?" he asked once Delilah disappeared through the hall.

I shook my head and dared to look up at him. *Damn*, he was close. I needed his presence so much before I forgot to freak out about his closeness. Even as I stepped back, I craned my neck to look at him properly.

He watched me for a little longer, before his eyes flashed to the call sheet, scanning the names. "Delilah Campbell," he whispered to himself.

I shrugged and kept my silence, this time not because of the game. I knew nothing about Delilah besides her sister, and Mr. Miller didn't know about that. He was already a teacher at the time of the *incident*, but I'd know if he knew. I got pretty good at spotting the pity glances people threw my way.

Yeah, no thanks. I'll keep that one to myself.

Like he was reading my mind, Miller's eyes scanned me up and down. I froze under his stare, telling myself not to show any reaction. After a second too long, he dipped his chin down and opened the theater's door for me.

Mrs. Carr was still in class, so we were the only ones in. I wanted to rush backstage and avoid everyone for the rest of the afternoon. My backpack hitched up my shoulder, I hurried my steps as he called after me.

"Would you tell me if someone was bothering you?"

I turned, feeling the blood rushing through my veins. He didn't know me, or he'd never ask for something like that. I wasn't the snitching type. My expression betrayed me once more, spilling all my secrets without my consent. His head hung low when he realized my answer. He took a deep breath before facing me again.

"Promise me you will come to me, Hallie."

A breath got caught in my chest. It was the way he said my name, the velvety quality of his voice. His eyes were fixed on me like nothing else mattered, even as the bell rang out there and the kids' footsteps filled the halls. Mr. Miller stood there, unwavering, jaw locked in place. My lips parted, I licked them and the lie rolled off my tongue. "I promise."

"Two milkshakes, fries and onion rings," I called as I pegged the order. Torres grunted from the kitchen, but I was already gone.

It was Saturday afternoon, and I'd never been so busy. Marian explained it happened every September. Summer was gone; people were spending less of their days on the beach, so they came around for food instead. I couldn't understand why they stopped going to the beach; it was still hot. It was so hot that week, I'd started wearing shorts instead of jeans, with my regular combo of a tee and Chucks. I wiped the sweat off my brow; I wasn't going to the beach anytime soon, but Bluehaven was a coastal town. There was little to do if not soak up the sun with toes dipped in sand.

Dad invited me fishing that morning, and it was hard to refuse. It was a while since the last time he tried, and it shocked me a little. So I told him half-lies: I needed to organize the shed he converted into a studio for me. I guaranteed it was something I needed to tend, even though I was actually more than happy to stay behind. My old Singer sewing machine was already propped in the right-hand corner and I couldn't wait to work on the soothing pedals again.

So it wasn't exactly a lie. I was busy. I also had to think of a way to turn the costumes into reality. Mrs. Carr approved all my drawings, but let me know our budget was so small. It was barely there, and I was sharing it with Mr. Miller for whatever he needed for the set.

Mrs. Carr's ideas for the set were Broadway worthy, but it was a play with fairies and magical creatures. The costumes needed money too. So I had to sit with Mr. Miller to see how much of the budget I could spend. Besides my promise the other day, I hadn't said anything to him in the weeks we worked together. I was going to break the spell, and I felt a little sentimental that our game was finally going to be over.

"How's school going?" Marian asked with her hip to the side of the counter, rooting around her bag for a cigarette.

I smiled. "I'm not in school anymore."

"Beg to differ, kid. You're there every day."

I shook my head. "It's going fine. Rehearsals are about to start."

"Painful. Do you have to stay there? Can't you do a few things from home?"

I shrugged noncommittally. Sure I could, but I wouldn't.

She arched an eyebrow at the lack of answer, and then sent me to table ten, as she placed a cigarette in her mouth and headed out. Looking down as I moved to the table, my pad and pen in hands, I called, "Hey, there. How can I help you?" quickly as I arrived.

When the customer didn't reply straight away, I looked up to find a smirk and brown eyes that waited for me.

"This doesn't count!" I gasped, placing a hand on my mouth like I could take the words back.

It didn't. I knew I was going to go to him for budget talk, but he wasn't allowed to surprise me at work. Miller laughed. His head tipped back, showing me the beautiful column of his throat as he acted like this was a victory.

"What are you laughing at, Miller?" Marian asked from outside, as she tapped on the glass beside Mr. Miller's booth. "The kid is not that funny!"

I raised my eyebrows to Marian in protest, but changed my gaze when he said, "Do you think I'm cheating?"

I nodded.

His eyes shone in mischief, lips curved. I felt my cheeks warming as I looked down at my pad and asked. "What can I get you?"

"Coffee," and a second later, "maybe pancakes, too."

I scribbled the order down. "I was about to ruin it, anyway," I confessed, feeling a little shy. "We need to talk about the budget."

"Oh yes, super fun. Can you take a break?" I wasn't expecting that. I'd imagine we had to go to the theater and sit on the far ends of the reading table while Mrs. Carr mediated. It seemed a little out of control to do this without supervision.

I bit my cheek and might have taken too long to reply, because he simply shook his head. His shoulders slumped for the first time around me. Mr. Miller expected me to refuse him. Something coiled inside my stomach, and an urge to prove him wrong surged within me. I couldn't disappoint the only person who was entertained by my personality, could I?

Even though it was too early to take my break, I marched straight to Torres, hung his order and threw my face outside, looking at Marian. "Can I take ten?"

She dragged her cigarette and watched me.

"Five might do." I bargained.

Marian tsked. "Go ahead. I'll send Torres with his order and something for you."

I beamed at her. "Cheeseburger with crispy onions."

"Aren't you tired of that already?"

I shook my head, and then went back inside, straight to his table.

He was sipping the coffee someone got him when I dropped on the bench opposite him.

"Do you know how much you need?" I went straight to the point, pretending not to be affected when he smiled warmly at me. I kept talking to distract us both. "I know Mrs. Carr wants to have this incredible scenery, but... It's a play about fairies. We need good costumes."

Mr. Miller nodded, his long fingers tapping rhythmically on the table. "What she wanted wasn't possible, anyway."

"Do I even want to know?"

Mr. Miller snorted. "She wanted me to construct a movable platform to rotate between the city scene and the woods."

"*Oh.*" My eyebrows rose. "That sounds silly when the city is only in the beginning. Isn't it better to concentrate in the woods?"

Mr. Miller took another sip and nodded.

"Did you change her plans?" I asked.

"I made them possible," he corrected me, but with a smile, stretching his arms behind him. I blushed straight away and held back the eye roll. I hated blushing, it was a dead giveaway. So I scratched my cheek and started talking about clothes before I lost my cool.

"I can convert Juliet's dress into Hippolyta's," I explained. "There's enough red fabric, and I can add golden bits and maybe rushing..." I closed my mouth and shook my head. Normal people tended not to care about rushing. He didn't need to know everything I was planning.

I looked up, and he was staring at me. Not in judgment, not impatient. Just looked like he had the whole time in the world to hear me blab about

Hippolyta's costume. I cleared my throat. "But for Helena and Hermia, things get a little trickier. I have white fabric, but it isn't as light as I wished for... for what I have in mind."

I waited for him to say something. But he kept his eyes on me and no words left his mouth. "What's wrong?" I wanted to know.

He shrugged. "Nothing. You're talking a lot."

My eyes widened, and I sat back on the seat, a little hurt.

He chuckled. "It's not bad," I was assured. "What else are you thinking?"

I chewed on my bottom lip. "What are *you* thinking?"

He rolled his shoulders back, looking comfortable on his own skin. "Paneling." Yes, he told me that before. "Get the kids to make a lot of leaves and branches from wire..."

"What diameter? We can use the same wire for the wings..."

"Wings?"

"Titania's."

He hummed. Honestly, being responsible for *A Midnight Summer Dream's* costume design was a dream come true. I was going to make wings. *Wings!* If I wasn't so nervous to talk to him properly for the first time, I'd have felt giddy.

"Your dad has a good bit from my list and he always gives the school a discount."

Good, that was one thing. But even before we got a quote from Dad, it still looked like an extremely expensive play. Mrs. Carr chose it right. It would look beautiful if we managed to turn the stage into a dream forest. Wings for the fairies, horns for Puck and Oberon. Stage makeup, glitter and all. It had enough charm to attract lots of people, and plenty of characters to involve many kids. But it was clearly more expensive than the other plays and I knew principal Anderson wasn't going to stretch the budget.

I fished my phone out of my apron's pocket and passed it to him. "I can try to get rolls in bulk and use whatever I have at home. But *that*," I tapped the screen at the end of my projections, "is the very least I need from the budget."

He glanced at my phone and then back at me, not worried that I was asking for more than half of the budget. "Let Anderson figure out that one," he replied.

I frowned, "Hm, I'm sorry Mr. Miller, but I don't think he cares."

The smile stretched his mouth, one of his thick dark eyebrows rose in question, "Mr. Miller?"

"Isn't that your last name?" I asked, terrified.

How could I have mixed it up? I remembered him from before and then Mrs. Carr introduced him all over again....

He laughed, "Yes, it is. It's just weird to hear you call me that."

"It's your name then?"

"It's my name. But Daniel is fine, ok? You aren't a student."

I crossed my arms over my chest. "Well, I remembered you from when I was a student."

For some reason, my comment made the smile disappear. He opened his mouth to say something, but we were interrupted by Marian with a plate of burger and fries for me and his order of pancakes.

"How's it going, Marian?" Mr. Mill—Hm, Daniel asked.

"Wondering why you are keeping my waitress during busy times..."

I was chewing on a fry, but wiped my hands on my apron quickly. "I can go back to work."

They both replied at the same time. "Eat."

Marian scoffed down at Daniel, and he smiled back. "Budgeting problems." It was his simple explanation.

"Tell goddamn Anderson to stop being an ass and let the kids do the play!"

They both laughed, and Marian moved from our table as Daniel called after her. "Are you coming to watch the play, Marian?"

"Fuck no."

I was giggling when he turned back to me. His eyes shone in my direction and I tucked my head down and ate more of my food from lack of knowing what to do with my hands.

"Maybe we need a bake sale or whatever. Put the PTA to work," He suggested, slicing through his fluffy stack. "They always manage to raise money for the swim team. They can do it for the arts."

I wanted to ask why he was involved in the project at all. He was the woodwork teacher, and as much as it made sense for him to work on the scenery, I couldn't see principal Anderson paying two teachers to manage the drama department. I doubted he was getting paid for the extra hours. I was gathering courage to ask him something that personal when he interrupted me.

"Go ahead and get whatever you want. Don't worry about me. Hopefully, your dad will give us enough discount to make this thing work."

I doubted that. So I added, "I can ask Dad to do a better price. I know he's holding the discount. He definitely can do better."

His lips turned up a little as he asked, "You think?"

"I know my dad."

Daniel shook his head, chuckled and then urged. "Eat up. Marian's going to kill me if I keep you one more second."

Marian, who never missed a beat, replied from two tables away, "Glad you know, Miller."

6.

"THE SWIM TEAM GETS a bake sale because people want to help them win," Anderson explained, glaring from the other side of his shitty desk.

I had very little patience with him. Teaching wasn't exactly a dream of mine, but when my ex-wife, Kelly, suddenly decided to move to the small town of Bluehaven, I knew I would not have enough customers to keep a furniture business going. I needed a steady income, and teaching sounded good enough. My students were creative kids using my class to relax, and troubled kids who needed at least one easy subject to keep them afloat. I graded them softly like a grandmother would, because to me, those walls were an escape too.

Things were almost too peaceful if it wasn't for the administration. If it wasn't for goddamn Anderson and his stupid mug. He was the type of guy who relished in the very little power he held. Besides finding him tedious, we never interacted much. In other words, I avoided him like the plague. And yet, I found myself in his office, asking for the thing he was more reluctant to give: money.

"They have a bigger budget than the whole arts department. And more incentive..."

"Again, you aren't listening to me, Daniel. They bring the trophies."

"They are boys in speedos. How much money do they need for that?"

"For competitions out of state, for starters," Anderson tapped on his desk, irritated, no doubt.

I rolled my eyes. "Do you want trophies? We can get you some."

Anderson laughed. "I doubt there's a trophy for a school play."

"There're competitions for anything, Anderson," I shrugged, not bothered. "You want the name of the school to shine, sure. You know Helen puts her body and soul in those plays..."

"Helen is a romantic. I appreciate it, but the lack of funding comes from the state. Don't pretend I'm the villain here taking money from the artistic kids."

I lolled my head to the side. "I'm past asking for money. I'm telling you, the PTA could organize something to raise money for costumes and..."

"I thought that's why the Delos Santos girl was around?"

For some reason, hearing Anderson call Hallie by her last name bothered me. Baring my teeth, I replied. "Yes, Hallie is making all the costumes, but she needs fabric."

Anderson was done talking to me, I could tell. He was right, the lack of funding came from the state, but he wasn't in the mood to do one thing about it.

I sighed, rubbing my hand on my face when he asked: "So you say there are competitions?"

I forced myself not to roll my eyes. "I'm sure I can find something. It's not bad to diversify the school curriculum."

He hummed. It was the most ridiculous conversation I'd ever had. I was trying to convince a grown man to do his job by pitting teenager against teenager in the battle of Shakespeare.

"Well, if you can get Sharon on board, then..." he waved his finger in a sign of go ahead.

"Sharon?" I was afraid to even ask.

He nodded. "She's the head of the PTA, and might have an insight into what can be done on short notice."

I didn't like the way he talked about this Sharon, like he knew she wouldn't help me. I said nothing. I got what I came for. Now I had to find this Sharon and get extra money so Hallie could buy fabric.

That was my life, apparently.

"Any competition?"

"Any we fit into the criteria."

Abby bobbed her head, looking down and going back to work. When I told Mark about my new side project to make Anderson interested in the arts, Abby took it into her hands to find a state competition for the kids. I was ready to just enroll the play in anything to shut him down, but it turned out that Abby had a friend of a friend whose kid loved the theater. One thing led to another, and now we were knees deep into extensive research with plenty of possibilities.

Thank god Abby took over. Without her, I'd have been lost.

I tried not to dwell on the fact that this was the first time I felt like having a purpose since Kelly left. We were together since forever. Where she went, I went. I got used to following her lead. Kelly was headstrong; it was something I loved about her. When she packed her bags and skipped town, she told me over her shoulder, "You don't care."

I had all the words to tell her off on the tip of my tongue. The billion reasons why she was wrong. Of course I cared. I married her, and I loved her. I promised her forever. I wasn't a bad husband, I told myself.

You don't care.

Time passed, and I started to believe in those words more and more.

For the past year, I tried my hardest to care.

About the girl I dated after Kelly left. Nice, fun, soft and beautiful. And still nothing.

About furniture, and the small projects I took to keep me busy. Nothing.

I tried. I didn't want to be the man Kelly left behind. A shadow of myself, someone just going through the motions.

It was grasping at straws for a long time. Watching life pass by without an ounce of want to join in. And after all this time, all of the sudden... I got that fire in the pit of my stomach again.

I blinked back to the present as I scribbled furiously, trying to find something we weren't late to apply for or didn't require a ridiculous entry fee. I was fuming at Anderson. I feared the Sharon character. I wondered about Hallie's past. It was so many goddamn emotions. My eyes got blurry.

"We have a couple of options here, Dan..." Abby's voice came from the computer like she was there at the kitchen table with me.

"Free?"

She chuckled and shook her head. "Cheap enough for you to pay from your own pocket."

I growled.

"Don't be silly. I'm sending you three options we can still enter this week. A warning, one involves a *camp*."

I was shaking my head before she even finished the dreaded word *camp*. "A theater camp? We wouldn't have money to send them, anyway."

"It's not expensive. They require teachers to accompany each school and—"

"Jesus, Abby, I'm trying to get things done, not make it worse."

"I think it would be cute if you went to a theater camp. Shake things up a bit."

"Sounds horrifying."

She chuckled at my resistance. "But it is the most prestigious one. Anderson would eat his words if you were selected. And they would select you, Dan. I saw last year's play. Helen takes it seriously. Everything turns to magic."

"It's a school play, Abby. Let's calm ourselves."

"Still," she insisted. "Just keep it in mind. There's cash for the winner. Anderson might need to accept that maybe Bluehaven High is an art school after all."

Just the thought made me chuckle. "He would prefer to choke on glitter."

"Not if the mayor comes to shake his hand."

I squeezed the bridge of my nose as I laughed. I told Abby about the time when the swim team won the state competition and the mayor came to campus. Anderson almost jizzed in his pants. It was something I never wanted to see again.

My phone pinged with Abby's email full of links. "Abs," I sighed, "Thanks for helping with this."

She shrugged. "That's all good, little brother. What else you need?"

"Nothing. I'll talk to Helen and then to the Sharon woman from the PTA."

Abby wrinkled her nose. "Never trusted a woman in the PTA. Call me whatever you want. There's something wrong with them."

My eyebrows rose in surprise. "Thought they were all good mothers baking for their kids?"

Abby shook her head. "There's loving and caring, and there's too much time on your hands. Just charm her pants off, but don't take her pants off, mmkay?"

I laughed hard at that one, tipping my head back. "Thought you want me to get laid."

"Absolutely not. I want you to date. I want you to date nice, fun women, not mistresses of darkness from the PTA."

I shook my head and skipped the awkwardness of reminding her Kelly was nice and fun. My last girlfriend as well. Nevertheless, I sat alone in the house.

"Who wronged you in the PTA, Abby?" I asked, keeping the subject light.

"Shush, I'm warning you. It doesn't come from personal experience or anything like that."

My lips twitched. "Sure." I glanced at my watch, wondering if I had time to drop a visit to the gym.

"Give me an update when you talk to the drama teacher?" she asked.
"Will do."

"Oh, that's marvelous, Daniel. Maybe next year..."

After carefully printing the three brochures Abby sent, Helen managed to dismiss it with a flourish of her hand.

She stood by the stage, looking over the script like it was suddenly different from yesterday's. I looked at the brochures, then at Helen, with a frown on my face. I thought Helen would be all over that. Not much for the money or sticking it to Anderson, but a chance to make the kids shine. She was that type of teacher.

Hallie sat on stage with her long legs dangling off the edge. All the kids were gone now, and Hallie finally appeared from backstage. She was a little thing, almost a foot smaller than me, but her legs seemed to go forever. Creamy white skin, shaped calves, delicate knees. Everything about her looked smooth to the touch. My eyes snapped to her face. She was watching me watch her.

I shook myself, cleared my throat, and turned to Helen once more. "We can enter *now*. For this year."

Helen waved me off. "It's too late for something like that."

I opened my mouth and closed it again. I wasn't prepared to convince Helen of anything. I actually imagined I'd need to stop her from entering all the three competitions.

"Helen..." I tried. "If we are in a competition, we can ask the help of the PTA for fundraising."

I knew if all failed, I was going to pay from my own pocket. But if we had a way to do things like they should've been done, I couldn't understand why she, of all people, was against it.

"We can do with what we have," Helen assured me. Which was a lie, and a tall order from someone with big dreams, while Hallie and I were supposed to make them happen. I turned to Hallie, practically begging for help.

"It would really help with the budget," Hallie started. "The play can be amazing. Daniel and I can work around many things but..."

Hallie said more, but I stopped paying attention. It was the first time she called me Daniel. It sounded perfect coming from her lips. I loved that she finally stopped calling me Mr. Miller like a student.

I threw a thankful smile her way. "We need money and this..." I waved the brochures in front of Helen, "is the way to get it. Anderson would get some publicity for the school. The PTA will get involved and if we win..." regretfully, I took the camp brochure to put on the top. "This one comes with a money prize at the end. We can save it for next year."

Helen looked at my offering like it was evil.

"I do think the kids will enjoy it, Mrs. Carr," Hallie insisted.

Hesitating, Helen took the brochures, her eyes glued to the one right on the top of the pile. I regretted the way things went; I felt the chill down my spine telling me the camp was what Helen was going to choose.

"We'll ask the kids," Helen accepted. "We'll see what they think." Turning on her heels, she left, closing the double doors behind her.

I dared to glance at Hallie, who was still dangling her legs off the stage edge like it was a swing.

"Do *you* know who's the head of the PTA?" she asked in a strange way.

"I don't exactly know her. But I'll deal with her soon."

Hallie arched an eyebrow and curled her lip. "You're in for a treat."

And even though I was dying to ask what she meant by that, I just stood there with a stupid smile on my face and didn't dare to break eye contact.

7.

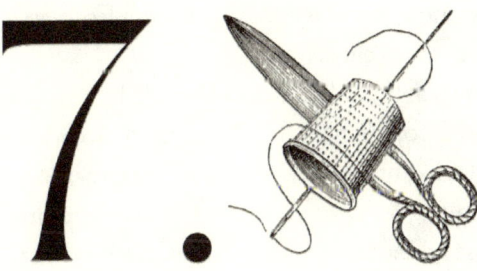

I SAT DOWN AT the sewing machine and moved the peddle absently, drained after a long day of human interaction. Taking a sheet of paper and charcoal pencil, I started sketching the dress of my dreams.

My costumes always had a purpose. I'd never indulged in making something simply because. Fabric costed money; sewing required time. But sometimes I had the urge to start something simply because I wanted to make it real.

My dream dress was a collection of things I missed, things I was. Memories of mom, trinkets of our lives together before she was taken from me. We used to collect shells at the beach, and my sketches always started with a skirt bottom full of attached shells. I traced a gown with a big enough diameter to keep me from others. A large circumference of fabric pooling at all sides like the waves. I thought about colors, but only the most delicate, almost like it was faded by time.

A soft curve to my breast because I liked them full and round. Draped fabric over my arms because I wished they were stronger. Fake lightness, the type of fabric which can flow, but is rough to the touch. *Linen, canvas, cotton.*

I lost track of time as I sketched the dress I might have never sewed, but as I tiptoed to my room at six in the morning the next day, I couldn't stop asking myself, why couldn't I have something that beautiful?

The next thing I knew, Dad's head poked through the bedroom's door. "Bug?"

I turned around, yawning. I probably slept less than two hours.

"Will you come to church with me?"

My heart was light, so I smiled and nodded.

I got dressed, feeling tired, but I wanted to accompany Dad. He was raised in church, and so was Mom. I had fragmented memories in the pew, and drinking tea after a sermon. I remembered my mother's nicest flowery dress and the treats I got at Torres' after each service. It was while thinking about Mom that I put a nice dress on, fixed my hair, and hoped to make her proud.

An hour later, I was listening to Father O'Neil talk about the prodigal son. I smiled at Dad when he arched an eyebrow in my direction, delighted by the coincidence.

This dutiful daughter, to home, returns.

Father O'Neil insisted it was all forgiven, but maybe that was where he and I disagreed.

I never felt true pressure on being the perfect daughter. People barely remembered I was Preston White's kid and when they ever made the connection, it was never expected of me to be anything but flawed.

I talked less than the other girls. I looked differently too, even now that my Filipino features weren't as prominent as when I was little; anyone could tell I wasn't Bluehaven through and through. I missed looking like Mom.

When the service was finished, Dad guided me out of the church, raising a hand to acquaintances, telling them how great it was to have me home. At the front, we were part of many conversations. I prided myself on chuckling and raising my eyebrows at the right cues.

"Oh, Preston, they told me your daughter was back. I couldn't believe it. I thought she was promised to make it big in the city."

The manicured hand held Dad's forearm and took him from a conversation. We both turned to find Sharon Campbell and her picture-perfect smile. Delilah Campbell stood just beside her, with a little smile on her lips like the good girl she was.

Dad blinked, startled by that conversation starter. He wasn't used to backhanded comments like the one Sharon just threw our way.

"She's back." His hand came to my shoulder. "I missed my daughter, so I'm happy."

I liked that he didn't explain why I was back. I didn't owe them anything. I left because I was accepted into a good school and I came back because I was free to do so.

Sharon's smile didn't reach her eyes. "My Katie's still out there. She's done amazing, of course. You remember Katie, don't you, Hallie? Were you friends?"

Delilah stifled a laugh. I frowned at them both. I didn't want to talk about Katie, especially in front of Dad. But I didn't have the chance to stir the conversation, Dad did it for me.

"Is she working?"

"She's a nurse." Sharon clicked her tongue. "It's a lot of work. But you know Katie, anything to help others."

There was a pause, but I didn't laugh. I didn't move or react. I didn't tell that Katie Campbell was the last person who should've been a nurse.

"That's great for her." I smiled brightly instead.

The blond women weren't happy, but I learned a long time ago nothing would make a bully happy. Years ago, I let Katie have everything. She owned the school; she owned the beach. She took me from extra-curricular activities when she was interested in them and didn't want to see my face around. I always gave in. I never fought back, not once. It was a war already won, and I couldn't understand why they were still trying to stab someone who was already down.

Dad heard his name being called and promptly turned after giving an apologetic smile to Sharon. I probably should have followed him, but I didn't. I stood in front of them in my nicest lavender dress and sensible heels. My hair brushed back, soft and shiny, but it didn't matter how pretty I thought I looked when I left the house. I could tell the Campbells weren't impressed.

"Fashion, isn't it?" Sharon asked. "Is what you've done to yourself?"

What I've done to myself? Like an accident or something? I had no idea why someone would phrase it that way, and I fought the urge to break eye contact. I refused to look weak.

"I guess we always have to wear clothes." She wrinkled her nose. "But I think is best to use our time to think about others. Use our skills to make the world a better place."

My eyes follow the small, almost imperceptible wince Delilah gave. She was fast to hide it, though, going for my jugular instead. "Don't you ever say anything?".

I shrugged.

"I'm glad you're back, Hallie," Sharon said. "I know some people think they are meant for greatness, but that's not true. It's best if you realize that now than in ten years from now. Being different doesn't equal being great."

"Isn't that a depressing thought?" Interrupted a voice a couple steps behind me.

I stilled. I wasn't expecting to hear his voice. I hadn't seen him inside, so it wasn't a big surprise when I spun around to find Daniel not in church clothes, but a tee and athletic shorts, sweaty and breathless like he just stopped by after a run. He was looking perfect, even though everyone was dressed in their Sunday best. Daniel made them look like ogres with his five o'clock shadow, floppy brown hair and perfect shade of hazel eyes. He was too handsome.

He extended his hand to Sharon. "Daniel Miller."

She took it, a little breathless. Of course, it was hard not to falter when Daniel was around.

"Sharon Campbell."

And I couldn't resist. "The head of the PTA," I said, only looking at Daniel. He flashed me a surprised look and licked his lips. He needed to ask Sharon a favor, and he just learned that she was a bitch. I bit my cheek not to laugh.

"Mr. Miller is the woodwork teacher at Bluehaven High, Mom."

Sharon shook her head, nodding. "Of course, of course. I only have girls, so I'm afraid we never had to meet in person," she joked.

Daniel's eyebrows furrowed. "There are girls in my class, too. We are open to all. Whoever is creative enough."

Ouch.

"Oh, well, Delilah is very creative. She's the protagonist in the new school play, isn't it, darling?"

Daniel was quick, "*Midsummer Night's Dream* has no protagonist. I'd say the closest to it would be Puck, and that's..." he turned to me in a question. "Scott Garcia?" I nodded, confirming it.

Sharon was watching us as we turned back, her tongue smoothing over her teeth. I didn't like the way she watched us. Like I was doing something wrong.

"Delilah told me you are involved in the play, Hallie."

Daniel took the wheel once more. "She's being kind enough to donate her time to help the school. We need all the help we can get. As you know, the funding for the arts department plummeted this year."

Sharon nodded, taking her proud stance. "Of course, it's a pity."

"And at the same time, the PTA organized nothing for the drama department. Not even a little bake sale." What he said sounded mean, but he spoke with ease. Sharon was careful to keep things light too, her fake smile in place even as she clearly felt cornered.

"The PTA helps to bring athletes to competitions. You know, it helps them with college applications."

Daniel didn't miss a beat. "So does diversifying."

When Sharon didn't jump to reply, Daniel turned to me. "Do you have your phone with you, Hallie?"

I nodded, taking it from my small bag. Before he even said anything, I knew what he wanted. The sketch of Delilah's dress. He knew the only way to convince the women was to use their vanity against them.

"Show Delilah," he gently instructed me.

I turned the phone toward the younger girl. Her eyes lit up the moment she saw it. It was all white, graceful fabric and golden details. It would look incredible on her.

"Did you draw this?"

I confirmed. She frowned, clearly conflicted between loving the dress and the dread of giving me praise.

"We need funding," Daniel hammered on, and took my phone from Delilah, giving it back to me.

"We have all fundraisers scheduled this year. It's not something we can decide last minute," Sharon argued.

Daniel rolled his shoulders back. A smile bordering on mockery came to his lips as he turned to Delilah. "Hope last year's costume fits you."

There was no way I'd ever let them reuse those *Romeo & Juliet* costumes for such a different play, but the Campbell women didn't know that. Delilah's mouth fell open, and she flashed her mother a murderous look. It was so entertaining, I almost missed Daniel's lips twitching as he said to my ear. "See you tomorrow, Cricket."

And jogged away.

"*In himself he is; but in this kind, wanting your father's voice, the other must be...*"

Adam scrunched his nose and brought the script closer to his nose.

"Worthier," Mrs. Carr helped.

He hummed, tasting the word between his lips. "Worthier."

"No, Adam, your full line please."

Adam rolled his eyes. He didn't want to be there. By his frame, I assumed he was a jock. By his wandering eyes, I guessed he was there to meet girls.

I sat in the shadows of the backseats this time. We had a full house and backstage bursting at the seams was the worst place to work. I was lost in thought, stitching a single silk flower and hearing Adam butcher Shakespeare's words. I had a vision for Titania's costume. As the queen of the fairies, I wanted her dress to carry flowers at the bottom, like she was flora itself. To accomplish that, I needed to be patient and sew as many little flowers I could make from a cheap imitation of silk.

After an hour of work, muscle memory kicked in, and I relaxed into my task. Something fell with a big thump upstage, drowning Adam's words, and I glanced at the front in time to see Daniel moving about, dismantling Juliet's old balcony. My cheeks warmed just from the sight of him. His sleeves rolled up to his elbows, the tension on his arms as he moved the wood around, oblivious to Mrs. Carr's frown. His muscles bulged as he worked, jaw set in concentration. My mouth watered, and I squeezed my eyes closed.

This was getting out of hand. It was one thing for me to logically see he was good looking; it was another to let him have such a powerful effect on me. I felt the silk between my fingers, wishing the soothing rustling of fabric could bring me back to my body.

He called me Cricket.

I was dying to ask why, but I wouldn't dare. For a fleeting second, I almost wondered if he forgot my name. But I was breathlessly aware of all the times he called my name. I bit back an annoyed groan. It was pathetic to feel like that.

I forced my eyes open and finished my work. When I had one flower done, I reached for the next. Wincing every time I heard the set move, I kept my eyes down and promised myself not to watch Daniel too much. My eyes blurred with the pressure of looking at the flower and the flower alone. I brought my thoughts to the edges of each flower and the loose thread rising because of the rough cut of the scissors. I was going to need to burn the edges, but I couldn't play with fire in the middle of the school.

Somewhere by the stage, Mrs. Carr's voice turned sour as she became exhausted. She was still kind, but I could hear the edge on every exclamation. Eventually, she gave up and told the kids rehearsal was over.

They cheered, of course.

"One last thing..." she uttered, mildly unsure.

I stopped my stitching and looked up.

"There's a competition we can enter," she told them with a grimace, like it was bad news. I held my breath. "I don't want to put anyone on the spot or anything. Winning would be good for the department. But it's up to you."

That was not how we should've delivered the news. I glanced in Daniel's direction, wondering if he felt underwhelmed by that delivery as well. I spotted him upstage, his arms crossed over his chest and I tried hard not to think how perfect his forearms looked in this light. I licked my lips and concentrated on his expression. He was scowling.

"What kind of competition?" Tommy asked.

"I don't believe in competitions," Mrs. Carr told them without answering. "Theater is supposed to be the expression of the soul, and true art is unique every time that is performed. So what value would a competition bring?"

Daniel cleared his throat. "Money for costumes and set design."

Mrs. Carr flicked her wrist in acknowledgement of his words. "Yes, I suppose that is something. But one has to wonder if it's worth the money for an answer that should never be given."

"And what's the answer?" Delilah asked, looking as confused as I felt.

"What art expression is the best?" Mrs. Carr blinked at her.

A few kids hummed distractedly, some kicked invisible rocks, a second away from bolting. I didn't blame them. Mrs. Carr wasn't making it appealing.

"How about a camp?" Daniel asked.

"Camp?" One kid asked, looking between Mrs. Carr and Daniel.

"What kind of camp?" Asked the other.

Daniel's gaze zoomed on Mrs. Carr. "That one it's not just about the competition. At the camp, they can get feedback. Isn't that a good thing? For them to get advice?"

"Still, measuring one's effort sounds horrific."

Well, Mrs. Carr and I had very different opinions of what horrific truly meant. I watched for Daniel's reactions. I hadn't read the brochures he gave to Mrs. Carr, and it surprised me he was pushing for a camp. I couldn't stop wondering what his motives were. But one thing I knew, Daniel was the practical side of the duo. He was trying to get the play off the ground even when he had to fight Mrs. Carr.

"Where's the camp?" the girl who played Helena asked when the adults kept glaring at each other.

"Spring's Harbor," Mrs. Carr finally replied.

My mouth fell open, and I leaned forward, my arms resting on the back of the seat in front of me. Spring's Harbor was a small town near Bluehaven, known for its lakes and hot springs. It was a beautiful and a popular destination.

"And what will we be doing at the camp?" Adam asked.

"Working on your craft," Mrs. Carr's reply made Adam twist his nose.

"The camp is not guaranteed," she addressed them all. "Once we enter our school in the competition, we'll have little time to work on our play and they'll send a committee to evaluate our progress. We have to wow them. It's a group effort."

The kids looked at one another. I heard them murmur between themselves and I held my breath. I was sure telling them about hard work wasn't a way to get teenagers involved, but maybe the promise of hot springs was enough to tip the scales. I bit down on my bottom lip as one kid timidly raised his hand, "And if we do a good job for the committee, then we'll go to the camp?"

Mrs. Carr dipped her chin. "There are teachers and theater experts at the camp. It's a good program," she offered.

"Can we swim in the hot springs?" another kid asked.

I held my breath and a laugh. Oh boy, Mrs. Carr did *not* like that. I could tell even from afar. But eventually, she tipped her head to the side. "But of course."

A second later, Adam spoke for them all. "I'll say we do it. What do we have to lose?"

He was the jock though, he was used to competition. I was watching for the shy kids. Tommy, Seth and the girl who played Helena, Nova.

But one by one, they nodded.

"Is everyone sure? I don't want you to feel pressure and—"

They interrupted her to say yes.

I chuckled. Mrs. Carr seemed finally convinced. When I looked up at Daniel, he was smiling too.

8.

I PARKED MY CAR eyeing the lone figure waiting by the backdoor. It was fifteen minutes before the bell rang and Hallie was waiting to venture through the halls. With a smile playing on my lips, I threw my head out the window, calling her attention.

"You should bring a book or something."

Her cute nose wrinkled. "I'm not a very good reader. I keep forgetting I'm reading something and then I forget all about the plot..." she waved her hands.

I grinned at her, tipping my head toward the passenger seat, begging her to take my offer. I followed her expression as she realized what I was asking, and I kept myself frozen, trying my hardest not to make sudden moves. Hallie was skittish. I won a little of her trust, and for a while it seemed amazing, but we still weren't progressing. She was wary, quiet and distant as she always was, but I wanted to be the reason she let those things go.

Ambitious of me. But I couldn't help but hope.

She had one leg propped on the wall behind her and when that leg moved back, removing her from the wall, I breathed in, relieved. Doing my best not to show how pleased I was, I unlocked the door and a second later it swung open and her sweet smell invaded my car.

"What about music?" I asked, going for the radio as she let her bag fall to the floor between her legs. "It must be better than social media."

I turned on a station I liked and glanced in her direction in time to see her smiling at me. "Do you think that's what I do on my phone?"

"Scrolling isn't what we all do?"

She shrugged. "At least you didn't say something about my generation..."

I feigned injury, my hand to my heart. "Jesus, Hals, don't make a man feel that old."

And she giggled. Fuck, she giggled and like a fool, I opened a smile the size of a continent. "Tell me what you do if you're not on social media."

She rolled her eyes at my request but didn't seem put out by it. Coming closer, she took her phone from her back pocket. "I make vision boards." She clicked on one on the front page. "This one is for the play, you see?"

I scrolled down. "I don't see the drawings you made."

She shook her head. "No, that's the inspiration before I get to work."

One picture grabbed my attention. She probably saved it because of Oberon's costume, but my eyes went behind the actor to the forest set. "I can do something like that."

"Can you?" she asked with doubt.

I scowled, making her laugh. "Not because I doubt your abilities. But money is short..."

"Now that we entered the competition, I just have to reason with Sharon." Hallie snorted. I chuckled too. "Don't be so skeptical."

"I'm sure you can charm her..." she said, and I was good at hiding my wince. I definitely had no plans for charming Sharon Campbell. "You're putting a lot into this."

Hallie threw it out there, her voice soft as usual, but I could feel the question wasn't that casual. She was right. I was trying more than I'd ever tried. It was embarrassing to think it took *A Midsummer Night's Dream* for me to wake up and take the reins of my life. I couldn't tell

Hallie it was the first time in the last three years that I woke up with a purpose. I couldn't tell her my ex-wife's last words to me still rang above my head, making me feel like the shittiest partner and the personification of apathy.

"I thought you wanted fabric?" I shrugged.

Hallie flashed me a look so intense, for a second I was sure I fucked it up. But then her expression softened, her lips parted, and she nodded.

"So, I'm getting you fabric, Cricket."

THE DAYS WENT BY in a blur. The kids who didn't care that much about theater suddenly were the first arriving at rehearsal. Everyone knew their lines. I would've said it was a miracle if I didn't know about the Spring's Harbor treat dangling in front of their eyes.

Cricket remained quietly working in the seats. She didn't dare to come over backstage now that the rehearsals were so chaotic and people were coming and going like it was their grandmother's backyard. Which meant I had to watch her from afar, her small smiles when someone messed up their lines, her tongue peaking out when she was concentrating too hard.

She was fascinating. Guarded and timid at first, but alive and full of passion, too. I couldn't help myself from wanting to discover more and more about her.

After a full week away from backstage, I was surprised to see her there. She sent me a small smile when I arrived, and we got into our backstage game of silence. I was happy to watch her work, barely concentrating on my own tasks until Delilah Campbell came in to take her measurements.

She arrived with her nose upright. She was the kind of student I hated. Kids who thought they knew better than everyone, who treated teachers and staff like we worked for them. Bluehaven High was filled with those.

It was a rich town with kids who were born into practical royalty and royalty was never afraid.

"Don't suck your stomach in, please." Cricket asked.

"I'm not," Delilah replied aggressively.

Silence.

"It doesn't matter, anyway. I'm going to lose a ton of weight before the play," Delilah announced. "So it's better if you make it a little tighter."

"I will make a corset," Cricket sighed. "It's better for everyone."

"So you can tie it real good? When I lose all the weight?"

Silence again.

"I asked you a question." Delilah practically stumped her feet.

A beat.

"I'm making the dresses with a corset because they can fit a larger range of sizes once this play is finished. It's better for the school." Hallie sighed. "You don't need to lose weight, you know?"

"What do you know? You don't care what you look like."

My hands closed in a fist. I wanted to say something, or put Delilah in detention. Sure, Hallie wasn't a teacher, but she was a school volunteer. But I held myself back. I had to give credit to Hallie and assume she didn't need a savior. Delilah started again as soon as Hallie turned her back to write the measurements.

"Are you going to screw this up on purpose?"

I almost groaned in frustration. What the hell was this kid's problem? This time I couldn't hold it. I turned into them and was surprised when I saw Cricket's hand making a signal for me to stay away. She didn't look in my direction, but her hand discreetly waved me back.

"Why would I do that?" Hallie asked sounded merely interested.

"Because that way you win," Delilah replied.

I frowned, wanting a clarification. What exactly was Hallie winning? What war did Delilah imagine?

"I will buy a dress on the side just in case," Delilah announced eventually. "Can't trust you."

"If you must." The reply had a sharp edge to it.

When Delilah left, Hallie turned to me. The pencil she was using to write the measurements pierced, secured in her ponytail. She arched an eyebrow, shaking her head slowly.

"Some people aren't worth words, Daniel."

"Some people are going to detention," I argued.

"I'd agree if she was going to sit there and rethink her words. She won't. I can't be responsible for her personal growth."

I laughed a humorless laugh. "You know that's not what I was planning. I'm not that girl's life coach."

Crossing her delicate arms in front of her chest, she stepped closer. "I don't care about what she says because I don't care about her. I don't care about what she thinks. I don't want her to have any piece of me, even if it's my hatred."

I rubbed my brow. "Maybe *you're* a goddamn life coach."

It made Hallie laugh and took the weight off my shoulders. I probably never understood the words she hid between her silent pauses, but I knew just there, I'd never stop trying.

"I HAVE A MEETING with Sharon," I told Hallie at the end of the day.

"Good for you," she replied, packing her things.

"You're getting quite mouthy," I observed.

She bit her cheek, trying hard not to give me a smile. I came toward her, helping her with the big plastic bag by her feet, full of small delicate flowers with jewels stitched to the middle. I grabbed one, analyzing it between my fingers.

"They aren't ready yet," she told me.

"Is this what you've been doing in the seats?" I asked. She nodded. "How come they aren't ready yet? They look amazing."

She came a little closer, bringing her finger to the edge to show me the loose threads. "I need a candle to burn these off."

I blinked at the single flower with many petals and then at the big bag by our feet.

"That will take forever."

"Yes." She chuckled.

"What..." I looked down again, the bag spilled over with flowers. I could barely believe she had done so many to start with.

"People will never see it from the stage," I argued.

She frowned. "I'll know."

I tsked, "Were you always a perfectionist, Cricket?"

"Do you always call people by the wrong name? It's Hallie."

I chuckled. Watching her packing up, I was brave enough to ask.

"What's between you and Delilah?"

She looked up at me, surprised. "I heard what you said about not caring," I assured her. "But I'm still wondering what the hell is going on."

"I don't know Delilah."

I lowered the flower down and stared at her. They seemed like they knew each other, but I didn't want to call her a liar.

"You don't believe me," she called it out.

I rolled my shoulders and stood up higher, pocketing a flower of hers before she saw it. "I said nothing. I just think it's odd."

"People know about me." It was the only thing she replied.

I scratched my cheek. How difficult was it to answer a question? Hallie must have tasted my exasperation in the air. In a flash, she turned to me, her eyes hard. "Ask what you really want to ask."

There was a hint of demand in her tone and a storm in her dark eyes. I didn't step back. I wanted to know.

"Is that anything to do with the people who bullied you?"

Hallie looked pissed. She didn't need to answer, but I still needed to ask.

"You cower every time a teenager comes your way. Delilah was a little brat today and you—"

"I explained why!"

"I know, I know but..."

"And Sharon Campbell is the head of the PTA," she added. "Why would I purposely piss her daughter off when we need Sharon?"

"That day in front of the theater," I accused. "We didn't need Sharon then, and I know I arrived when something was going on between you and Delilah. It's not a big deal; I already think very little of them. I just want to know what else to expect."

Her shoulders sagged as she shook her head. "I have no answers for you, Daniel."

"I'm sorry." I brushed my hair back with my fingers. "I was only curious."

"Why does it matter, the reason she hates me?" she pressed. "Do you think I did something to deserve it?"

"No. Of course not."

She took her backpack and placed a strap over her shoulder. I couldn't shake the feeling we just had our first fight. "I shouldn't have asked anything..." I shook my head.

"You're not the first or the last person to ask me why," she replied with a melancholic edge to her voice.

And right there, I felt like the biggest asshole in the world. I'd been asking myself a lot what happened for Hallie to be so reluctant to be around people, and most importantly, where were the adults when she was a teenager. And now I was doing the same. I was putting it all on her to understand something she hadn't done.

I stepped closer and tried to not be offended when she stepped back. "I'm sorry."

"It's ok."

"I'm sorry, anyway," I insisted.

"You're late for Sharon."

"Let her wait." I looked down at her as she craned her neck to match my stare. "You have to start answering back."

"No."

Firm, decisive.

I arched an eyebrow. "If you don't, I will. And you don't need a defender."

"I don't want one."

For someone who hid from teenagers, she was quite ok in holding her own against a thirty-six-year-old man.

"But the thing is, Cricket, if I hear that damn Delilah having a fit one more time, I will go off on her. I will say things I shouldn't and I will call her names."

She watched me for half of a second. "You could just give her detention."

I smiled. Smart-ass.

"So you want me to fight Delilah? A sixteen-years-old?"

"You don't need to jump her, Cricket, stop being crazy." I was pleased when I saw her relax a little more. "But I'll expect you to reply when she starts again. Cut that shit off. Leave no space for argument. You cut me off all the time. What's the difference?"

She thought for a second. Hallie took her bottom lip in her teeth, rolling it slowly. And I watched because I was insane, following the movement with my eyes, pretending that all my blood hadn't run to my cock. "It's different," she announced, taking me from my dirty thoughts.

"How come?" I asked, cracking my voice.

"Because it doesn't matter how I am with you; I know you would never be mean."

I blinked, trying to bring myself back, even though Cricket's lips were now burned into my eyelids. "But you said it doesn't matter. Water off a duck's back."

"I said I don't waste my time schooling them. No one likes when people are mean to them."

"No, they don't. But we established the Campbells are shit so let's not worry about them, ok?"

She stood there, a smile on her lips. "You're late to see Sharon."

"I'm not looking forward to it."

"Take one for the team." She shrugged.

I glanced down at my watch and, of course, I was ten minutes late. I had to go, so I stepped back once, and then again. It became clear that I had to work hard to be removed from Cricket's orbit. Like a jackass dying to be involved in things I shouldn't, I pointed to her bag of flowers. "Will you let me help with those?"

She looked down at the bag and then up at me. "If you convince Sharon to let us have a fundraiser."

I smiled. "Challenge accepted, Cricket."

THE DEVIL WEARS PRADA and all that but they forgot to mention the sweet perfume, bleached locks and long nails as she typed on her phone. Sharon Campbell was right in the middle of my classroom, perched on a bench with her phone glaring on her face like she wasn't completely there.

My heavy boots on the floor announced my arrival and Sharon looked up at me with a sugary smile that gave me the hives.

"Sorry for making you wait, Mrs. Campbell."

"Sharon." She smiled, looking more like a predator. It was the same smile of Delilah, which made me dislike the teenager even more.

"Sharon," I accepted because I wasn't allowed to start this meeting antagonizing the woman. "I wanted to talk to you about the fundraiser for the play," I said as I sat down.

"Directly to the subject..." Sharon raised her eyebrows. "But I have to say, Mr. Miller, there's no fundraiser for the play."

"Yet."

"Yet."

She watched me in a way I didn't like, even though it was way more docile than the way she looked down to Cricket Sunday past.

"Principal Anderson must have told you we are enrolled in a competition. There's a committee arriving in a couple of weeks and we might be invited to a camp at Spring's Harbor." I put all my cards on the table. "Not having money to proceed with costumes would hurt the kids' chances."

Sharon licked her front teeth. "So we are all running around so Hallie Delos Santos gets what she wants?"

Don't ask why she hates Cricket.

Don't ask why she hates Cricket.

Don't ask why she....

"There's any problem with Hallie, Sharon?" I winced as the words left my mouth.

She sucked in a breath, tugging her lips inside. I waited for her to tell me she was secretly in love with Preston White, or Hallie actually killed someone before I arrived in Bluehaven. Something, anything.

"She isn't a student anymore. What she wants and needs shouldn't matter."

"And it doesn't," I cut it in. "The money isn't for her and what she needs. It's for the kids."

"The school survived before." She pondered. "The theater department never needed its own fundraiser."

She was right. But then again, Helen was never so ambitious, but I wasn't about to throw Helen under the bus.

"You know about the cut in the budget." I did not know why she would know, but something told me she did. "And it's good we have so many kids involved in the play. It looks good for college applications. It looks good for the school. The competition could bring money for next year. It's a win for everybody."

Sharon put her phone down, leaning over the table. "The school year is full. The fundraisers are planned in advance. There's no way to do something on such short notice."

I knocked on the table between us. "Come on, Sharon, there must be something you can do. If anyone can do it, it's you." I had a wild guess that flattery would get me anything.

She twisted her lips. "There's the carnival. I could get you a booth, but Mr. Miller..."

She shook her head as we both realized that, unlike her, I never asked her to call me by my first name.

"All booths are taken. Baking goods, drinks, games and anything in between. All departments fought over the booths last year."

I straighten my back. "So it's a question of coming up with something new."

To my surprise, she smiled. "Yes. Something new that won't take business away from other departments. If you can think of something, you get your booth. I'll give you the space and we can talk prices, but anything else is up to you. And Mrs. Carr I'd imagine."

"E-mail me what booths we have in place." And I rattled off my e-mail address.

"Surprise me, Mr. Miller."

9.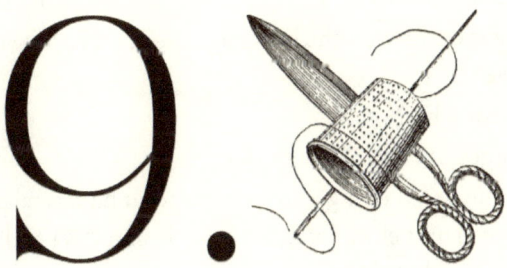

"*How now, my love? Why is your cheek so pale? How chance the roses there do fade so fast?*" Tommy's voice ricocheted through the theater.

"*Belike for the want of rain, which I could well. Beteem them from the tempest of my eyes.*" It was Delilah's reply.

"You have to feel it, Delilah!" Mrs. Carr called. He asked about your feelings and you aren't giving it to him."

"Well, because I don't know what *beteem* means!" Delilah whined, and I tuned out.

It was an hour into the rehearsal, and Daniel wasn't anywhere to be found. It was ok, I told myself, even though I looked at the door every five seconds and then winced at my own pathetic eagerness.

I had no business getting attached to Daniel Miller.

I shook myself from my stupid thoughts. I was working backstage, gathering a piece of fabric to a mannequin's right shoulder to drape and pin it. I could've just sat and cut the fabric right away, but I liked to see the rushing beforehand. I wanted to make the perfect dress, regardless that it was Delilah who was going to wear it.

I refused to think about Delilah and my quasi fight with Daniel, because when I thought about that, I had to think of why I bothered sharing my reasoning with him. I've been quiet all my life. I was considered a doormat by many and I never cared to correct them. Until him. I didn't want him to think I was stupid. But why did I care so much what he thought of me?

"Are you ready?"

I turned around to find the devil himself watching me. I frowned, tracing my eyes through the backstage, wondering how the hell was he able to sneak on me.

"Ready for what?"

"You forgot our deal?" he faked outrage.

I racked my brain trying to remember what he was talking about, but he interrupted me before I reached a conclusion. "What did you promise me if I got a fundraiser?"

My eyebrows soared. "You did it? You got us a fundraiser?"

With a devilish smile, he walked straight to the plastic bag full of my silk flowers and took them, extending his hand to me. "Come on, Cricket. Let's go."

I closed my hand, scratching my palm to relieve the need of reaching for his stretched hand. "Tell me about the fundraiser," I asked instead.

Daniel swung the bag left and right, bringing down his outstretched hand, making me feel lost. Why didn't I take his hand? What was wrong with me?

"I got us a booth in the carnival," he was saying. "We just need something to sell..."

"Like cupcakes or something?"

He shook his head. "Everything was taken. She'll only let us have it if we bring something original to not take business from other booths."

I crossed my arms over my chest. "So you partially did it."

"No. I know we can beat the challenge. I brought reinforcements already."

I arched an eyebrow. "What reinforcements?"

"My sister-in-law."

I laughed. He seemed to like that. "So, what's our booth for?"

"That is all on you." And he looked so excited, it almost infected me as well.

"Abby had an idea. I imagine you have costumes lying around, don't you? Besides the ones here?"

I lifted a shoulder. I wanted to know where he was getting at.

"That could be our booth. You can bring the costumes and dress up the little girls in Princesses' dresses and..."

In a second, my mind was already racing. "I have cosplays too, for the older kids. But then maybe we need to get a backdrop and a camera too? Still, we couldn't print the picture straight out... that would cost..."

He interrupted me. "Not a bad idea. I will get the details. But that means you have it? The costumes?"

I nodded, distracted. "I have a few things with me. I can go to the city and ask Ms. Handall to lend the things I left with her..."

"Who's Ms. Handall?"

I was already cataloging costumes in my mind. "She's a theater teacher just beside the place I used to live. I started helping her with costumes and donating a few things."

Daniel smiled, shaking his head. "You think she'll be ok to lend us for a day? We guarantee to bring it all back. I can drive you."

"My dad can give me a ride. Don't worry." And I regretted the minute I said it. I preferred much more going for a day trip with Daniel. I still hadn't got over the amazing smell of him and leather all over his truck.

His left eyebrow twitched for a second, but he unfortunately didn't push. I tried to get past the disappointment and concentrate on the plan. If we could let the parents take the pictures without getting them printed, we could run the whole thing for nothing. I knew I had enough costumes to cause a little stir. From beautiful princess dresses and fairy wings to cosplays of the best fantasy worlds; I knew it would please a crowd and most of my clothes were made to fit many people, anyway. I designed it so Ms. Handall could use them over and over again.

"Ok, come on then," he broke the silence.

"Come on, where?" I asked, forgetting all about the promise for a second.

He shook the bag in his hand. "You can't have an open flame in the theater."

"I can't have an open flame at school," I agreed.

Daniel flashed me an excited look. "Imagine if there was a place where even on school grounds you still could use a saw, tools... and..."

I widened my eyes, understanding what he meant. "Your workshop."

He didn't confirm, just smiled, jerking his head toward the exit. And I followed him this time. Neither of us told Mrs. Carr where we were going. She had enough trouble as it was, trying to teach archaic English to high schoolers.

I followed him down the empty hallways to his classroom and when we arrived, Daniel opened the door and stepped back, letting me in first.

The workshop was like I imagined it'd be. A whiteboard on the side with instructions from a previous class; I saw his handwriting for the first time. Long wood benches instead of chairs, and several lockers which was where I imagined he kept the tools.

Right at the far end, I found small sculptures. Some clumsy, some in rich detail. I touched them without thinking. "Be careful with splinters," his voice called.

I retrieved my hand and turned around. He was waiting, sitting on the middle bench, flower bag on the table.

"Do you really only need a candle?"

I nodded.

"Don't go silent on me now, Cricket. We are over it."

I stepped closer to the table. "I'm always quiet."

"Yeah, I know. I like it, but I like when you talk too."

I closed my eyes trying to not get affected by what he said. It was overwhelming how attractive he was. I still remembered when he started teaching at Bluehaven High and all the girls went insane. His presence alone stirred their minds. His long legs ate the halls as he didn't notice the whispers and sighs that followed him around. I'd be one of the infatuated students if I was dumber. But at that point, with the amount of things I had to deal with, I didn't have time to have a crush. Not a crush on a boy my age, and especially not a crush on a teacher.

I blinked at the man in front of me and wondered if the crush was just bubbling on me since I saw him for the first time.

I dropped into a seat across from him and reached for a flower from the bag. Covering all petals but one I showed him. "We have to be careful or we might burn the whole thing. Just separate each petal and carefully pass the flame close to the edges. It will curl and burn the loose thread. "

Daniel listened to my instructions attentively and with a stiff nod stood up to grab a box of white candle sticks and a yellow lighter.

He passed them to me. "Show me how you do it."

I lit the candle and closed my fingers in all petals but one sticking out. When the flame came close to the fabric, it sizzled into a hard line, burning the loose threads away.

I finished one petal and started the next, Daniel's gaze burning and warming my cheeks. When I finished the third flower, he decided it was time to try.

"How mad would you be if I screw this up?"

"Not mad at all. I'm expecting shitty results on your first or second try..."

He tsked. "Don't you trust me?"

"It requires grace." I taunted him.

"I'm a graceful man, Cricket."

"Tell me about it." I had this undying hunger to get to know him, but my awkwardness always stopped me. It never bothered me, yet now, I shifted in my seat and ignored the tingling awareness as I shamelessly pried.

"I make things," he told me with eyes glued to the flower between his fingers. "I made a chessboard once. And I like to find branches so I can carve them into canes."

"What do you do with the canes?"

"I donate them to the nursing home." He hissed when the flame got too close, making a hole in the petal. I reached for the petal he held, still warm, my fingers touched its hole. "Looks authentic."

I sent him a small smile so he wouldn't feel bad, but his eyes were intense. Too serious and fixed on me. They traced my face; jaw, cheeks, and eyes. Eventually, he cleared his throat, looked down and started on the next petal.

"Tell me about your time in college and Ms. Handall."

"College was fine," I replied fast.

"Enthusiastic."

I shrugged. "It was fine. I liked to learn... And I love sewing..."

"But?"

"There's no but."

He kicked me lightly under the table. "Come on, Cricket."

"I liked my degree. But..." I frowned a little, reluctant to admit. "I'm not exactly your regular fashion graduate student."

"What's that supposed to mean?"

"It means I'm... Hallie." While the rest of my classmates were mile long legged girls and guys with a perfect bone structure wearing designer clothes, I was painfully still me.

"There's nothing wrong with that."

I tipped my head in thought. "Sure, there's nothing wrong with me. But it also meant I made no friends because I was a little different from them. I had no interest in the things they talked about. So yes," I breathed deeply, "college was fine. I learned what I needed to learn."

"You don't have to like the same things to make friends. I know nothing about what you do, and look at us now, huh?"

I lifted one shoulder, giving him that. "I made a friend. Not a friend. I mean, we talked enough times, and she invited me to a party and I went."

I stopped myself. I wasn't supposed to tell him any sappy story. Just the fact that my mind wandered that far annoyed me. I wasn't supposed to be thinking of that.

"Tell me," he ordered.

"It wasn't for me."

And for a while, I thought he was going to let it go. We went back to our work, silently burning the edges. I let a calming breath out.

"If you're not ready to tell me things, that's ok," he finally spoke. "But sometimes I have the sense you never tell them to anyone."

"I told you I was quiet."

"That's more than being quiet. That's keeping what you have no business keeping."

"Like what?"

"Resentment. Pain. Why are you collecting it?"

I blinked at him, flustered by how I let the conversation turn in that direction. I opened my mouth, but closed when he talked again. "You said to me you don't want them to have any part of you and that's why you don't engage. But I don't know if it works that way. If you still feel it and you just don't let it out..."

He said nothing else, but I finished his sentence in my mind. If I didn't give them my resentment, it meant I kept it inside all the time. I sighed, annoyed.

"A friend of theirs asked if fashion students weren't supposed to be hot." I rolled my eyes. "It was stupid and not a big deal..."

"What's wrong with these people?" he roared, his breath blew off the candle. I took his lead and blew my one off too, placing it down on the table.

"It's not like he said it to my face. I heard them talking. It's easy to sneak up on people when you're quiet." I was trying to make things light, but Daniel's face looked like thunder. "They were drunk and stupid."

"It's rude. And not true."

"It doesn't matter. I should know better than to care about what people think."

"And why's that? Why is it your responsibility to take on this as well?"

I splayed my palms on the roughness of the wooden table. It surprised me that mean people annoyed him that much. He lived in Bluehaven for years now.

"I grew up here. I lived through enough..." I swallowed and shook my head. "I shouldn't care. I never even tried to be like them. I could've tried."

And not because I had aspirations of being as beautiful as them. I could've done it just to fit in. But I didn't. I had no regrets, but I didn't feel like a victim either.

"Good! You're not supposed to change for people."

I rolled my eyes. "You're missing the point."

Daniel crossed his arms over his chest. "Explain it to me then."

"If I'm so adamant about being myself, I should take pride in it. It shouldn't be so easy to shake it. I'm not saying they weren't rude; I'm not defending anyone. But I can't be a shaky house in the wind."

That calmed him down, his expression softening. He dipped his chin, tapping quickly on the wood like someone who's processing a thought.

"You're right. I just told you the other day you have to stand up to Delilah. Still, I'm going to be annoyed when people are dicks."

I smiled. "Ok. You can do that."

"And you'll start cursing them out, huh?"

"I won't promise anything." But I bit my cheek to hide my smile.

We lit the candles again. We wouldn't be finished today, but I didn't care how long it would take. I liked his company. I felt safe in his workshop even though it was still inside the school grounds. One petal after the other, we worked in silence once more.

"Tell me about school now."

I chuckled, shaking my head. "Why don't we talk about you for a change?"

He shrugged. "I'm an open book. What do you want to know?"

Everything.

I arched my eyebrow at him. Instead of replying, he nodded and started. "I was born in a small town and dated the same girl since I was fifteen."

I frowned at myself, but didn't interrupt. Was he still dating her?

"We went to college in the city and then moved around a little more. Five years ago, she got a job in Bluehaven and we moved here."

I swallowed dry, not sure if I was allowed to ask questions about this girl.

"Are you married?"

He flashed me a look. "Not anymore."

I nodded. Of course, yes, I should've known that.

"Were you always a teacher?" I decided to stir the conversation away from his ex.

"No. I had a furniture shop, but I figured I couldn't keep it up when I moved here."

Hmm. I wanted to ask a billion things, but all of them were about his relationship. I fixed my eyes on the flower and kept working.

"Do you have a boyfriend, Hallie?"

I whipped my head up in alarm. "What? Why would...? No."

Daniel chuckled. "I assumed if I asked something personal it would show I don't mind you asking the same?"

I nodded stiffly, licking my lips. "What happened to your wife?"

"Left. And after her I dated only one time, but it wasn't very serious. Anything else?"

He replied it all so matter-of-factly it got me dizzy. He called himself an open book, but it felt like I was only reading the badly written summary.

"Nothing else," I decided to say.

"Ok, then. So tell me about school." He tried again with a grin.

I chuckled at his persistence. "School was hell."

"Tell me one thing," he pleaded. "If it's too broad, just tell me one example. One thing they did."

A little movie played in my head. Of all my sins, the one I regretted the most was to let it interfere with my relationship with Dad.

"I used to go fishing with my dad," I told him. "It was our thing. The kids started going to the beach... playing around at first, but they would stay the whole day and..." I measured my words. "They made me uncomfortable, and I gave up. I took it during class and in the hallways, but the weekend was supposed to be my time of peace and..."

"What did you do?"

"I stopped going. I told Dad I wasn't into fishing anymore. And that was the end of that. We never went again; we have nothing in common anymore. School was a string of mistakes, fear and regrets."

Daniel took what I was saying, his eyebrows furrowed. The candlelight burned and brought dancing shadows to his features.

"You have to take it back."

"Excuse me?"

"That's it," he said, looking at me, forgetting all about his flower. "These things you just gave away because people were horrible. The college you didn't enjoy. The hallways you walk in fear. The damn beach. It's time for you to take them back, Cricket."

I chuckled. "There's no need for a take back."

"You'll feel better if you do."

I cocked my head to the side. "You think so?"

"I know so." His confident voice resonated. "You're used to be quiet, but what if you took it back? You don't need words, just actions."

"Do you mean going to the beach and demanding to have it back?"

Daniel blew off his candle and leaned on the table. "Tell me about the last time you went."

I bit my cheek, stopping myself from replying. Last time I went was a week before the *incident*.

"Just go. It's your town too. It's your place to be. It's your goddamn beach. I'm not saying to go over and make a speech, Cricket." I chuckled, and he did too. The idea of me arriving at the beach and saying any words was comical. "What I'm saying is go over, bring earphones and that's it. Nothing else. Just sit there."

"Just sit?"

"Just sit."

I thought for a second.

"I'm going easy on you," he pressed, and I laughed.

He was just asking me to take space once again. And I was tempted.

Because I hadn't told Daniel it was at that college party when I decided to go back to Bluehaven. When I realized it wasn't the school or my town. It was me. I let them talk down to me. I let people walk all over me and they had done it in Bluehaven and they did it everywhere I went.

Moving hadn't fixed me.

"Take back?" I asked again, uncertain.

"Take it all back." He nodded.

10.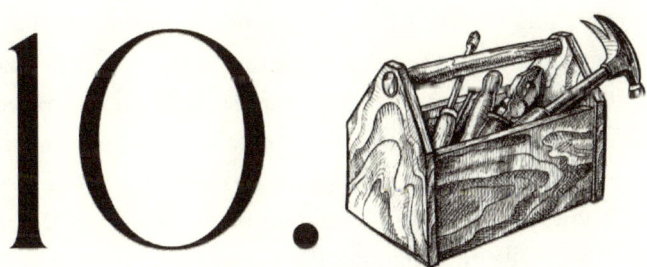

"How's it going, Mr. Miller?"

Cole Thompson was a reluctant presence in every class but mine. Bold, intelligent, but never compliant. He was a teacher's nightmare with the eye rolls and bad boy attitude. But he excelled in my class, so if I was going to have a favorite student, he would be it. Not exactly the person I had in mind when I arrived at the White Hardware store, but I took it.

"Good. Working hard?" I came to the counter, my extensive list of supplies in hand.

He scoffed. "Not more than I should." He pointed to the paper. "Should I have a look?"

I handed it to him. It was a mix of supplies for my personal projects and things I needed for the set. I was still unsure about spending money before the fundraiser was finished and we knew for sure how much extra we had. So I decided to donate a few things and hoped Preston was in a good mood to hand out discounts.

It wasn't a surprise that Hallie wasn't here, but my eyes searched a perky ponytail and a curious frown anyway. I shook myself off. I knew well that thinking about Hallie was a bad idea. She was young and clearly going through things. I couldn't help myself when we were together, but I knew it had to stop. I could pretend all I wanted was that I had just a mild interest in her, but it was the most obvious lie I'd ever told myself.

While I busied myself with conflicting thoughts, Cole jumped into action, fetching the items from my list in the aisles along the store. I leaned against the dated counter beside the till and waited. Preston once told me the store was originally his grandfather's and was passed on to his father, and now it was his. He'd probably sell it to retire, since his daughter would never be interested in the family business. I thought it was odd how at peace he was about losing his family's legacy. But that was before I met Hallie and understood the quiet force of nature she was.

"Daniel!" boomed the blond-haired man coming from the back.

"Hey, Preston." I straightened myself and stopped all thoughts about his daughter. "How are things?"

"Good, good. Have you been taken care of?"

I confirmed, jerking my thumb in Cole's direction. "Kid is grabbing a few things for me."

Preston nodded, seeming satisfied with Cole. "Hallie tells me you're both working a lot."

Guilt pricked my skin. Guilt, why guilt? I had done nothing with his daughter. Still, it was hard to look in a man's eye when you imagined driving your cock in and out of his daughter a couple of times. It was another reason why I should've tamed things with Hallie.

"You know how Helen works..." I shrugged. "She wants what she wants."

"Huh." Preston's reply made me frown. "I'm glad Hallie is helping," he said, rubbing a hand to his chin. "But maybe she should put more work on herself? The diner already takes too much of her time."

"Would you prefer her not to work at the school at all?" I pried.

He tipped his head left and right. "Hallie isn't the type of person to sit idly by when everyone else is working. I'm happy she's there with Mrs. Carr, but she's my daughter, and I want more for her."

I considered what he was saying. "I gathered that everything she's doing can go to her portfolio."

It was a massive speculation on my part, but I didn't need to hear from her to know that she enjoyed working with theater. She wasn't wasting her time like Preston was suggesting.

He nodded, but still insisted. "With the diner, theater and that secret dress, I hardly see her."

"Secret dress?" I asked at the same time the bell chimed by the entrance.

I turned to my right to find no one but Cricket there, blinking at her father and then quickly at me, like she caught us doing something we shouldn't. I swallowed my ill placed guilt once more and tried to smile.

"Hey, Hallie."

Not Cricket today. I couldn't call her by a nickname and get away with it. I barely thought I was getting away with the way I looked at her, but I couldn't control it. Hallie had the kind of beauty that knocked the air out of my lungs every single time. It was the regal way she carried herself. Gentle, delicate all over and in the occasional times she actually spoke, I was transfixed by her sharp tongue and wit.

Christ. It was stupid how much trouble I was in.

Cole placed a shopping basket on the counter between me and Preston with a thud and took my attention from Hallie. I felt her stepping closer, craning her neck to have a good look at the items inside the basket, and frowned.

"Those are supplies for the theater," she accused.

"No," I lied.

She grabbed the packet of thin wire from the basket. I doubled my original order so she could have extra for the wings. She waved the package in front of my face.

"Are you making fairy wings, Daniel?"

I couldn't stop from chuckling. "I use wire in my day to day, thank you very much. Can you stop touching my shopping? I will call the manager on you."

Hallie's eyes warmed. I'd take being silly any day of the week if I was going to be rewarded by her laugh each time. She licked her lips and shook her head, putting the package back in its place and then crouched under the counter to pass to the other side. Going on her tiptoes, she kissed Preston's cheek. I observed them lip tied, especially when I noticed the dumbfounded expression on the man's face.

"Those are the things I told you we need a better discount for, dad," she told her old man.

I opened my mouth to talk, but she held a hand up, stopping me. I laughed and let her continue. "What can you do for us?" she pushed.

Her dad seemed to be completely perplexed by his own daughter. I knew sassy Hallie didn't always come to play, but by his reaction, I would think he never saw that side of her.

"Family discount, bug?" he finally said.

She tilted her head to the side. "Not your usual family and friends discount, dad. Let's say daughter's discount."

Preston glanced down at my basket. "That's his shopping, though." And I wasn't sure if he was just against giving me the discount or if he was digging into whatever it was between his daughter and me.

Hallie shook her head. "That is mostly for me." I got a small smile as she turned her back and left for the backroom. But we both heard when she murmured, "That's Daniel being Daniel."

I watched her go, doing my best not to follow the swing of her hips. I looked back to Preston, his gaze burning into my skull. Damage control, I guessed, trying to look as calm as I could.

"Any help with the school supplies is appreciated," I told him.

Preston grumbled, crossing his arms over his chest; he suddenly looked taller. We were mostly the same height, but his chin went up and his eyes narrowed. "You are both getting close."

I had no idea how to reply to that.

"Yes." I had the urge to add "sir" to the end of that sentence, but he and I were closer to age than me and his daughter. Just that realization made me shift on my foot. Preston was in his forties, built like a truck, even though I wasn't far behind. I thought about Mark and how he'd feel if someone close to his age was hanging out with one of the girls, but I stopped myself in that line of thought.

"I guess it's good she's making friends," he finally said after watching me in silence for a terrifying thirty seconds.

I cleared my throat. "Sure."

His eyes narrowed again. "*Friends*, Miller."

I nodded since I couldn't give him the verbal confirmation. Nothing I felt toward Hallie was very friendly, but I wasn't ready to advertise it. Eventually, Preston stepped back, calling Cole to finish charging me for my shopping and telling him the amount of discount I was given.

Daughter's discount was very generous after all.

He disappeared through the back door, and I breathed again. Cole came behind the counter and scanned the first item as I kept my gaze pinned on the door which Hallie disappeared to.

"Teach?" Cole called.

"Hmm?" I replied, distracted.

"He's gonna kill you if you fuck his daughter."

And for the first time, I understood why no other teacher liked Cole Thompson.

I WAS UNDER CONTROL. I wasn't stupid. I wasn't a child. I knew Hallie wasn't for me and by Monday I knew I was done with my moronic ideas.

But then I parked in the staff parking lot and she was leaning against the wall, all legs and dreams. I got stiff just by looking at her. I knew there were no legs in the world I'd rather be in between.

Unrequited lust. What a stupid thing to feel.

I swung the car's door open, striding toward her as she tilted her head up for my arrival.

"Vision board?"

Hallie lifted a shoulder, pocketing her phone. I wasn't offended by her silence. It comes and goes, I noticed. Sometimes she seemed to be too much in her head, like her thoughts were so great she couldn't express them in words. I glanced down at my watch; it was already after school hours. Usually, Hallie went straight to the theater if school wasn't in session. Which made me think she was waiting for me.

"The bell already rang," I observed.

"I know," she agreed, her hands twisting in front of her body.

I watched the motion for a second and flashed her a look. "What's going on?"

The next thing she said was really fast and rehearsed at the same time. "I have a favor to ask."

I couldn't stop my eyebrows from going up. I didn't want to poke at her awkwardness, but I couldn't keep my expressions neutral.

Her lips parted, and then she shut them at once in a thin line of determination. "Never mind," she decided, turning toward the door.

I grabbed her arm before checking myself. The second I had my hands on her, I regretted it. The pads of my fingers felt extra rough in comparison with her smooth skin. She was warm and perfect, looking as startled as I felt when we touched. With an alarmed frown, she turned to me, almost in panic, and I let go of her arm, my voice soft. "Tell me what you need."

Her eyes traced my face, from my eyes to my mouth, just a second, like she didn't have the willpower to stop herself.

Good, relief flooded me. I wasn't the only one suffering.

"Dad is busy with inventory this week and I needed to get the costumes from Ms. Handall…"

"Do you want me to drive you to the city?" I tried.

"I know it's too much." She shook her head quickly. "Forget about it. I can wait until Dad is free or get a bus…" she raked her hands through her hair, a few strands got loose from her ponytail. "I should get a car."

"Oh yes, you should," I agreed.

"Dad enjoys driving me around," she told me. "It's like our little time together."

I nodded, understanding. It made sense for Preston to grow attached to that time when he said himself Hallie was so busy, it was hard to see her even though they lived together.

"Do you play car games or something?" I asked.

"Car games?" she wrinkled her nose. "All our trips are five minutes. It's Bluehaven. Nothing is far enough for a car game."

"No, I mean, do you know any car games for our trip?" I asked as I turned on my heels and walked to my car.

"Our trip?" she asked behind me. "Where are you going?"

"To get the costumes," I replied over the shoulder. "Chop, chop, Cricket, time is money," I mocked. We both volunteered our afternoons. Our time was anything but money.

As I unlocked my door, I heard her steps coming after me. "Are we going now?"

I glanced at my watch. "I can make it in two hours. Will Ms. Handall be available?"

When I looked in her direction, she was standing right in the middle of the lot, her anxious little expression in place. "We can go another day if you like," I offered.

I didn't tell her I wanted to go right away because I was afraid Preston would become available or someone else would volunteer. Helen and the damn bus became my enemies. No, no, I wanted to drive her and steal that little time with her in my truck. No rehearsal, no kids coming and going.

She nodded to herself and came to the car, opening the passenger's door. I guessed we were going today. I got inside; we both put on our seat belts and she started texting on her phone. "I'll let her know we are on our way."

I took us from the lot, switching the radio on when she finished texting.

"You can choose the music," I told her, glancing to her side.

I nudged toward the glove compartment. "Open that." She did what she was told and gasped as the contents fell down the second she opened it.

"Tapes?" she snorted.

"What the hell is wrong with tapes?" I complained when she reached down and grabbed the ones that had fallen over her bag.

Shaking her head, she read the titles. It was mostly old rock from when I was a teenager. I wasn't a very exciting person; I liked what I liked and my taste in music hadn't evolved since. Hallie gathered the tapes on her lap, looking from one to the other, not answering my question.

When she made her choice, she put a tape in the slot and arched her brow at me. "How old are you?"

"Old enough to put you in detention if you ask me that one more time." I huffed. She laughed.

She selected a *Guns N' Roses* album. I nodded to myself.

"Do you like my choice?" she asked.

"Yes," I replied, lost in the song, my fingers tapping on the wheel.

"I know that album because my dad listens to it. My *dad*."

I scoffed, daring to look in her direction just as I entered the highway. "Good music is timeless, Cricket."

"But you aren't. How old are you, Mr. Miller?"

"Old enough to spank you."

She sucked in a breath and I chuckled, pretending not to be affected by my own words. Maybe it was a bad idea to relax that much in her presence. All the work of convincing myself to stay away was going down the drain.

I turned up the radio to have something to do. I sped on the road, the music pouring through the speakers. Hallie turned to the window and watched in silence.

"How much are we bringing?" I asked when I couldn't take the silence anymore.

"I left a lot with her, but I'm not sure what she kept. Have you talked to Sharon to see how much we can charge?"

I winced. Talking to Sharon Campbell was the last thing I wanted to do.

"It's ok. I can talk to her if you prefer..." Hallie started.

But I interrupted. "God no. If anyone has to suffer, it has to be me."

"Another one for the team?"

"Always."

When she giggled at my answer and looked relaxed again, so I asked. "What's the secret dress?"

"Hmm...?"

"Your dad said you have a secret dress. What's that?"

She rolled her eyes. "It's not a secret dress. I've been working on something for the last couple of weeks and Dad calls it the secret dress. It's not a secret."

"What's the dress for?"

She shrugged. "For me?" Bringing her hand to rub her face, she angled her body toward me. "I kept drawing the same dress, but I did nothing about it. I guess I just finally did. Not that I will wear it anywhere or..."

"But it is for you?"

Hallie nodded. I glanced her way. "Tell me about it."

"No."

So firm it curled my lip a little.

"Will I ever see it?"

"You're so curious." It wasn't a no.

I smiled to myself, stealing furtive glances. She kept her body turned to mine, her head tilted to the side and cheek to the seat. Relaxed with a leg bent, she looked so right inside my truck.

Ms. Handall jumped up and down when she saw Hallie. This school was completely different from Bluehaven High. Not just because it was obviously in need of help, but Hallie's reactions were completely different. Back home, even when the halls were empty, Hallie still found difficulty negotiating them. Here, she walked in confidence, her step firm as she led me to the small room where she knew we could find Ms. Handall.

The teacher was another surprise. She wasn't a woman in her fifties rocking a mullet like our Mrs. Carr. No, Ms. Handall was young; younger than me, but older than Hallie. Curly hair piled on top of her head, glasses and mismatched clothes with the strangest patterns. Maybe it was a regular thing for drama teachers to be a little bit odd.

The woman squeezed Hallie, who didn't cower or tried to escape the embrace. She actually hugged her closer and smiled when Ms. Handall let it go.

"I miss you so much!" she said, holding on to Hallie's hand.

"I miss you too." Hallie's cheeks reddened.

"God, it's like the only person who gave a damn left!" Ms. Handall gushed.

Hallie bit down on her lip. "I'm sorry."

"Oh no. I'm not saying for you to feel guilty. Jesus, you had to get away from that horrible place you used to live." And she turned to me, still with the same breath. "Have you seen her old apartment? It wasn't safe. I'm telling you. It wasn't."

"You live in the same building." Hallie pointed out.

Ms. Handall waved her off. "Yeah, but I know how to take care of myself. I'm glad you're out of there. Even if I miss you."

Hallie smiled, glancing at me quickly. "This is Daniel. He came to help me collect the costumes."

"Oh, yeah!" she nodded like it finally explained my presence. "I'm Spencer." She extended her hand to me.

I took it, wondering why Hallie always referred to her as Ms. Handall and not Spencer. It was clear they were friends and living in the same building. But then I wasn't sure if Hallie ever opened up enough to consider anyone a true friend.

Spencer moved on from our introduction. Quick on her feet, she brought over the bags with costumes, chatting to Hallie as she did it. I tuned out, looking around the room as they kept going over the costumes. There was a wet-looking cardboard box with lost and found written in running ink. A couple of broken instruments leaning against the wall, and many other things that looked like broken pieces of an old theater set and, right in the middle, chairs in a circle. The room looked like a dump, and clearly where Spencer worked. I understood why Hallie wanted to help. Compared to Bluehaven High, it was ridiculous to think we needed money.

I turned right in time for them to finish talking about the costumes, as two big back bags were beside Hallie. "Should we go? I don't want to arrive late. Dad will worry."

I stuffed my hands in my pockets and nodded. We still had a couple of hours together, but what I really wanted to ask was to Hallie to have dinner with me. I wanted to keep her, but I knew tonight wasn't the night.

"Thank you," Hallie told Spencer. "I'll be back once we finish. Dad will give me a ride or,.."

I opened my mouth to say I'd definitely drive her back when I noticed Spencer's cheeks warming with the mention of Preston. "Whenever you like, Hallie," she said in a weird voice.

Huh.

"Do you know Preston?" I poked.

She looked flustered and scoffed. "Only saw him once. When Hallie was leaving." She clapped her hands. "Anyway. They are yours, Hallie. Take your time."

"I'll bring them as soon as I can," Hallie guaranteed.

I took the bags over my shoulder even when Hallie protested, saying she could carry them. I ignored her and stalked through the halls, Spencer on our heels. We said our goodbyes once more as I loaded the bags on my truck, waving to Spencer Handall and her rundown car. A cloud of smoke rose when she turned it on. Hallie and I watched her disappear into the street.

"Don't get a car if it's one like that." I warned her.

She looked at me over her shoulder, laughed, and rolled her eyes. Sassy, just how I liked her.

11.

"SHOULD I BE WORRIED?"

Dad asked, after turning on the coffeemaker and leaning back on the counter. I felt his gaze weigh on me as I absentmindedly drew one of the costumes. My feet curled up under my body and my back hunched over the kitchen table.

"Bug?"

I finished tracing the shoulder and moved my eyes to him. "What do you mean, dad?"

"I'm worried," he sighed, rubbing one hand on his face. "I've been waiting for you to open up to me. I'm giving you space but..."

Uncurling my back, I slid the drawing to the side as my feet fell on the floor with a thud. "I told you I was ok."

"Since you were a teenager, you talked about leaving, Hallie. Jesus, I wanted you to stay, but I was trying to be a good dad. I knew if your mom were here, she would like you to fly high."

I licked my lips. "Are you disappointed I'm back?"

He was quick; in a second he was leaning on the counter, in the other he was rushing to sit on the chair across the table. "Of course not."

"I don't understand, then."

"You were out there in the city and then one day you called me and asked if you could come back home. Hallie, you can always come back home. But..."

I wasn't sure what could I say. I didn't want to upset him, but the truth was, that wasn't me who was so adamant about leaving Bluehaven. People kept saying it was my best shot. Every time a kid was mean to me, all the times I felt isolated in the middle of a crowd. There was always a teacher there, with kind eyes promising me that things were going to get better. I was going to a good college and would find my own people and forget all about our small town.

I didn't want to confess to Dad that leaving wasn't my idea. I was lost and alone and in need of direction, and that was the direction they gave me. Not because they were mean, no. Mrs. Carr was one of the people who told me things were going to be better once I left. They were just trying to be kind.

"I just want to know what's happening," he insisted. "What's next for you? I want to know."

"I don't know what's next, dad," I told him sincerely. "But nothing bad happened. I went out there, I lived whatever was to be lived and..."

"Was it good?"

I opened a small affectionate smile. To my widowed father, who paid my college fees with his hard work at the hardware store, I would never say college wasn't what I thought it was going to be. I would never say I felt alone most of the nights and wrong most of the days.

"Yes, it was perfect. But at some point, I needed a plan, you know? And I didn't see myself living there in the long run."

"So you came home." He nodded, calming himself.

He had a reason to be worried. I simply called him one night and told him I was giving my apartment back and asked if it was ok for me to stay in Bluehaven for a while. He went to the city, saw the building I was living in, and then helped me bring a few things to the school and say goodbye to Ms. Handall. On our way back, I was quiet and stiff. I was scared.

Moving back to Bluehaven after five years away felt like a lot and a little at the same time. My stomach lunged when I saw the town's name on the signs. I bit my cheek until it hurt when the car passed Main Street.

It took me five years away to understand I wasn't a reflection of the town I was raised in. Five years for me to accept myself, love myself in the shyest way, and right when it was still raw, I came back to face my biggest fear. But it had to be done, because I needed to see that I was Hallie Delos Santos and that was enough anywhere in the world. And the only way for me to be at peace was if I came back.

But I said none of that to him.

He didn't deserve to hear how this town treated me. I feared the day he'd find out about the *incident*. My dad was just forty-five years old, and he already lost the love of his life and raised a child all on his own. He was born and raised in Bluehaven; the store and this house was all he had. He didn't deserve to resent it as I did. I wanted him to see me as the kid who left for college because she was smart enough to be accepted, not because she needed to run away.

"I don't know what my plans are moving forward..." I said carefully. "I like working with theater, though. I know I'm only sewing a few things for the local school, but I really enjoy making costumes. I'm taking pictures of my portfolio. So, you know, I'm not here wasting my life."

Not that I'd ever think working at Torres' was wasting my life. But Dad was proud of my diploma and he wanted me to do good things with it. I knew he didn't want me to give up, so I would never.

Dad grunted. "Daniel Miller said the same."

I shot my eyebrow high. Daniel was smart. Of course he knew I could use all that experience, but I was still surprised he thought of it and even more that he was talking with my dad about it.

"Why were you both talking about me?"

Dad shrugged. I didn't push; it would've been easier to ask Daniel than dad. That small realization hit me like a ton of bricks. *When did Daniel become someone so easy to talk to?*

Like he was reading my mind, Dad asked. "Are you both getting close?"

"We work together." I retrieved my drawing to work on it again.

The coffee finished brewing, neither of us got up to get it.

I decided to ask. "Is there any problem with that? Is he a bad person?"

Of course, I knew he wasn't a bad person, but I wanted to hear from Dad. I wanted to know what he thought of Daniel.

"No, of course not."

"Ok, then." I finished another part of the drawing while Dad moved and got us coffee. I mouthed a thank you when he placed the mug in front of me. I sipped with a content smile.

"I'm going to finish a few things upstairs," I announced. "Lasagna for dinner?"

Dad nodded, and I stood up, heading for the stairs. When I turned my back, he spoke again. "You never had a boyfriend, did you, bug?"

I stopped in my tracks, turning around and controlling my frown. "No."

Dad sighed, shaking his head and pinching the bridge of his nose. "God, I miss Cecilia. She'd know what to do."

I SPENT MY DAYS until the carnival organizing the costumes I got from Ms. Handall. I separated them into piles of style and age and then placed them in boxes for easy transport. Mostly, I had to eyeball what ages it would fit and then I tried to make labels to help Mrs. Carr and Daniel identify each collection. It was good to have them with me. Not just because I knew they were going to help the play, but because I felt good when I looked at my work.

From the oldest to the newest, I could see my skills evolving. I was proud of myself, I recognized. I wanted to show off my art at the carnival. I wanted people trying on my creations and taking pictures of it to bring it home.

My phone beeped with an incoming message, and I put a medieval dress aside to grab it.

Mrs. Carr: The committee is arriving in three days.

It took me a second to understand what it meant. I had almost forgotten about the committee, who was supposed to come to the school to evaluate if our kids deserved a spot at theater camp.

The kids and Mrs. Carr hadn't forgotten, though. They had been working non-stop to get everything ready for the committee's arrival. The lines were repeated, the feelings were checked. And maybe I would've been more excited or even involved if I didn't spend my days worrying about Daniel Miller.

Daniel was older, wiser and too good-looking for me. Every woman he came into contact with fell for him. All the students had a crush on him; all the mothers looked too long at the definition of his muscles perfectly visible through his shirt.

It worried me I was one of them. My own lingering looks. It was a silly crush.

I had a friend in Daniel. Probably the first real friend I ever had. I laughed when I was around him, and he never asked me to be different. Did I want to have a crush on my first friend ever? No. Did I want my first friend to be ruggedly handsome and almost fifteen years older? No. But I was grateful for Daniel anyway, crush or not. Ridiculous gawking or not. With that thought, I told my heart to relax when the next message came through:

Daniel: Are they ready?

I held the phone in my hands, uncertain what to do. I had nothing to add to the conversation and no qualms about leaving it unanswered, but having access to Daniel's phone number did something to me.

I scoffed. I was being silly. We joked around most days. He brought me to see Ms. Handall. *Friends* stuff.

But he also said... I felt my cheeks warming. *Old enough to spank you.*

God, I rubbed my cheeks, hoping to make the red disappear. I hated being that shy, that inexperienced. I wanted to be the kind of girl who replied with something witty and sexy, but no. I said nothing, just blushed and looked at the window. Even as my ears warmed, even as my heart thumped. Even as I pressed my legs together, trying to ease the throbbing between them.

Old enough to spank you.

I squeezed my eyes shut, and the phone beeped again.

Mrs. Carr: No.

I had to chuckle at Mrs. Carr's theatrics. Her reply was one worded, but I read it in the way she would've said it; a low rumbled whisper while she braced herself with her cardigan. She wasn't a fan of what she called "pitting kids against kids" but without Daniel's ideas, we wouldn't have been able to carry her vision.

Daniel: It is what it is.

Of course, he was going to reply like that. Daniel never fell into Mrs. Carr's drama.

Daniel: Everything's ready with the costumes for the Carnival, Hallie?

I twisted my lips. Daniel was always trying to get words out of me. Biting my lip and stifling a laugh, I couldn't resist. I searched on my emojis, selecting the one with the woman shrugging.

Sent.

I opened a smile, thinking I was very clever. That was, until the phone started to ring in my hands. He was calling.

Calling *me*.

Eyes wide, I had no idea what to do. Answer? Yes, I should answer, but talking on the phone weirdly felt more intimate than texting. I steadied my shaky hands, refusing to let it ring out.

"Hello?" I hoped I didn't sound out of breath.

"Shrug?" he asked, his rich voice in my ear, so perfect I shivered.

"People always struggle to show their personality in text."

He laughed, big and rich. I relaxed a little and sat on my bed, trying to avoid the costumes.

"What are you doing?" he asked.

"Organizing the costumes."

"I'm going to chaperone," he told me.

"Where?"

"The camp." I could hear the frustration in his voice.

"Of course you are." I frowned. "Who else would be?"

He grunted. "Yeah, that was what Helen said. We need to bring a teacher to sleep with the boys and a teacher for the girls."

I nodded, even though he couldn't see it. I moved to get comfortable, my back to the headboard. "How long you'll be away?"

"Four days." He sighed. "Four days of camp, teenagers and theater."

I chuckled. "Stop being dramatic. This is good."

"Good?" he scoffed. "You should go then. Will I tell Helen you're interested?"

"No!" I couldn't stop from wincing. "I don't exactly inspire authority, you know? Teenagers need discipline."

"Maybe you do. You're quite serious."

"Can you see me scolding someone?"

He laughed. "No. But I couldn't see myself being a teacher until I started."

I closed my eyes, trying to imagine. The first time I saw Daniel, he was a teacher stalking the halls, lost in thought. Big, muscly and handsome. They never had to tell me he was the woodwork teacher. He was built for the role. His hands were big and powerful, his worn jeans fit him perfectly. He moved like a man, he smelled like a man and the women fell to his feet.

The authority fit him right. His voice was strong and deep to never be challenged. It was weird to hear him saying that he never imagined his life going this way.

"Tell me what you wanted to do instead."

"A cowboy when I was six. A firefighter when I was eight. Your turn."

I chuckled. "A ballerina. A biologist."

"A biologist?"

I made a face. "It was a weird time when I started watching too many nature documentaries. I thought I could go around exploring the world."

"That doesn't sound bad. How did you end up with costumes?"

"My grandmother liked to sew, and I learned from her. I was good at it and I liked to have a project. I liked to be good at something." I shrugged. I was young, and it was right at the time when kids started to make fun of me. Two years after mom died, I wasn't the quiet kid mourning anymore. I was just plain weird, and they noticed. Sewing gave me a reason to be.

"You're very good at it. You're creative and passionate."

I smiled. Sometimes people confused shyness with indifference. I liked how Daniel saw I was passionate in my own strange way.

"Ok, so little Hallie already knew how to sew. What's next?"

And for the rest of the night, I told him. What I liked to do and what caught my attention. I made a list of movies with the best costumes for him to watch. He laughed at things I said and I let myself say things just to hear him laugh.

It was almost three o'clock in the morning when I fell asleep with the phone still in my ear, and my bed full of costumes.

12.

"THEY ARE SO NERVOUS."

Her voice was low and barely a murmur, but I heard it perfectly. We hid in the last row of seats, in the dark, so we wouldn't interrupt the committee. The first man was talking to Helen, gesticulating to the stage, had a long ponytail and a goatee. The second, with unruly curly hair, scanned the theater with a frown like he couldn't wait to be away from us. And the committee's third member was a woman in her sixties with a huge amount of red hair.

"They will be fine. They know their lines."

"Still," she whispered back. "Sometimes you can mess it up from being so nervous."

She had a point. The kids were jumpy before the committee arrived, even the ones who had a natural swagger. I was worried, especially because we put all our eggs in that one basket.

We watched in apprehensive silence as Helen showed them the front seats. I heard Hallie suck in a breath when the lights dimmed. Wait, silence and Adam opened the play as Theseus.

"I thought he was confident," Hallie commented, when Adam's voice wavered. "Being a jock and all."

"Not all jocks are confident..." I argued.

She turned away from the stage to give me a look. "Not all jocks, huh? Were you one?"

I shrugged. Something told me she wasn't a fan, and even though it was twenty years since my school days, I didn't want her to think I was one of them. Whatever *they* were to her.

"You can tell me. I won't judge."

I flashed her a look, not believing it for one second. She giggled.

"Ok. But I'll just judge a little."

I opened a smile, getting bolder by the minute. I captured her fingers on mine. "Shhh, Cricket, I'm trying to listen to the play."

After a while in silence, it was Hallie who talked again. "I finished getting the costumes ready. Separated by age and... theme."

"Theme?" I glanced her way.

Hallie nodded, tucking her legs under her body, and turning completely toward me like it was the easiest thing in the world. The seat barely fit my body. Imagine if I tried to bring my legs up, but Hallie was a cute little thing.

"I separated through the ages; medieval, 20s, 50s, 70s..." she explained. "And cosplay. *Star Wars, Game of Thrones, Lord of the Rings...*"

"Did you make them all for Ms. Handall?"

She made a face, thinking for a second. "Not all, no," she finally replied.

"Why did you have to think about it?"

"Where art thou, proud Demetrius? Speak thou now!" Tommy yelled from the stage.

"Because I made some of them for me. But I'd never wear them."

"Why?"

Hallie twisted her lips, arching an eyebrow with a teasing glint in her eyes. "I don't know if you noticed Daniel, but I'm a little shy."

"No shit? You shy? You're always picking on me."

Her mouth fell open. "I never pick on you!"

I shook my head. "Sure. You tease me a lot. Is that better?"

Hallie bit her lower lip and I wished she didn't. I liked when we were goofing off, but when she did something like that, I remembered how much I'd been thinking of the other parts of her.

Like that bottom lip, she insisted on chewing. Those legs that were always on display because of the hot days. Even her hands were perfect. Long fingers, trimmed nails, precise movements.

"I never teased anyone before," she confessed, and I couldn't stop myself from feeling proud that she chose me to be the first one.

"You saved all of it for me?"

I was hungry for everything she had to give. First her words, then her laughs and truths. It was endless, took me apart as much as it put me back together. Thirty-six years old and sometimes I felt brand new.

"You're easy to talk to," she breathed, leaning her head on the chair, still watching me rather than the kids on stage.

"And there was a time you didn't want to talk to me..."

She shook her head. "I always wanted to talk to you. But I liked our game. I never had a game with anyone before."

"I like taking all of your firsts." Rolled off my tongue before I could stop it.

And then I froze. I meant it in the most innocent way, but once it was out of my lips, it hit Hallie at once.

All of her firsts.

She stopped, lifting her head, looking at me with wide eyes. I should've told her I meant I liked being her first friend. Or I should've deflected and changed the subject. But I did nothing. I stood there, watching as she worked a lump in her throat. I couldn't stop myself from wondering—shit, not even wondering —*knowing* that Hallie was a virgin.

I had no business knowing that. And I definitely had no business insinuating that I was going to take her virginity.

Christ, it was bad.

My eyes traced the delicate round of her cheeks. I rasped, "I'm sorry."

She shook herself off, turning away from me. "It's ok."

"I didn't mean it..."

She cleared her throat. "Of course not."

"It's none of my business, Cricket."

She winced. Clearly the wrong thing to say.

"Unfortunate choice of words. I will take some of your firsts. How about that?"

She said nothing, and I sighed, deciding to give her space. We watched a full act in silence. Not a companionship kind of silence, a damn uncomfortable one like there were spikes between our chairs.

"Can people tell?" Cricket finally whispered so low I missed for a second. Her eyes were glued on stage, and it took me a minute to understand what she was asking.

"No!"

It wasn't like she had a huge virgin sign over her head. It never crossed my mind, actually, but now that I knew it made sense. Hallie was reserved. She let no one in. Why would she open herself up enough for a boyfriend? No. I couldn't imagine even being high on her priorities.

"It's no one's business," I said again because I didn't want her to feel weird about stuff like that.

"The girls walk so confidently," she talked again. "Even when they are young."

I followed her eyeline to see she was watching Delilah and the girl Carmen who played Titania.

I wasn't equipped to have that conversation. I cleared my throat and shifted on the seat. "One thing has nothing to do with the other."

"But people build confidence from interacting with other people. And I never cared to do much of that..."

I waited in silence. I could tell her mind was working fast, and I didn't dare to interrupt.

"You know the costumes I'm too chicken to wear?"

I barely nodded.

"I have one of Mystic from *X-Men*. I know they do it with body paint, but I found this amazing stretchy blue latex and those little green beads and I couldn't stop thinking about it. So, I made it and it fit me like a second skin. You can trace my body through it..."

Christ. I closed my eyes and begged not to imagine anything, and I nodded quickly to see if she kept going. She did.

"I never had the courage to wear it. Even when I'm alone, it's too much. And I have Princess Leia's golden bikini, of course..."

Kill me now.

"Monica Bellucci's Matrix, get up too..."

At that time, I groaned out loud. She turned to me quickly with a frown.

I cleared my throat. "So, you have a lot of costumes."

"I feel my mind is freer than my body. When I see a fabric, a pattern, a texture, my mind starts working and I create these things that my body can't carry."

"I'm sure your body can."

I knew she could because my imagination was already showing me all the ways she would look unbelievable in the costumes she mentioned. And many, many more that kept popping into my dirty mind. But besides that, it was wrong that she couldn't see herself wearing whatever she wanted. I wasn't sure what she was scared of, but I made a vow to find out.

"Some things grow from the inside out," I told her.

"You think?" She glanced at me.

I nodded. "You're already thinking about it. Give it time. One day, you'll show everyone what's inside."

"IT'S NOT BAD," THE voice behind me announced.

It was the morning of the carnival, and the last person I wanted to see was right behind me, ready to criticize my work. I turned around from the booth to find Sharon with her arms crossed over her chest and a fake smile on her lips.

"I'm sure Hallie and Helen will do a nicer job when they arrive."

Her eyebrows rose as she circled the booth, taking notice of everything. Sharon Campbell was exhausting. I never met her before this, and if I never saw her again, it would have been too soon. She was demanding and so difficult to please. I couldn't help but to feel bad for her children.

I waited patiently for Sharon's verdict while I regarded the booth as well. Hallie categorized the costumes in a way it was impossible for me to screw it. We agreed I was going to take the first shift, and Hallie was on the phone with me until odd hours again, trying to guide me through her costumes. Plus, the wands, swords and hats Helen took from the theater's trunk to be used as props.

Yes, I did my best to keep Hallie on the phone for the longest time. But I actually needed the help.

The only part I didn't struggle with was to put together the six feet tall white backdrop so the parents could take pictures of the kids all dressed up.

Right across from us was a cotton candy stand and now that I thought about it, it couldn't be more perfect. The kids in line would have the perfect view of Hallie's dresses.

Sharon nodded to herself, taking a costume and feeling the fabric between her fingers. She wrinkled her nose like there was shit under it. What the hell did she expect? School play costumes weren't made from silk. Of course, some of them were rough to the touch. They were made to last and weren't tailored perfectly to just one person.

"I hope it works," Sharon said, but didn't really mean it.

I managed to dip my chin in acknowledgement and she finally left me alone.

My phone beeped with a voice message from Mark telling me they were already en route. I heard the girls singing happily as he talked, Abby's voice the loudest in the background. I pocketed my phone and turned my attention to the families arriving. I knew none of them were coming to our booth. The school never had something like that before, but I hoped the backdrop would pique their curiosity.

It took an hour of people just watching at a distance with mild interest until a little girl ran straight toward a pink puffy dress displayed on the biggest rack.

"Would you like to try it on?" I asked with a smile.

The mother rushed after her, taking the girl by the arm with an apologetic smile. The little girl was younger than April, maybe about seven or six. She was completely ignoring her mother, her little sticky fingers clutched on the pink dress. I did my best not to wince.

"I'm sorry..." the mother said to me. "Anna, what did I say about running off?"

"Look, mommy!"

"She can try it on and you can take a picture." I pointed to the backdrop. "And maybe get some props from the trunk?" I offered, trying my best to be a smooth seller.

I never sold anything before. Even with my furniture, I simply made them. Kelly was the one who put up a website and dealt with customers. She was a people person.

The mother blinked at me, and then down to her daughter. I kept going. "We are trying to fund the drama department. This is all Mrs. Carr's idea."

No, it wasn't, but Mrs. Carr was known and liked in Bluehaven. It was good to have her endorsement. The mother opened a smile and nodded. She took two tickets from her purse, which I stuffed into our little money box by the side.

I left them alone to decide on a dress and props, only offering my assistance when the kid wanted the mother to be in a picture with her. After them, a line formed. Soon all costumes were requested, and I even got a couple of parents to try one thing or another. An older couple requested a picture together dressed like 70s hippies. And another wanted as Daenerys and Jon Snow from *Game of Thrones*.

Time flew by. I distracted myself by dealing with the tickets and keeping Hallie's costumes intact. Almost at the end of my shift, I saw Mark's big head above the crowd and five seconds later I heard the children's shriek as two little things threw themselves on my legs.

"Uncle Dan!" they yelled.

I chuckled and crouched down, giving a hug to April and then Rose, who was much tamer than her younger sister.

"How was the trip, kid?" I asked Rose as I stood up. April kept her arms around my neck, so I scooped her up in my arms.

Rose shrugged. "It was ok. Dad wouldn't let us stop."

I gaped at them in fake outrage. "Are you kidding me?"

"And he knows the stops are my favorite!" April whined.

"They are her favorite because she wants candy and a soda from each stop. And then she wants to go to the toilet and..." Mark said, coming closer to us, Abby just beside him, smiling brightly.

I gave Abby a one-armed hug since I had her kid in the other. She patted my chest with familiarity and then stepped back to look at the booth better.

"What do you think?" I asked.

"I think I'm a genius," she replied.

I laughed as Mark patted me on my back. "It'll go to her head."

"I always knew I was a genius, darling," Abby quipped.

I shook my head, chuckling, as Rose asked, "Can I try any of them?"

"Of course," I assured her. "There's more over there..." And I put April on the ground to go help my other girl.

I showed Rose all the possibilities, her eyes paying attention like it was the most important decision. Rose finally decided on a *Star Trek* uniform and April the puffiest pink dress around, and they dragged Mark to take multiple pictures in all the poses they could think of.

"Where is she?" Abby whispered as the pictures were being taken.

"Hmm?" I replied, not taking my eyes off the girls.

"Come on, Dan. Where's the girl?"

I flashed her an annoyed look, making her laugh. "Hallie. Where's Hallie?"

"Why do you want to know?"

"Dan." She sighed, rolling her eyes.

Yes, I was going to downplay it as much as I could. I wanted to scan the crowds for a glimpse of a high ponytail, but I wasn't ready to confess how much Hallie affected me.

Mark and I were just two years apart; Abby was a year younger than him, and Kelly was my age. Abby and Mark started to date when Abby was fifteen, Kelly and I started a few months after that.

The four of us were close. We did everything together. Abby and Kelly were best friends practically all their lives. I was the best man, and she was the maid of honor at their wedding. They did the same for us. Kelly and I were Rose's godparents.

The reality was, I felt guilty for breaking up the group.

Kelly left because I wasn't a good husband. She left because she thought I didn't care enough for her and because of me, everyone suffered.

The four of us weren't planning vacations together anymore. We didn't bring the girls to the zoo and the planetarium on Saturdays. I fucked up and broke our group.

The rational part of me understood that what we had was gone, but the irrational one? I wanted to show off Hallie and make Mark and Abby like her. I wanted Abby to be her friend. I wanted her to be one of us.

But it wasn't fair. Hallie was younger and clearly not someone very interested in making tons of friends. She was shy and quiet and completely different from Abby and Kelly, who were loud and unafraid.

Still, I ached for them to love Hallie, but I couldn't say a word. So I didn't. I pretended it wasn't a big deal.

Eventually, Abby let the subject go when the girls were done with the costumes and begged for a snack. The four of them left, and I busied myself with other customers.

I glanced down at my watch to see I had another ten minutes left on my shift when I heard the voice to my side, raising the hairs on my arm. "Tell me we are rich."

I knew she was at the diner in the morning, but now she smelled like citrus and something girlie. A slow smile came to my lips, and right there, I knew I was going to be garbage at hiding my feelings.

She looked amazing. Mini shorts with golden buttons, a cropped sweater that showed just a sliver of skin. Her hair was down for the first time, shiny and longer than I expected.

Yeah, I wasn't hiding crap from anyone.

"It's been busy," I croaked.

"So rich?" she joked.

"Super rich, Cricket," I confirmed, making her giggle.

"Walk me through it." She requested, coming closer, her nose up, looking at everything.

"You know your costumes," I said. "Just get the tickets, put them in the locked box, and then let the kids play around."

The parents from the family who just took pictures gave me back the costumes with a smile and a thank you. I straightened the clothes and hung it on the rack.

"Easy-peasy."

"Are we taking pictures of the whole family?"

I shrugged. "If someone asks."

She watched me work in silence when another family came. I dealt with them, showing all I was doing to her, and once they left, Hallie twisted her nose.

"Shouldn't you be in costume to attract more people?"

"No, thanks." My answer was direct.

She went to the rack, passing her hands on the costumes. "Don't you like my costumes?"

I laughed. "Don't start, Cricket..."

"Don't start with what?" My brother asked as they came back. Hallie turned, blushing straight away, clearly embarrassed when someone caught her in her teasing mode.

"Hallie thinks I should wear a costume to attract more people," I told them, just because I wanted them to see her fun side. "This is Hallie, by the way."

She didn't have time for a shy wave. April was already jumping up and down. "Yes, Uncle Dan, that's so cool! Can we match?"

I was about to reply when no one but Hallie interrupted me. "I'm choosing his costume now. Do you want to help me?"

April had no problems in partnering up for my misery. Rose took a second longer, watching the situation unfold, but she eventually stepped closer to them.

"I'm April, and this is my sister Rose," April promptly introduced.

"Nice to meet you. I'm Hallie."

I grinned like a fool, whipping my head to the other side just to catch Mark chuckling as Abby made a kissing face to mock me. I rolled my eyes. With those guys, it was like we were back in school.

"I know, right? He would look great in that uniform. What about the bald cap? What do you guys think?" I heard Hallie talking to the girls.

As I looked at them, Hallie was holding a *Star Trek* uniform in one hand and a bald cap in the other.

I groaned, "I would watch it if I were you. My shift is almost over."

Hallie fluttered her eyelashes. "I thought you could walk around in costume and call people to our booth."

She delivered in such an innocent tone, I believed it for a second. It was Abby who laughed first, clapping her hand, delighted with herself.

"Oh, I like her!" she chuckled.

I pointed at my sister-in-law. "Traitor." And I called Hallie, "Come say hi to Abby, the reason why this is here."

"Ok, you guys keep our search going." She directed the girls in a serious tone. They nodded, accepting her as their leader, and I tried my best not to fall in love with Hallie Delos Santos.

"Hi, sorry I got caught up with..." Hallie tried to explain herself, jerking her thumb toward the girls.

Abby had the biggest, craziest smile. "Don't you apologize. I'm so excited to meet you!"

She shrieked.

I watched for Hallie's reaction. Abby was overwhelming, actually the whole family was a lot to take in at once. I was on the edge, afraid Hallie would feel cornered. But she smiled at Abby. "Nice to meet you. The girls are amazing."

"I'm Mark, Dan's brother. The good-looking one."

I scoffed, but Hallie looked at Mark and then at me, like she was actually comparing us both.

"Can you correct him, please?" I asked when she said nothing.

"Be more confident, Daniel," she said. "It comes from the inside out, you know?"

I burst into a laugh. She was beyond sassy today and it was a joy to see it out in front of Mark and Abby. Everyone laughed, and I tried not to react too much to how happy I was. Eventually, she touched my arm, calling my attention. "You can go relax with your family," she bounced on her heels. "I can have the booth from now on."

"You sure? Do you want me to stay a little longer and help you out?"

She scoffed. "I think I can manage. Go have fun." Turning to the other two people in the circle, she smiled. "It was great to meet you."

"Ok, I will be around anyway. Just text me if you need anything, Cricket."

The term of endearment slipped off my lips, and I knew I should've held that one. Hallie nodded, joking. "Yes, of course, the many emergencies that happen at a Carnival."

But my eyes were on Abby. Her eyebrows rose, and she mouthed *"Cricket"* to me and elbowed Mark.

I was going to kill them.

I rolled my shoulder back, looking at Hallie and ignoring my family. "There're plenty of horror movies starting at Carnivals."

To that, my two nieces gasped.

"He's joking," Abby said quickly. "Aren't you?"

"I'm just messing with Hallie," I confirmed to the scared children.

April crisped her lips. "You shouldn't mess with Hallie. She's cool."

I turned to Hallie, and she had a priceless expression on her. "Don't mess with Hallie, she's cool," Hallie mimicked.

I chuckled, stepping back. "See you soon." The girls raced toward us, April and Rose taking my hands while waving goodbye to Hallie. Abby and Mark waved too, and soon we were moving from the booth, the girls jumping up and down and telling us all the things they wanted to do.

I felt a slap on my stomach, and I looked at the woman responsible. "What?"

Abby's lips curved in a smile. "Tell me everything about *Cricket*."

13.

People were trying on my costumes.

My creations.

I tried to keep it together, but I had a silly grin was splattered all over my face for the whole day. Yes, sometimes I got a little fearful with the most delicate dresses, but when I saw the look on people's faces when they put it on? There was nothing like it. The wonder of the kids when I dressed them like their favorite character? I couldn't stop myself. I was... *happy.*

Twenty minutes before Helen was due to come for her shift, Daniel was back with an easy smile and two ice-cream cones. He handed me one; I mouthed thanks while taking two tickets from a woman and shoving it in our money box.

When the woman stepped away with her kids, he said: "What's the first thing you want to do when Helen gets here?"

I arched an eyebrow at him. "Go home and sleep for twelve hours?"

"Aw, Cricket!" he looked disappointed. "Just one ride?"

I looked around, taking the Carnival in. For what it was worth, Sharon and the PTA did an amazing job. The bulky fairy lights were on now, making everything even more magical. I chewed on my bottom lip, tempted. There were bumper cars, a vintage-looking carousel and a big Ferris Wheel right in the middle.

"Which ones did you go to already?" I asked, knowing it was many if April and Rose had a say in it. They were the absolute cutest.

"All of them, But I'll go again with you. Actually, I'm insisting."

I chuckled, shaking my head at his silliness. I knew he got a weird satisfaction in pushing me more each time. I licked the ice-cream and dodged his question. I was weighing how tired I felt and how excited I was to spend time with him away from the school.

"So..." his voice lowered, "What are you going to ride?"

I blushed straight away and words died in my throat. I opened my mouth to reply, but I was cut off by Mrs. Carr jogging in our direction. "Am I late? I feel late!"

"You're fine." Daniel assured her.

She breathed easily as she reached us and then looked at him like he had grown two heads. "I thought Hallie had the afternoon shift."

"I'm just the ice-cream man." He explained easily.

I shifted on my feet. Why every time someone saw us together, it felt like I was doing something I wasn't supposed to do?

"Oh, ok." Even for Mrs. Carr's standards, she looked extremely distracted. "And of course, you both know already?"

"Know what?" I asked, but Daniel dipped his chin.

"I saw the email." Turning to me, he explained, "the kids were invited to the camp."

My mouth fell open. "That is amazing!"

"Isn't it?" Mrs. Carr flickered her wrist to nowhere, like she wasn't following the conversation. I found myself frowning again. Before I had time to ask if she was all right, we heard the calling of *"Uncle Dan!"* and soon Daniel's nieces were on top of him.

Daniel winded, with the power of their little bodies throwing themselves. "Meet my nieces, Helen," he introduced.

Mrs. Carr opened an honest smile when the girls said their hellos. Another customer approached with her family. I finished my ice-cream while showing off the costumes. The girls jumped up and down holding hands with Daniel, and Mrs. Carr laughed at something in the background. Eventually, when I came back to the circle, we were joined by Abby and Mark.

"Daniel says it's going well," Mrs. Carr beamed at me when she saw I was free of customers.

I nodded and opened my mouth to agree, but April and Rose jumped on me, not interested in the adult's small talk. "Hallie! Come with us!" April demanded.

I was fascinated by April's bossy tone when her sister shyly added. "The rides are cool. Do you want to go on one?"

If I wasn't able to say no to one Miller, I knew for a fact I wasn't going to say no to the cutest ones either. They clutched their hands on mine, tall girls, but the excitement made them sound and look younger than their age.

"Are you afraid of heights?" April was saying as she pulled me away from the booth. "You can't be because the coolest thing is the Ferris Wheel, and that's very high."

"You can see the beach and all!" Rose seemed as excited as her sister.

I let myself be dragged, but I turned to look at Mrs. Carr to confirm if it was ok. She smiled and gave me a thumbs up. "Have fun, Hallie, you deserve it."

Grateful, my attention went back to the two little menaces. "Do you need to eat or something?" April asked, like she was confused how people worked.

"I don't think—" I started.

"Adults always need to do something before something fun happens," Rose explained.

I bit my lip not to laugh and shook my head. "No. I'm fine, thanks."

My burger with crispy onions was hours ago, but I wasn't that hungry to spoil the girls' fun.

"Ferris Wheel first then? Do you think they would let the three of us go?" April wondered.

Rose twisted her nose. "I don't think that's allowed."

"So I will go first with Hallie and then you can have her," April decided. I widened my eyes and looked over at Rose to see her reaction.

She didn't seem to like the idea. "What about me first and then you?"

They started bickering, dragging me over the Ferris Wheel's direction; nothing was settled but the fact I was apparently going on the same ride twice. Confused about how to handle the situation, I turned around, trying to look for their parents. Abby, Mark and Daniel were strolling after us, talking among themselves.

"Dan! Help me!" I called.

He stopped in his tracks. He flashed me a hungry look and then opened a stellar smile, jogging the distance between us. "Why are you two little monsters scaring Hallie?"

April seemed appalled. "We're just deciding who goes on the ride with her first."

"First?" Abby asked, catching up.

"It's established I'm going twice."

"Oh, dear..." Abby said, but the little smile tugging her lips gave away how funny she found the situation.

The girls waited patiently, as if their mother was going to be the tiebreaker. We stood in line, the girls first followed by me, Daniel, Mark and Abby.

"I see I lost my chance," Daniel said behind me, his voice tickling the nape of my neck. April and Rose were still trying to figure out how we were going to proceed, so I wasn't worried about them eavesdropping.

"You should have dragged me along. It seemed like the way to do things."

He chuckled. "I will definitely remember that trick next time."

"Or maybe the Miller family can calm down and wait for me to make my own decisions?" I teased.

When he said nothing, I turned a little to the side, trying to get a glimpse of his face. He was rubbing his finger on his mouth in thought.

"I'm not upset," I felt the need to add.

"Hm," was his reply.

I frowned, tugging my hand from the girls. They let me go, which probably wasn't a good sign for the whole silent fight they were having.

"It was a joke," I insisted, turning to him.

He gave me a small smile. "I know."

"You said nothing, though."

"Maybe I haven't thought of a comeback yet."

I looked him up and down. "Impossible. You love to rile me up."

Daniel laughed, throwing his head back and showing off his gorgeous neck. I bit inside my cheek to stop my goofy smile. I glanced at Mark and Abby, who looked transfixed by Daniel's laugh. *Odd.* Daniel was always joking around, always with a funny remark, trying to make me laugh, but the way Abby was looking, it was like Daniel hadn't smiled in a while.

"Tell you what, Cricket, I'm not even sorry."

I rolled my eyes. Impossible man; of course he wasn't sorry. I was lost in him when I heard my name being called in the crowd.

It was the way he said, "Hallie!" There was only one man in the world who said my name like that. I opened a smile to Dad cutting through the crowd, his eyes bouncing from Daniel to me and then zeroing on Daniel's back again.

"Hey, Dad." I stepped toward him, trying to block his view of Daniel.

"I went around the stand, but only Mrs. Carr was there."

I nodded. "My shift ended. I didn't know you were coming."

He kissed my temple. "Of course I was coming. I was just finishing with the store."

Taking his eyes off me, Dad looked over at Daniel and dipped his chin. "Miller."

Miller?

A few weeks ago, Dad and Daniel were best friends and now he was Miller? I fought the urge to roll my eyes or ask what crawled up his butt.

"How's it going, Preston?" Daniel offered. At least he sounded natural.

"Are you Hallie's daddy?" April asked, stepping closer.

"Yes, ma'am," Dad replied with a twitch on his cheek.

"You don't look old." April frowned. "Just as old as my dad. That's weird."

We all exploded in laughter, of course. I heard Mark grumbling behind us, and my dad looked like he liked April much more than he liked me at that moment.

"Why thank you. That must be because Hallie here isn't much older than you," Dad said, as his eyes slid to Daniel.

Not much older than an eight-year-old?

"Oh, burn!" Abby whispered somewhere to my left.

"Excuse me?" I protested.

"Not that long ago you were that little," the man who raised me insisted, pointing at April.

I scoffed. Rose asked; "How old are you, Hallie?"

"I'm twenty-two."

Mark whistled and then coughed. Dad arched an eyebrow at me like he made his point. And Abby commented, "Damn, this is better than daytime television."

"Thank you, Abby," Daniel cut in.

I wanted to say something more, but I really didn't want to talk about my age. Instead, I cleared my throat, "This is April and Rose, Dad," I introduced. "Daniel's nieces." Dad took both of their hands in his like they were important business partners. "And this is Abby, the girls' mother." I turned a little to the side to let Abby come to us. "And Mark, Daniel's brother."

Dad shook hands with them both, but then turned to April. "You're right, your daddy definitely looks older than me."

April giggled and Mark groaned as Abby patted his chest. "I love your dad-bod, honey."

Dad seemed satisfied with the mess he was causing. He was just forty-five, and by looking at him, no one would have guessed he had a grown daughter.

April tugged my sleeve to show the line progressed a little. I followed her as Mark asked, "You own the hardware store, am I right, Preston?"

Dad nodded. "I never saw you around, and I can't seem to get rid of your brother."

"We don't live in Bluehaven," Abby replied. "Just here to visit Dan."

"Even if you did," Daniel mocked, "Mark is shit with repairs. You wouldn't catch him dead in a hardware store."

"Excuse me?" Mark protested. "I know my way around, you know..."

"Tools?" They all laughed, but in my defense, he seemed to forget the word *tool*.

"Are you good at fixing things?" Dad asked Abby.

She shrugged. "I'm better than him. But we are all very grateful when Dan comes to stay with us."

Mark tried to defend himself just to have Abby tell everyone a story involving him and a leaking faucet. The faucet won.

"I was going to go for a ride with them," I jerked my thumb toward the Ferris Wheel. "But I can do something with you after?" I'd have gone with Dad first, but I didn't want to disappoint the girls.

"No, no, bug. You have fun. I'll move along and see if Marian can feed me."

I smiled. Of course, even at a Carnival, Dad wouldn't just eat anything. He was a creature of habit, and he loved the things he loved. With a last kiss on my temple, he said goodbye to the rest of the crew, leaving us just one couple away from our turn.

"What's up, Cricket? Are you afraid of heights?" Daniel taunted, taking me away from my thoughts to fix it all on him once more.

When he smiled, the corner of his eyes wrinkled in the most handsome way. His body was so big, I wondered if I could fit perfectly just under his chin. I stepped closer, craving Daniel all of a sudden. Maybe it was Daniel's family who was so easy to get along with, or how happy I was because people liked my costumes. Whatever it was, when I breathed in and out, I wanted to wrap my arms around him.

"You look worried," he observed, serious once more.

"I'm not." And I laid a hand over his heart.

I never touched him before. His warm body burned through the clothes, and I looked at his chest, fascinated by how it felt under my fingertips. Deciding it wasn't enough, I stepped closer again, and as if we did it one hundred times before, he enveloped my body in a hug.

I inhaled deeply his warm scent, that was all wood and male. He rested his cheek on top of my head, and I wrapped my arm around his waist.

My heart thumped as he lazily stroked my spine up and down. Up and down. It was the best hug of my life.

"Do you have a death wish, Dan?" Mark asked behind us.

I tried to move my head, but Daniel kept me in place. "Shut up, Mark."

"He's going to kill him, Abs," Mark told his wife, and then louder again. "He's going to kill you."

"Who's going to kill Uncle Dan?" April wanted to know.

"Hallie's daddy, of course."

"Is that true?" she asked me, and this time Daniel let me move away from his body to answer his niece.

I chewed the side of my cheek. "Maybe."

THE LITTLE GATE OPENED as soon as the Ferris Wheel stopped, and two people left the cart. I sat quickly on the further side instead of being the one who decided which child was going to follow me first. I was sure Abby would come with a solution.

I slid in, immediately looking up, my gaze following the highest point of the Ferris Wheel, where we were going to be soon. I gulped. I was asked twice if I was afraid of heights and until now, I was pretty sure the answer was no.

A warm body slid in a second later, taking me away from my newest fear. I turned, surprised by the size of my companion, definitely not a small child judging by the strong, warm thigh plastered to mine.

My eyes followed the denim-clad legs up to the thick plait shirt to finally meet Daniel's gaze as the Ferris Wheel jolted into move.

"Did you steal a child's turn?" I asked, looking behind him to find the family still in line.

He smirked. "Abby thinks is better this way. Less fighting. You don't mind, do you?"

"I guess I will survive your company." I grinned right when we halted at a stop and swung just enough for my lips to melt into a cringe.

"Are you *really* scared of heights?" He sounded worried.

I squeezed my eyes shut. "It might be my new thing." He chuckled, and I peeled my eyes open when the Ferris Wheel started to move once more. "Distract me, Dan."

"I love when you call me Dan."

His boyish smile made my stomach flutter. His gaze was intense and attentive. His arm brushed on mine, the muscles straining the fabric of his shirt. I bit back a pathetic sigh. The Ferris Wheel stopped once again, and I closed my eyes out of instinct.

"So tell me, Cricket. How do you think your dad is going to kill me?"

"He will not kill you." I told him, opening one eye.

"Shot? Boulder?"

My close my mouth in a line. "He's not going to kill you."

"Do you think so?"

I lifted a shoulder and made a noise that wasn't really a reply, so he bumped his shoulder into mine. More like his upper arm to my shoulder because of our height difference. "Cricket?"

"I never had friends," I croaked out. "Probably I had friends when I was little, but I don't remember them. Dad never had to deal with sleepovers and people around me."

"I see."

I licked my lips. "It was always me and Dad. He doesn't even have close friends or anything. He's nice to everyone but..."

"He keeps his distance."

I nodded. Telling him this made me think how lonely Dad really was. I felt bad not to realize sooner, to push him to get out more and look for companionship.

"Do you think that's the reason your dad was acting like that with me?"

I stopped my rapid thoughts, focusing on what he was saying. "I don't think he knows what to do with people in my life. He never saw me loosen up and..."

"So this is you loosening up?" he teased.

"Oh, that's me going crazy."

"Hallie's gone wild?" I heard the laugh in his voice.

"Of course."

I glanced down just once and regretted it straight away. We weren't all the way to the top yet, but it was still a long way down to the ground.

"How the hell did people miss out on you?"

Laughing, I rolled my eyes. But when I faced Daniel, I saw how serious he was.

"Don't be silly." I shook my head.

"I just don't get it." His intense gaze pinned me in place, "How stupid are they?"

I chuckled at him being goofy. There was nothing special about me, nothing bad, but it wasn't like my friendship was a big deal. But before I could tell him so, he read my mind and was already shaking his head.

"It seems like I'm your only friend, so I'm telling you, Cricket, they are missing out."

"Thank you," I accepted and turned to look at the view because his intensity was raising goosebumps all over my skin. Bluehaven's white sand was barely visible in the night. Still, I got a glimpse of the beach, the immense ocean, and the crashing waves.

"Can I get one truth?" He asked, making me look away from the view.

"I always tell you the truth."

He smiled, satisfied by my reply. His eyes flickered from me to the ocean as he breathed in. "You're like the sea. When the tide is far away and you barely can reach the waters." His eyes focused on me again. "That's how you usually are. And don't get me wrong, I like that you are your own person. I love that you're full of thorns, Hallie. But sometimes..." his mouth opened in a devastating smile.

Sometimes the tide rose. I understood him without the words. Sometimes I let him come close and those were the best moments.

"Are you asking for one of those rare moments?"

His eyes on me, he licked his bottom lip. I'd never been so aware of someone. His scent was strong and powerful, so Dan. His leg searing hot under the rough denim, scratching my naked legs. He was taller than me, stronger than me, older than me. And at times, it felt like we were one.

Daniel read my mind flawlessly, always had. And suddenly, I wanted the tide to come in too. I wanted to give him everything. All the truths, all my fears, all my reasons and all my firsts. I wanted him to have me in the palm of his hand.

So I gave him the most vulnerable part of me.

"In my senior year, I started swimming. I know the swim team is a huge thing in Bluehaven, but definitely wasn't for me. But I needed the credits..." And I loved swimming even though I wouldn't dare to return to the beach. I always liked the water, and I thought, why not? It would help me.

"Ok..." he said, just to acknowledge what I was saying.

"There was this girl. She..." I wasn't even sure how I could start to explain her. "She didn't like me." I chuckled miserably after the biggest euphemism of the century. "She picked on me a lot. I always avoided being around her, you know." I felt my neck getting hot. I didn't want Daniel to know I left extra curricular classes when she asked, that I made myself smaller than possible because I couldn't deal with her cruel words. "But this time I needed to stay, and I thought I could handle it. I was so close to graduating; I was going to leave Bluehaven for good."

The irony. My eyes flickered to the town spreading underneath us. I would never escape Bluehaven. It followed me in my memories, every Christmas and every time I had to walk down Main Street. I didn't get stronger as I left, I just became haunted.

"I thought I could handle it." I turned away from Bluehaven to the warm eyes of the only person I trusted besides Dad, Marian, and Torres.

Daniel wasn't just my only friend. He was the first one to know the new version of me. The scared, trembling Hallie who ran away in fear was long gone. I was quiet and shy now, but it took years for me not to be afraid.

"You don't need to share if you don't want," he said in the gentlest voice.

If I wasn't going to talk to him, then who? I shook my head, determined. "One day after a class, I waited until the changing room was empty so I could have a shower in peace. And I did." I gulped. A prickling sensation went down my spine, it brought me right back to that day. That stupid day when I let my guard down. I always just threw a t-shirt on and left with my bathing suit still wet underneath. But that day I thought I was being silly, that day I believed I was being overcautious. "They caught me after my shower."

"They?" I heard the edge in his voice.

"She got everyone together, and they waited for me." I drew a calming breath. "I'm going to say it all at once and matter-of-factly because I think that's the only way I can talk about it. Is that ok?"

"Of course." He rasped.

"They took my towel. They made fun of me like they always did. But it was so much worse, because I was naked and..." I stopped again, breathing in and out. "She had a Polaroid. It took me long to realize I was trying to hide and there were at least ten of them. And a couple of guys."

Daniel froze beside me. I kept going or I would've stopped completely.

"They took the Polaroid pictures and passed them along. They wrote what I needed to change, and..."

They laughed and joked, then they left for college and moved on with their lives. I was the one who carried the scars. I remembered everything that was said about my body. I heard it every time I was standing alone in front of a mirror. I knew how stupid, cruel they all were. I refused to be guided by their mistake. But I couldn't forget. It ran through my mind more times than I should've let it. Dad wanted the reason I came back to Bluehaven?

It wasn't because of the expensive rent back in the city.

It wasn't because I had no friends and was alone beside by Ms. Handall.

It was because their voices still followed me and I needed them to stop. I came back to the Hellmouth because hiding wasn't an option.

"Hallie..." his tone was so different from the one I grew used to. "What happened with the pictures?"

"They had it. When I got my clothes back, I just wanted to leave. I didn't think..."

"I know," he agreed. But I still felt stupid for not staying and demanding the pictures.

"What happened?"

"I don't know." I shook my head. "But I was called to the principal's office a week after and he insinuated he had them."

Daniel growled. I ignored it. "He asked if I was giving them to..." I sighed. "If I was sharing them with the boys."

"He asked what?!" And this time he let it go. The cart swung with the force of his reaction, and I placed my hand on top of his leg.

"I'm done with it."

"I'm starting!"

"Dan..." I shook my head.

"Hallie..." my name on his lips was a plea.

"Do you want me to keep talking?"

He nodded stiffly.

"I just wanted to go. They always told me how much better things would be once I got into college..."

"Who are they?"

I lifted a shoulder. "The teachers."

"So after all of this..."

"Principal Anderson somewhat believed I wasn't passing naked pictures around." And I almost laughed at the possibility. "And then I left."

Silence. The Ferris Wheel kept going, Bluehaven in its most beautiful picture mocking me.

"What did Anderson do after..."

"I hope he didn't keep the pictures." It was a joke but by the way Daniel tensed, it wasn't very funny to him. "I left school. He said it was better to leave it as it was and... I agreed. I just wanted to go."

"So Preston doesn't know?"

"No, he doesn't." I drew a breath. "I hope you keep this between us. I have no idea who saw the pictures and who shared, but... It never got into Dad's ears. And I don't want him to hate everyone."

"Like you do." His hands closed in a fist, his body vibrated with rage.

"I'm sorry. I wished I was stronger at the time. I wished I planned revenge or something cool. I don't know." I scratched my nose. "I'm sorry."

Daniel let out a raggedy breath. His arm curved on my back and in the next second, my head was on his chest, his arms warm around me.

"You're killing me, Cricket."

"Please don't die."

He huffed a laugh. I stayed in his arms, no more words to be shared. I felt raw and exposed, but light and warm. I hated remembering. I couldn't do it without wishing I did something different. That I was braver and demanded the principal to call their families. Or if I was stronger and fought them more for my clothes. It was the what ifs that killed me.

But Daniel never asked me if I fought them enough, and for that I was grateful. I watched the Ferris Wheel move, happy it was Daniel by my side. When it started to halt because people were coming off once again, Daniel brushed my hair off my face and tipped my chin up.

"Why did you agree with Anderson to bury this?"

I winced and put a little distance between us, but Dan captured my hand, not letting me move. "I'm not judging. If it's because you just wanted the pictures to disappear and you didn't want to talk about it, or if it was because you were protecting Preston, it's all valid. You had your reasons and I respect that. I just want to know them."

I nodded. He was so good, of course he wasn't judging me. "All of those reasons. I wanted to forget the second it was happening."

We were almost on the ground again, sobering me up. The quiet Hallie wanted to come out, but I enjoyed being honest with Daniel, so I told him. "But also because I knew nothing was going to happen with a Campbell."

Daniel frowned. "What? Delilah?"

I shook my head. "Her older sister. Katie Campbell. She was the one with the Polaroid."

Daniel paled. His forehead creased with a frown, his body froze in shock. I grimaced. "I know I told you I don't know why the Campbells hate me and it's true. I never knew why Katie hated me and I have no idea why Sharon and Delilah do. Maybe they also believe I passed around my pictures? But that's my best guess. Katie probably told a lie to cover her ass." I bit my lip, trying to get it out of me before we hit the ground. "I'm sorry I lied to you."

It took him a second to react. It was like the lights went out on him and he needed to shake himself off. "You didn't lie," he grunted out. I wasn't sure about his reaction. The cart stopped at the exit, and Daniel raised the metal bar straight away, unfolding his big body in a second.

I was still wary as he led me out. Suddenly, Daniel turned, taking my face between his rough palms. "You did nothing wrong, ok?" I nodded as much as I could with him holding my head. "I just want you to know that. Everyone failed you. Everyone."

"Not you." It came as the biggest truth of my life. Daniel Miller would never fail me. He took a deep breath, and then rested his forehead on mine, mingling with our breaths. Our noses brushed. His hands fell from my face to my neck. And he called my name like a tortured man, "Hallie..."

"Uncle Dan!" called a little, a voice tearing us apart.

We turned to April, jumping our way, with Abby, Mark, and Rose following. And I smiled, ready to hear all that the little girl thought about the ride. Daniel crouched down and raised her in his arms. Rose took my hand in hers and we went to the next ride.

14.

ALL I WANTED WAS Bluehaven to burn.

I rubbed my face, my own skin feeling too tight over my bones.

Katie Campbell.

Rage coursed through my veins, but I had to keep myself in check since I had to be on my best behavior to bring the kids to the camp. My eyes traced the school parking lot in search of the usual cars. But it was too early. There were no teachers around or students but the ones heading to Spring's Harbor. My rational side thought it was better this way. The other part of me?

I wanted nothing but to meet Anderson face to face. I wanted to tear him apart, limb by limb. I always thought he was an incompetent fuck, far more interested in his own ego than what was best for the kids. But I shouldn't have underestimated him. He could've gone lower. The thought of him holding Hallie's pictures between his stupid clammy fingers... I released a shuddering breath.

I tried to calm down the entire weekend, happy that Mark and Abby stayed for a bit because the girls' presence helped me to relax. But the second I arrived in the parking lot, all reason flew away.

My hands shook the clipboard, ticking names as the students got in the bus, taking the permission slip and keeping them safe. How did Hallie take it? How did she just stand there in all her grace and not succumb to binge murder the entire town?

I couldn't handle a weekend of knowing. I had no idea how she handled it for years. She was resilient, and pride swelled in my heart. My appreciation for her was almost constant as the anger I felt toward Anderson.

I spent so long trying to control myself, I didn't notice the obvious thing we were missing. It was Alan, who played Nick Bottom, who asked first, "Where's Mrs. Carr?"

I opened my mouth and then frowned, checking my watch. We agreed to meet ten minutes before the kids were supposed to arrive, but she never showed up. And then I got busy and enraged and...

I nudged Alan toward the bus as I fished my phone from my front pocket and tried Helen's number. More students arrived. I called Helen with the phone between my ear and shoulder as I ticked names. It rang out twice, and I was officially worried. All students had arrived and were now waiting inside the bus. The bus driver got in, dipping his chin and grumbling "good morning" as he sat behind the wheel. I was trying Helen one last time when a new car arrived.

Not Helen, who I was waiting for. Not Anderson, who I wanted to murder.

But Preston, with Hallie in his passenger's seat. I placed the clipboard on the bus' steps and jogged toward them as Hallie jumped out of the car with agility. She looked frazzled, her pony tail not as perky and her clothes wrinkled.

"I'm so sorry it took me so long to get here. I never packed so fast in my life." She flung open the car's trunk and retrieved a duffle bag.

"Are you coming?" I felt confused and just the right amount of trill.

Four days in a theater camp wasn't exactly what I called fun, but if Hallie was coming, I was going to enjoy it much more. Like he could read my mind, Preston came out of the car and watched me with narrowed eyes.

"How's it going, Preston?" I was determined to kill him with kindness. The man muttered his answer, but it was good enough for me.

"Mrs. Carr didn't call you?" Hallie asked, bringing my attention back to her. I shook my head as I tried to take the duffle bag off her hands, but Preston was quicker and got in my way, taking the bag himself.

"Oscar is in the hospital," Preston explained as he left to bring the duffle to the bus.

Oscar was Helen's husband. I knew little about him, but I knew his health was fragile.

"I wondered why Mrs. Carr was so distracted the other day." Hallie brushed her hair out of her face adorably. She turned and went for the trunk again, taking a much bigger suitcase out of it. I helped her set it on the ground without damaging Preston's car. "She called me this morning in a rush. I'd assume she called you first."

"I was calling her just now. Do you know if it is serious?"

Hallie shook her head. Poor Helen, she was probably overwhelmed and still had time to check if Hallie could take her place.

"I'm coming instead of her if that's ok."

"I think I'll survive." I smiled.

She rolled her eyes, tucking a strand of hair behind her ear as she followed me to the bus. "Two bags?"

"One of them is for my supplies. I can't afford to stop working on the costumes right now. I'm making horns and wings this week. I brought whatever was small enough to fit into one bag." She winced. "Sorry again for being late."

"Don't worry, Cricket. I'm glad you could get all your things in order."

I forgot for a second her dad was in earshot. Preston held his arms crossed over his chest, watching us intently. I remembered what Hallie told me about how lonely she and Preston had been. I tried to be sympathetic to the man. It wasn't just the fact I was clearly salivating over his daughter, but there were much more things to consider. Like I was older and Hallie was fragile.

Well, she *looked* fragile, but I knew better now to let her appearance deceive me.

I opened the bus's luggage compartment, and we tossed her bags in. I turned to tell Hallie she could get inside when I caught her looking up to the windows. Most of the students were fast asleep already, their heads resting on the glass. But a few faces watched us. My gaze zeroed in on Delilah Campbell straight away.

The rage came back.

All the soothing Hallie's presence was able to do was gone in a flash when I remembered the name Campbell.

"Are you ok?" Hallie asked beside me.

I gave her a stiff nod. I wasn't sure if I was ever going to be ok, but if she could do it, so could I.

"Bug, you call if you need a ride back, all right?" Preston interrupted my thoughts. His daughter nodded, and I left them talking between themselves as I knocked on the side of the bus to get the driver's attention.

"Ready to go, chief?" he asked, putting his phone away.

"Yeah, in a minute. Thanks."

"No problem," he said as he turned on the engine to heat a little.

I grabbed the clipboard I left by the steps and went back to Hallie's side. She was watching her dad's car disappear, holding herself with arms around her stomach. I came close, taking a rogue strand of hair between my fingers and brushing out of her face. "Will you survive four days of teenagers?"

She snorted. "I survived much longer than that."

I tried not to show my anger. I didn't want her to feel like she needed to comfort me. She had confided in me and I should've been the one holding her hand, not the other way around.

"So you're excited as me?" I joked.

She faced me, a little smile on her lips. "Yes."

Her voice was melodic, she sounded so happy and content. I had to leave my anger behind. She wasn't dwelling on the past anymore, so maybe killing Anderson wasn't the answer. I moved my hand to the small of her back, guiding her to the bus.

"Delos Santos?"

"Oh..." Hallie stopped in her tracks, faltering on the bus's step. "Hi, Ryan," she greeted the driver.

Her body tensed, her fingers trembled. I traced her face for an explanation, but she ignored me, her gaze pinned on the driver, Ryan.

"You teach?" I hated the way he looked Hallie up and down.

My possessive hand on her back spread even more, like I could protect her somehow. I hated her reaction to whoever he was. She recoiled like that first day when she had to walk the halls of Bluehaven High.

If I knew how hard it was for her, I'd have carried her in my arms.

I didn't give her time to explain herself to him. I didn't want her to ever talk to someone she didn't feel comfortable with. My irrational side won, and I cut in. "Let's go?"

Hallie looked up at me. I was happy to notice her eyes softened, and she bobbed her head up and down quickly. "Good to see you, Ryan," she said as she slipped out, but I couldn't help but notice how robotic she moved.

Ryan's eyes followed her ass. I growled. "Eyes on the fucking road."

I was barely over the weird interaction between Hallie and our bus driver when a voice rose in the middle of the students. "Where's Mrs. Carr? Why is *she* here?"

Delilah, of course. I wanted to bark that she didn't have the right to talk to Hallie, to breathe the same air as my quiet girl, but I had to refrain. I was feeling overprotective, but I needed to remember I was a teacher and my job was to protect the students, not yell at them. There was also the possibility Delilah knew nothing about her sister's mess. Like Hallie said, Katie probably lied to cover her ass.

Katie Campbell.

I had to pause and regroup every time I thought of the name. It made me sick, disgust curling in the pit of my stomach, my hands closing in a fist. And how I was supposed to remain calm when every time I looked at Delilah's face, the only thing I saw was her sister?

I bit back my anger. "*She* is here in a teaching capacity and disrespect toward her can land a detention, Ms. Campbell, so I would tread lightly."

My eyes scanned the bus to check if they all understood me clearly. By my side, Hallie was frozen in the spot. Her spine was rigid, her hand clutched to the seat by our side.

"Mrs. Carr had a personal issue, and we had to ask Ms. Delos Santos to take her place," I told them loud enough to wake up the sleeping ones. "Goes without saying that even though Ms. Delos Santos isn't a teacher, she's being respected as such. She's involved with the play, so whoever is caught being disrespectful will face detention, but I'd say she can apply her own version of punishment with your costumes. That goes for your low hanging pants, Morales," I said to the kid playing the carpenter.

People laughed, and I relaxed a little. They quickly lost interest in us, turning between them to talk or going back to their naps. The bus pressed forward, jolting in movement. I grabbed Hallie's waist to help her stand, ignoring the glances in our way. I nodded to the seat to our left, and Hallie sat down by the window.

It was only eight in the morning, and I was already exhausted. I'd planned on skating by this week. I was there just to be responsible for the boys' bunk, probably preventing one or two teen pregnancies. But without Helen, I was the teacher in charge. For the first time since Hallie came to the parking lot telling me the news, I realized I was going to be the one responsible for the rehearsals.

Shit.

I groaned, rubbing my hands on my face.

"What's wrong?" her voice sliced through my thoughts.

"Thinking about how much work I'll have."

"I'm sorry. I can help."

"Oh, you will."

She giggled and all the heaviness of my chest left with the simple sound of her laugh. "Are you ready for this?" I teased.

"God no." She shook her head. "I don't even know what I packed, Dan." She paused, chewing her bottom lip. "What if my clothes make no sense?"

I couldn't stop myself from laughing. "Do you have something tragic in your wardrobe, Cricket?"

She wrinkled her nose like the cutest thing she was. "Things are a little messy since I've moved back home. I left a bunch of clothes when I moved out and Dad kept them. So now it's a mess. My teenage years might come out this week."

"It was only five years ago. I don't think the fashion changed that much."

She swatted me on my arm, a smile tugged her lips. "Don't start with the age thing."

"I never started with the age thing." I shrugged, pretending I wasn't bothered. "I prefer to forget I'm ancient."

"You're not." She rolled her eyes, resting her temple on the headrest so she could face me. "Maybe I'm the one too young."

"We can meet in the middle. What's the age between ours? Thirty?"

She nodded. "But if I was thirty, I hoped to be a little more put together."

"Like what?" I pried.

Hallie sighed. "I'd like to know who I am. And I want to figure out this whole career thing, because going to college wasn't enough to get things going. And I don't know... I'd imagine thirty-year-old Hallie to be secure and... an adult. You know?"

"God, Cricket, I have bad news for you." I smirked.

She groaned. "You're going to tell me being thirty won't guarantee any of those things, right?"

I shook my head. "I'm sorry."

"You suck." She pouted.

I wanted to taste that pouty mouth of hers. "You can work toward those things regardless of your age. You can learn about yourself today. You don't need to wait."

Hallie thought about it, brushing her hair away from her face, and got just a little annoyed when it returned a second later. Blowing a raspberry, she pulled the hair tie, letting her hair fall over her shoulder. I watched, transfixed, as she gathered all her hair once more, putting it together in a neat ponytail. I could watch her doing that forever, I decided.

"That's what I'm trying to do," she told me.

"What?" I asked, pretending I wasn't hypnotized by her hair.

"I'm trying to understand myself and fix the things I don't like."

"I can't think of a single thing about you that needs fixing." True. It was the rest of the town who needed ass kicking.

"I let many people get away with many things, Dan. I just let them take things from me. One by one, it slipped through my fingers. I let them mistake my quietness for weakness."

"That's on them," I told her at once. "It says much more about them than about you."

She lifted a shoulder. "I know. But I let them." I could see her lost in thought, trying to explain something I wasn't getting. I wouldn't have gotten it, anyway. I would not have sat there and agreed that what happened to her was partially her fault.

"One day I'll know how to act," she was saying.

"How do you want to act with the people who did it? If you ever saw them again?"

My questions were somewhat innocent. I wanted to know where her head was, but I also wanted to know if she saw any of them in town yet. She was very careful not giving me any names, and I suspected it was because she knew how violent I'd feel. I couldn't protect someone from their own past, but I felt like trying.

Maybe if I wasn't watching her reaction so carefully, I would've missed the signs. The unsure way she licked her lips while twisting her hands over her lap. The tiniest way her breath caught and the flicker of her gaze from me to the bus driver.

The fucking bus driver.

My body realized what it meant before my brain was completely on board. My fist closed, my spine erected. Hallie's hand covered mine before I said anything.

"Don't," she whispered.

Her eyes pinned me, a fierce expression on her face as someone who just gave an order.

"Hallie..." my voice wavered, even I couldn't trust what I was going to do.

"You asked me how I wanted to deal. It's my choice, isn't it?"

"And you told him it was nice to see him?" I growled.

Hallie's mouth closed in a line. "The way I deal with my ghosts is not of your concern."

She was angry. Good. I was furious too.

"How about asking him to stop on the side of the road and leave him there? How about you give me two minutes alone with him? I just need two minutes."

She rolled her eyes, not taking me seriously. "Stop. And what? Walk to the camp?"

"I can drive." I tipped my nose high.

"Can you?" she arched an eyebrow.

"No." I didn't have a fucking license to drive a bus, but technicalities were the last thing I had in mind.

She kept watching me, and the realization I couldn't do anything washed over me. I hated it.

Hated it.

"Did he see your pictures?" I strangled out because I wanted to torture myself.

She took a second to reply. Watching me with those intense dark eyes like I couldn't be trusted. Good, I couldn't. I was a second away from ripping another man's throat. That couldn't be normal.

"He was there," she whispered.

That... That destroyed me.

He was there.

He laughed while she was what? Being assaulted. Yes. He stood there and laughed while she was being humiliated and assaulted. He pointed and laughed and he probably shared her pictures with his friends. My eyes were frozen on Hallie as my whole body shook with rage. I couldn't breathe, I couldn't move.

I wanted to do something.

Yes, I wanted to take this Ryan guy and teach him a lesson, but more than that, I wanted to go back to the past and punish them all. I wanted to be there when she needed me the most. I wanted a time machine to bring me to that moment so I could run the halls and save her. She proved again and again she was strong enough to deal with it. But I sure wasn't.

"Dan. Dan. Come back to me," her voice called.

She was right. I was long gone. Angry, disappointed, appalled. I was going to wait until we arrived at the camp and then get him before he returned to Bluehaven. Yeah, I was going to let the kids get in the camp and leave Hallie to get on with that and then...

Well, I actually had the camp forms with me. And Hallie would hate to be the one to bring them in. Until this morning, she had no idea she was going somewhere. Plus, if anyone saw me destroying our own bus driver's face, they would think I was violent and probably not want me to stay in a camp with a bunch of kids.

That wasn't going to work. Ok, fine. He was the driver, and I knew his first name. It wasn't going to be hard to search for him, right? Yeah. It was Bluehaven, after all. I was going to find where Ryan lived and hopefully after an incentive, he'll give me the name of his other buddy who was there and--

"Dan." Her warm palm touched my face. "Look at me."

My eyes found hers, melting a little of the icy rage I felt inside.

"Look at me," she said again. "It's over."

I opened my mouth to disagree, but she shook her head and said it again. "They didn't break me."

My heart racing, every breath hurt. It wasn't fair that I got so worked up about it, and now she had to calm me down. I should be there for her and not the other way around, but I was blinded by my anger. I trembled beneath her palm.

"Don't let them take a piece of you. It's not worth it."

I wanted to argue, but before I could, her lips were on mine.

15.

I REMEMBER RYAN'S EYES on me.

I remember the way he watched me when Katie took my towel and laughed at my helplessness. He snickered behind his hand while nudging Jack Williams. And even though they mocked, I remember the feeling of his eyes on me, devouring every inch of my skin. It took me months until I could see myself naked and not trigger flashbacks.

Sometimes I cried without noticing, tears running free down my face. I felt small and trapped. I couldn't ever trust anyone.

My mind was filled with questions. What kind of person planned something like that? Who sat around, texted the details, thought about it and gathered the people? They walked down Main Street every single day. They ate at Torres' and went to Dad's store. They were out there lurking, and the thought alone was terrifying.

But one day, I stopped crying in the shower. One day, I stopped looking behind my back. And because of those days, I thought, one day I'd see them face to face and not cower.

Life is hardly the way we imagine. I didn't confront Ryan when I saw him, but I said it was nice to see him. Daniel could think whatever he wanted, but that was *my* victory.

I looked at Ryan's face, and I did not fall apart.

That meant something. And that impossible man, Daniel Miller, got so angry on my behalf. So ready to take my sorrows for himself.

My past finally caught up with me, and all I wanted was to leave it behind.

So I took Dan's face in my hands. The scratch of his beard in my palm, the warmth of his breath over my cheeks. The kiss was chaste at first, his firm mouth on mine. My hands slipped from his cheeks to his neck. He brought me closer, his rough palms skating from my hand and up my arm. Tipping my head back for a new angle, I licked his lips lightly and trembled with the fierceness of his groan.

"Be quiet. There are teenagers everywhere," I whispered.

I felt his smirk on my lips. "Let's see how much we can get away with, Cricket."

I tasted his mouth. Goosebumps rose as his hands found my leg and hip, bringing me closer to him. He tasted like toothpaste and something warm, his tongue dominating mine in the most delicious and intense kiss of my life. And it was on a school bus, with a bunch of half-sleeping teenagers.

I bit down on his bottom lip. He growled, sounding unhinged.

"You are going to wake them up," I taunted.

Instead of replying, his hand took the back of my neck, tilting my head to the side, taking my lips like a starved man. And I lost myself once more. Everything was Daniel. All my thoughts, my body and the present.

I was too far gone, but I didn't find it in me to care.

I nipped his lip once more. His hand held my head in place as we opened our eyes to each other. "I'm too hard to be allowed on a school bus."

I widened my eyes, afraid to look down at his crotch, but then suddenly, laughter bubbled off me. I laughed, and he followed my lead, my head sagging as he took me and cradled me to his chest. I heard his heartbeat while we chuckled.

"Of all the places... Here is where you decide to kiss me?" He asked.

I shrugged. "You seemed like you needed an anchor," I explained no further, afraid to say something else and make him remember the whole ordeal again.

He drew a breath. "You're incredible."

I rolled my eyes, even though he couldn't see it because my face was still on his chest. But as usual, he knew me enough. His finger reached down my chin and he tipped my head up, nudging my nose with his.

"Do you have any idea how lost I've been? How much I needed... an anchor?"

I frowned, my hand touching his jaw. I didn't know he was unhappy.

"And you just needed to exist," he kept saying. "And I'm full of life again."

I held my breath, afraid if I moved I was going to start crying or something just as embarrassing. Was it bad that I liked he was lost too? It made me feel less broken. It made me wish we could heal together. I threw my arms around his neck, hugging him for dear life and hoping he could understand all the words I wasn't saying.

And my bubble of happiness was destroyed a second later, when I opened my eyes and caught Ryan watching us through the rear-view mirror.

"Welcome to Camp Nightfall! I'm Pandora, your guide and teacher."

A round of applause, some more enthusiastically than others. But I was pretty impressed by Pandora. Wasn't Pandora a drag queen's name? Jewelry brand? Or that girl with the box? Either way, the Pandora in front of me carried the name flawlessly. She looked impossibly ethereal and magical, with a chain of daisies on top of her curly blond hair and a long lacy dress. Her voice had an actor's quality to it. She enunciated each syllable. It reached all sides of the food hall.

Five schools were selected to be part of the camp, which meant around seventy people—kids and staff—listened carefully to Pandora's words. In the four days we were staying at Camp Nightfall, the schedule was handled religiously. Dan handed me a calendar with breakfast, lunch and dinner times, plus the exclusive time on the main stage being coached by Pandora herself.

Apart from that, the kitchen was opened for snacks throughout the day, and the teachers were required to rehearse separately with their school to work on Pandora's feedback.

A couple of hours a day was left for leisure, which meant, of course, to bring them to one of many hot springs since the kids weren't allowed to go without adult supervision.

It was only four days, but I had ten pages of instructions in my hands.

Ten pages with times of meals, instructions to the cabins and the hot springs, the name of the other teachers working with Pandora and the name of the schools and the number of each teacher responsible.

It was a lot.

I wasn't adult enough to supervise teenagers in a hot spring. I doubted anyone was. And my suspicions showed correctly when I looked to my side at Daniel and saw the grimace on his face.

"We'll call Helen and have a talk about the program," Daniel whispered to me.

I nodded numbly. Pandora kept talking about the rules and what was expected from the groups. I hoped a few kids were interested in theater because it was a once in a lifetime opportunity. Pandora talked about stage coordinators, voice coaches and everything they could imagine.

After her speech, she wished them all to break a leg. Everyone clapped again, and we were dismissed from the food hall. Dan jumped into action, passing along the camp's map to all our kids.

"Girls with Ms. Delos Santos in cabin seven, boys with me in cabin five." Everyone shuffled to stand up and follow each of us. "Meet you back here in thirty for breakfast, Hallie?"

I bobbed my head, feeling just a little overwhelmed. As the girls waited for me to move, I took it as a sign and led the way, only checking the map once until I found cabin seven.

Our luggage waited in front of the door with a huge padlock. I unlocked the door with the key that came with my welcome pack and let the girls go in first. It was only later when I thought maybe I should be the one to go first to check if it was safe of bears or axe murders.

The room had a single bed to the side and four bunk beds, the perfect size for us. We had seven girls, four from the main cast; Carmen who played Titania, Anna as Hyppolita, Nova as Helena and Delilah as Hermia. The other three played Titania's fairies. They all decided between them for the bunk beds, so I took the single bed and dragged my two huge bags with me.

I took the biggest suitcase, the one I dumped all my craft supplies in, and decided to sort through that first. Opening the zipper with care while the suitcase laid on my bed, I took one thing after the order, trying to find calm in the chaos. When an annoying piece of wire refused to come out without spilling most of the bag's contents, someone called my name.

"Ms. Delos Santos? Do you want help?" Nova's eyes darted from me to the mess in my bag.

"I put it all in a rush when Mrs. Carr called this morning," I explained, tugging the wire. "It's all tangled now."

"My mom has a trick to unravel Christmas lights..." Carmen interrupted from the other side of the cabin.

She reached for my suitcase and started the wire with one hand, using the other to block the stuff tangled. Nova and I worked on her instructions, pushing, pulling, and unraveling. Titania's flowers, the leaves for Hermia's and Helena's dresses, it all fell on top of my bed and floor, and I tried my best not to cringe because the girls were trying to help.

We freed the wire, and I worked on a bundle in my hands so it wouldn't be a problem anymore. Nova caught one of the flowers between her fingers and looked closely.

"What's the flowers for?"

"That's for Titania's dress." I smiled a little, remembering it was Daniel who helped me burn the edges.

Carmen reached for the flowers. "That's so beautiful, Ms. Delos Santos!"

"Hallie, please." I couldn't deal with people calling me Ms. Delos Santos. I was literally five years older than them.

"What's this for?" Nova was a curious one. I usually tried my best to escape talking with people, but I loved talking about costumes.

"That's the material for Puck's horns." I looped the material to give the shape of a horn. "I think it will look good for Oberon as well."

One by one, they all approached, asking what my plans were for each character, demanding to see my drawings and gasping in awe when I showed them. Titania's fairies, played by Olivia, Emma and Sophia, couldn't handle themselves when I showed them the soft material I was going to use for their wings.

Glitter, glue, wire and ingenuity. I loved that part of the creation and it warmed my heart they liked it too. By the time we had to go to breakfast, all of them were sitting around me, and the only one unpacking was Delilah.

"Helen... hm... can you be more specific than that?"

I bit my lips into my mouth, trying to hold myself not to burst into a laugh. Our time with Pandora wasn't until the end of the afternoon. The kids were nervous and jumpy after breakfast when Dan guided us all to the second theater between cabins one and three. It was pretty much a reformed barn, but perfect for rehearsal.

But Daniel and I understood very little of what was needed for a rehearsal.

After breakfast, I went back to the cabin just to get a few things to trace Puck's horns while the kids practiced, but now I felt guilty because I needed to be a bigger participant in all this. Daniel called Mrs. Carr for advice, but whatever she was saying had him rubbing his own face so hard I would think he was trying to peel the skin off.

"I understand..." he said over the phone while all the kids and I watched him like hawks. "That's a feeling though, not a direction so you see..." a little pause and he nodded, squeezing his eyes tight. "Ok, thank you Helen. You give Oscar my best."

Knowing well that the phone call did not help in the slightest, I left my materials at the table by the side and joined him at the front.

It turned out Nova took pity on him, too.

"Mr. Miller?" she asked tentatively.

"Yes?"

She flicked through the pages of a worn script. "We were having problems with Act 3. Maybe we should go from there so you can have a look?"

Daniel's shoulders sagged in relief. "That sounds great, Nova, thanks."

She nodded, but besides Nova, Carmen was the only one getting into position, taking the script in her hands. The rest of the kids remained unblinking, waiting for Daniel's next instruction.

I cleared my throat, and he looked at me straight away. I arched an eyebrow, nodding to the kids waiting. That was enough to spring him to life.

"Yes, of course. Let's start with Scene 1, Act 3. Er... From the top?"

I held myself not to laugh. He was really trying. I circled around the chairs and sat beside Daniel just in time for Nova to hand us scripts. She was definitely way more prepared than we were.

"Are we all met?" the kids started.

It took me a second to watch them and understand what the problem was. Since it was decided to have them in the competition, the rehearsals became about knowing the lines by heart. It was a mechanical work for a while. I remembered that made Mrs. Carr very unhappy.

The people who started the act set a pace, but Act 3 specifically was led by the people with the least lines, which meant they spent less time with the group.

Of awkwardness, I knew a lot, and that was the problem. Their lines were delivered with an apology. They barely trusted the words coming out of their mouths. Eventually, the scenes picked up pace, when Carmen arrived, but was still wooden.

They finished the act and Daniel looked utterly lost.

"How about you guys go for a drink of water or..." I shrugged, not used to addressing a room full of people. "While Daniel and I have a talk?"

Everyone nodded, their faces sad and downcast. I felt bad. They couldn't come all the way from Bluehaven to suck. We needed to do more for them, like Mrs. Carr would do. But copying her ways wasn't going to work. Daniel was a completely different kind of teacher, and for him to be confident to lead, we had to find his way.

"So, you were a jock, right?"

His eyebrows shot up. "Is now the time...?" He trailed off, confused.

I shook my head, raising my hand. "What I mean is, you were on an assembly team before."

Daniel's lips quirked up. "The way you say it sounds like I was a part of *Ocean's Eleven*. But sure, I played ball in school."

I nodded.

"And college."

I winced. I had to keep my prejudices in check. "What's happening is that the main cast got so much work done they can carry a scene. But the rest of them... They need practice. They need to interact with the rest of the team."

Look at me, speaking sports.

"I think for some of them it's still a little awkward to be on stage." I thought out loud. "Like thread going from one texture to the other. The transition needs to be seamless, but right now, most of them barely belong."

"They need to feel like they are part of the team." He repeated, thinking about my advice. "Will we call Helen and..."

"No." I was firm. "I think you should do things your way. We know the problem. We won't be able to do things like Mrs. Carr, because we aren't her. And I could tell the last phone call was a nightmare."

Daniel sagged his head down. "That's an understatement. Helen works on feelings, emotions and whatnots. I wanted directions, and she told me parables of the bible."

"Really?" I scrunched my nose.

He lifted one shoulder up. "She might as well."

"One more reason for you to take the reins. Just get them acting like a team, use an exercise, involve everyone. I don't know. But don't do it Mrs. Carr's way, because I'm sure we will suck at that."

He nodded, looking away as the thoughts formed in his mind, and then turned back to me. "Were you always that smart, Ms. Delos Santos?"

"Yes."

That made him chuckle, and I did too. "After dinner... when they go to bed... Do you want to meet?"

He asked like I was ever going to say no. My body has been buzzing since our kiss. I looked him up in his eyes and nodded. We were lost in each other when a throat cleared, bringing us back to Camp Nightfall. I gulped when I found the kids back, all of them watching us with smirks.

Great.

Just... ugh.

16.

I RUBBED MY MOUTH when I looked out front, determined not to get distracted.

Hallie was wearing one of her denim shorts over a swimsuit. Black and backless. It was tame, sweet and perfect for swimming with teenagers, but my dirty mind was too far gone. Her legs were long and perfectly shaped. Her skin was pale and smooth. I couldn't look in her direction. I simply couldn't.

We brought the kids to the hot springs. I prepared myself for the worse, so I lectured the boys non-stop before we even left the cabin. I told them they weren't allowed to lurk on the girls, to make them uncomfortable or comment on their bodies. I said it so many times, I was pretty sure they were now avoiding all eye-contact.

I didn't think about how Hallie would affect me, though. I brought the boys first, and then a couple of minutes later, the girls came along, guided by Hallie.

My mouth went dry when I saw her. Her hair was piled on top of her head, and all I wanted was to taste her long, graceful neck. The swimsuit had a small dip in the front and I wanted to drag down and expose her tits. So I did just like the boys and avoided eye contact.

I brought my sunglasses further up my nose and kept as far as I could from Hallie as we both watched the kids frolicking in the water. They were all in a good mood since our first disastrous rehearsal. After I came up with a few silly exercises, they relaxed and the next time we tried was a tremendous improvement.

Later that afternoon, Pandora had them for a full hour and she seemed thrilled. Her advice was much more technical than I could understand, and she seemed to take a shine to Delilah.

Sure, I hated the Campbell family, but even I couldn't deny that Delilah was a good actor.

Scott Garcia, who seemed to decide he was Puck reincarnated, jumped in the water again, splashing everyone, including me.

"Scott, you're banned!" I roared.

He stood right in the middle of the pool of water, brushing his wet hair off his face. "Banned from the hot spring?" he asked, gutted.

"Banned." I repeated because obviously I wasn't going to ban him from the hot spring, but I was annoyed anyway.

A girl named Carmen splashed water on him, scoffing. "Yeah, Scotty, get out of here!"

The girls were annoyed he splashed all over them. They were content with just relaxing and talking in a group. I couldn't help but notice the group had Hallie sitting on the edge, her legs dangling into the water as three girls circled her, talking.

My lips tipped up from the image. I hardly saw Hallie with other girls, definitely not in a little group like that. And for a second, I forgot I wasn't supposed to be watching her. My eyes were glued on her when she brushed a strand off her face, wet because of Scott's splashing. She was talking to the girls, nodding to whatever Carmen was saying, when she stood up and I noticed her shorts were wet.

I gulped.

Hallie undid her button and slid the zipper down, and I stopped breathing. It was ridiculous. I was behaving exactly the way I told the boys not to behave. I was thirty-fucking-six years old, but when Hallie lowered her shorts and jumped out of them? I was just like a teenager.

She threw the shorts to the side, probably to dry, and instead of sitting, dove underwater.

I looked up at the sky, breathing through my mouth.

"Hey, how long until the next rehearsal?"

I groaned. I was trying to avoid her, but she wasn't going to let me. I was trying my best to be a teacher first and foremost, but it wasn't possible with her like that.

I looked down and there she was, looking the way she always looked, but now fucking wet. Sunglasses perched on top of her head, she had the smallest smirk on her lips. It dawned on me. She knew what she was doing. She knew how much she affected me and loved it. It was sassy Hallie coming out.

"In an hour." I rasped.

"Already?" someone complained in the background.

"Aren't you going for a swim?" Hallie batted her eyelashes.

I cleared my throat. "You better behave, Ms. Delos Santos."

"Only if you do, Mr. Miller." And she swam away, on her back, and I watched her wet swimsuit outline those damn perky nipples.

Jesus Christ.

"ALL I'M SAYING IS that she has a bright future," Pandora told me, her smile perfectly in place as she served more herbal tea, first to me and then Hallie.

"Thank you," Hallie replied in her smallest voice.

"I'm glad." I wasn't. "But I'm afraid I'm not sure what you liked me to do, Pandora."

She tilted her head, regarding us as she sighed. "Delilah tells me her parents don't approve of her pursuing the arts."

I exchanged a quick look with Hallie. We were called to Pandora's office after dinner during our third day at Camp Nightfall. I was so sure someone did something dumb, before I left the cabin, I scanned the boy's faces trying to find who looked guilty. But surprise, surprise. What she wanted to tell us was how *good* Delilah was.

"Her mother is very difficult," I offered.

Pandora nodded. "It's very common for kids like her to have to fight their parents. I told Delilah I'm recommending her name to a few theater troupes that will help with scholarships. This kind of commitment usually makes the parents realize the kids are serious." She clicked her tongue, showing her disapproval. "But we need your help, too."

"Help Delilah?" Hallie asked, clearing her throat. "How?"

"You say you know her family, don't you? Bluehaven High is such a small High School."

Hallie opened her mouth, but no sound came out of it. I gritted. "Yes, we know her family."

Pandora nodded. "It would be great if you called her parents in a meeting to tell them of Delilah's success. I can nudge her in the right direction but..." she frowned to herself. "It would be awful to see talent wasted."

"Awful? Awful?" I repeated as I cruised from Pandora's office back to our cabins. "Dealing with the Campbells is awful!"

Hallie sighed dramatically on my heels. "She was just doing her job. Delilah probably told her about her busted college plans and Pandora felt bad. I feel bad too."

That stopped me in my tracks. I turned to Hallie, wondering if she had gone insane. "You will not feel sorry for the Campbells, Hallie."

"It's not for the Campbells... Exactly." I scoffed and walked again as she followed me. "Can you imagine if my dad forced me to go for accounting or something?"

"I'm not talking to Sharon Campbell about her amazing daughter, Cricket. Don't even start."

Hallie looked shocked. "But of course you are!"

Pandora's office was far from the cabins, which meant we had to pass through the woods on our way back. The trees were sparse and tall, the smell of nature fresh. I really enjoyed it. Even though it was late, the camp's lights at a distance were enough to illuminate our paths, and the moon was full tonight.

"You're her teacher!" Hallie said, outraged.

"Wrong. I am the woodwork teacher."

"You're her teacher now!"

"It's not going to happen, Cricket. I think I'm being quite reasonable. I'm holding myself not to blow that town up. Not to tell the whole of Bluehaven how horrible they are. And you want me to help one? To praise her?"

After everything that family put Hallie through? I could easily blame it only on the older sister, but Sharon and Delilah were deliberately being horrible to Hallie since the beginning of the term. I couldn't excuse that. Sharon used her power over and over again to do things her way. Of course, it now made sense why she wasn't jumping on the possibility of helping the theater department. She was head of the PTA and was obsessed with the swim team, even though her child wasn't on the swim team. No, she was ignoring her child and...

And now I felt sorry for Delilah.

"You won't be praising her. You're just going to deliver a message."

I stopped, turning to Hallie, making her stop too. I stalked over to her, shaking my head, annoyed. "Why do you want to do this? Don't you take just a little relief in righting a wrong?"

"I won't be righting a wrong. I told you, it's the past."

"My anger at Sharon and Delilah goes beyond... that. It's about how you were treated this year."

She sighed. "She's a kid."

"She knows..."

Hallie shook her head. "She's a kid. And clearly there's stuff going on there we don't know. The Sharon I remember when Katie was in school? Super overprotective parent. She was cheering for Katie every time the girl breathed. If Delilah is so sure she isn't being supported, so sure she confided in Pandora after only three days, don't you think it's worth to believe something is going on there?"

I hated when she was right. I told her that. She laughed, "Well, get used to it, because I'm very wise."

I took her hands in mine, and then her wrist and up her arm. I loved touching her skin. It was always hot and soft. Hallie stepped close, putting her arms around my waist. "Think. This is clearly something Sharon doesn't want. This will definitely upset her. Does that help?"

I hummed under my breath, forgetting all about the damn Campbells and focusing only on Hallie. She looked gorgeous under the moonlight, her eyes sparkling and her smile easy. My palms touched her face. I wanted nothing more but to taste her again.

"Are we about to make out in the woods, Mr. Miller?"

I nodded slowly and bit down on her bottom lip. Hallie shivered in my arms and I took great satisfaction in her reaction to me.

"You have been teasing me a lot these days."

"I would never." She shook her head, sounding serious.

"I know you better now, Hallie Delos Santos."

"Do you?" she asked, almost sounding innocent.

There, in the middle of the woods with her, everything was perfect. The breeze, her perfume, her little bold smile. I loved that she was herself with me. I loved that I was the one to discover that side of her. I grabbed her by the waist, need shooting over me when she gasped. My eyes traced her perfect features, my leg fell between hers as her hands rested on my shoulders.

I kissed her slowly, my hand buried in her hair, taking strands off her ponytail as she whimpered in my mouth. Our touch turned frantic, starved and took us too long to hear the *"ahem"*.

But someone cleared their throat again, so I let Hallie's mouth go. I prepared myself, cursing under my breath as I turned slowly to the side. Wide eyed and smirks in place. Watching us were all the kids from Bluehaven High.

Boys and girls, all of them together.

Then Adam-fucking-Brown snickered. "Damn, Mr. Miller, go get it."

17.

"WHY IS EVERYBODY OUT of bed?" Daniel wanted to know.

The kids blinked at us. "Because it's like nine o'clock and we aren't farmers?" Carmen replied.

"Or really old ladies," added someone in the back.

I would've usually been flustered by being caught like that, but Daniel was so frazzled I couldn't fall apart too. He was standing weirdly, his knuckles white from squeezing his hand together. His whole body was bent forwards probably to hide the hard on that was carving on my hip just a second ago.

"Still doesn't make it ok for all of you to wander in the woods!" Daniel replied.

"Our curfew is at ten," someone pointed it out.

"And this is not against the rules."

"Maybe what is against the rules is for Mr. Miller to suck face with Ms. Delos Santos." Another helpful point.

Daniel groaned. "It is not against the rules." He cleared his throat. "Although, I'd appreciate it if you don't tell your parents you saw this."

Everyone snickered.

"You're making it worse," I pointed out.

"Can we all appreciate this? The lovers? All of us in the woods...?" Nova started.

"Lovers?" Carmen feigned gagging.

"That's how old people call each other," another helpful student said.

"*Old people* is definitely about you, not me," I whispered to my supposed lover.

"Anyway, I was talking more about the whole escaping couple in the woods," Nova said, rolling her eyes, but everyone shook their heads. "Guys! *Midsummer Night's Dream*!"

"OH!" they collectively nodded.

"I mean, right?" Nova seemed thrilled about it, so I twisted my lips in her direction, making her wince and say, "I'm sorry, but isn't this perfect?"

"No, because there'll be no changing up couples..."

"So Mr. Miller is against swapping," Adam chuckled.

And the girls squealed, "Ew!"

I clapped my hands, my boldest move yet.

"All right, why don't we all go back to our cabins? Let's go, girls with me, boys with Mr. Miller."

They all followed. It surprised me I had some authority, even though the only official title I carried was "Mr. Miller's Side Squeeze." Hopefully, Main Squeeze. As we separated, each to their cabin, I heard one boy asking Daniel how old I was, which earned him a slap behind the head. *That* was definitely not allowed.

The girls filed in for the cabin one by one as I waited by the opened door. Until only one was left, and she looked me up with those big blue eyes. "Can we talk?"

Daniel would've probably told me it was a bad idea, but I found myself nodding and closing the door, leaving Delilah and me alone on the porch.

She was a little thing, Delilah, even smaller than me. Her manicure was perfect, her hair shaped around her face and her nose was the cutest. She hugged herself, swallowing and asked. "Did she talk to you?"

I didn't need to ask who. "Yeah."

Delilah nodded, looking down. It broke me a little how fragile she looked just there. I've been reminding Daniel she was just a kid, but I only truly saw it right then that she looked exactly like her sixteen years old of age.

"She told us you were great and you should pursue theater."

Delilah's stare changed, turning fierce and strong. "I know you hate me. And there's no reason for you to help me. But I really need this."

I did not hate her, still, I didn't correct her. Katie changed my life for the worse; she changed the person I was and how I saw myself. But Delilah? I wasn't sure if she was cruel or ignorant. I wasn't in the mood to ask which, so I said nothing.

"I need all the help I can get. Not having Mrs. Carr here fucks my plans a little bit." She laughed to herself, brushing her hair with her hands, making the perfect golden waves a little wild. "Pandora is a big deal."

I could tell Pandora was a big deal. I knew nothing about theater but I could see the program was good. I wondered if any of the kids were taking it seriously, and my answer was just there in front of me. Five-foot nothing, blond, mean, and hated my guts.

When I said nothing, she rubbed her temple. "Never mind."

Her hand was on the knob when I spoke again. "We're going to talk to your mom. I don't know how much she'll care for it, but we're going to do like Pandora asked."

Delilah looked back at me, staring hard like she was ready for me to announce I was messing with her.

"Can you tell me something, though?" I asked.

She shrugged.

"What does your mother want you to do?"

Her shoulders relaxed. She tried hard to bite back a little smile, but I saw it. "Law school."

A trained lawyer? Delilah? No thanks. "Well, let's make sure that doesn't happen."

THE LAST DAY AT Camp Nightfall passed in a blur. From breakfast to lunch, the kids rehearsed non-stop. After lunch, they had a session with Pandora. Normally, it was the time Dan, and I had to relax, but he was called by another teacher to help with a falling tree blocking a track in the woods. By the time Daniel was done, the kids were back from Pandora's rehearsal and they were more than ready to relax for a couple of hours. Some of them wanted to go for a last dip in the hot spring, but some didn't. We decided to divide and conquer. I stayed behind with about a handful of students, and Daniel brought the rest for a swim.

I gathered my craft supplies outside and put them on top of a picnic table. Nova followed me, with a book in her hands, which she devoured as I worked, proving to be a great companion. The rest of the kids stayed around doing other things, some on their phones and a couple of girls—Olivia and Emma—even asked to help me glue a few small stones to their own wings.

In the last four days, I forgot to be anxious. Between seeing Ryan again, kissing Dan for the first time and being the responsible adult at a camp full of teenagers... I forgot to be that Hallie always with her guard up. I relaxed in the sun, finishing the things I had to finish as the warm breeze brushed my cheeks.

By night, I was ready to be back in Bluehaven. I was feeling stronger than I ever was, and I was ready to go back to town and live my life.

The lights were out. The cool sheets between my legs were a constant reminder of how muggy the air inside the cabin felt. The girls were all sleeping now. I could hear their breathing slowing down and turning heavy. The silence was so comforting, I almost jumped out of my skin when my phone vibrated under my pillow.

Daniel: Come out. Bring a swimsuit.

I rolled my eyes, even if he couldn't see me. And then I texted back.

Hallie: Dan...

Daniel: Let's go, Cricket, I'm waiting.

That made me pause. Was he outside waiting for me?

My fingers hovered over the phone. I should've texted telling him to go to sleep. But no. I sat up in the bed, careful like the girls could awake just by the rustling of my sheets. My feet found the floor, and I waited a little longer to see if anyone moved. They all seemed to be sleeping deep, or they were *that* good of actors. So I dared to move again, to reach my duffle bag and take a swimsuit, shorts and a t-shirt.

I got dressed slowly, half expecting to be stopped by someone, but eventually I sneaked out of the cabin and the girls didn't stir.

The door moaned opened, and I almost shushed it. I went on my tiptoes, afraid of the sound of my flip-flops. Going down the porch, I scanned left and right, trying to find Daniel. I was almost certain he was messing with me until a pebble landed just by my foot, coming from the shadows.

My eyes narrowed. I went one step further to investigate. Another pebble came from the darkness and landed just a hair from missing me. My lips curved. "So you woke me up to throw rocks at me?" I asked.

From the shadows, Daniel came to light. Dressed in swimming trunks and a white t-shirt, he brushed his hair off his face, sending me the most delicious boyish smile.

It wasn't fair how good he looked.

"Where are we going?" I wanted to know. "We can't swim."

"Why not?" he challenged.

"Because... I don't know. Can we?"

He didn't reply, but took my hand and led me to a trail I knew would end in the hot springs. I put a swimsuit under my clothes as he requested, but still felt naughty going to a swim at night. I followed in his footsteps, his hand on mine. We kept going for a few minutes until the trail opened to the right to reveal the smallest of the hot springs at Camp Nightfall.

It was perfectly centered among thick, tall trees that danced in the light breeze.

I shivered. To my side, Daniel was peeling his shirt off; hot golden muscle came into view, and I lost all words. I licked my dry lips as he stepped into the water, relaxed and perfect like nothing was a bother to him.

That was what attracted me the most about Dan. He always looked like he belonged. He knew how to act around people. He spoke with ease and was never awkward. He lowered down into the water, and I watched him swim to the center. Only then, he turned back around with a smirk on his lips.

"Come in."

His voice was a hot liquid dare. I tossed my shirt to one side and my shorts to the other. Leaving my flip-flops behind, I fell into the water. It was the perfect temperature, so incredible, I groaned. "I'm going to miss the hot springs."

His arms stretched for my waist, bringing our bodies together. "We can visit on the weekends."

"Camp?" I arched an eyebrow.

"No. God, enough of camp. Spring's Harbor."

I laced one arm over his shoulder, grabbing the hair on the nape of his neck. I kept my other hand on the water, right on the surface, watching as it rippled. He brought me closer, his lips brushed mine; in an instinct I didn't know I had, my legs closed around his narrow waist.

"Camp wasn't that bad. Actually, I would argue it was much better than I imagined. I think I made friends."

He groaned. "Please don't make friends with the kids."

I shrugged. "Maybe that's my thing. I make friends with people younger or way older than me."

"Just older is enough, Cricket. Leave the *way* behind."

I giggled. "Maybe the lesson here is that I don't get along with people my age. Younger and older are game."

"You said you wanted to learn who you are," Daniel reminded me.

"Is it weird if I say Camp Nightfall helped with that?"

He chuckled. "Sure, just don't tell anyone."

"Oh god no. I can't be in a brochure saying '*Camp Nightfall changed my life!*'"

We both laughed at my silliness, then I arched an eyebrow. "It might change Delilah's life."

He stilled under me. "Not this again."

I held his face between my palms and nipped his bottom lip. "She came to talk to me."

"Did she?" he asked, half annoyed, half interested in kissing.

"Told me she really needs this."

"No snarky comments?"

I shook my head. "Nope."

"No insults as she talked?"

I bit my cheek not to laugh. "No."

"She was genuine and nice?" He looked skeptical.

"She was genuine."

Daniel growled, shaking his head, but I kept it in place. "She is what she is. But is one more artistic kid out there and one more obnoxious parent disappointed? Isn't it worth it?"

When he wasn't convinced, I pressed. "If you do it, I owe you one." I winked.

His smirk was back. "Own me what?"

I took his mouth, but after a second it was clear he was the one in charge. Each time I kissed him was better and better. His mouth felt perfect against mine, his body searing hot under me. His hands sprayed under my ass as I squeezed my legs around him. His kiss ravished me, he licked me from inside out. It was overwhelming how perfect everything was, the warm water, and his sun kissed chest with droplets all over waiting for me to lick it one by one. I whimpered, feeling his body against mine.

His mouth fell to my jaw, neck, then ear. I started to move, like my body knew what to do even when my head hadn't caught up. I rubbed my core against his hardness; I had no idea what I was doing, no idea if that would make me look sexy or insane, but I spent so long overthinking things, I was ready to do them.

In the water, it was easy to move. I raised a little and then dropped, causing friction, and we both moaned in sync. He ceased kissing me, our faces a breath apart. We watched each other. I licked the seam of his mouth and dragged his bottom lip with a bite.

"Jesus, Hallie," his voice was restrained, like he was holding together by a thread.

And I really - *really*- liked that. I went for his ear, taking an earlobe as I moved on top of him again.

"You need to stop." If his husky tone showed anything, it was that he didn't really want me to stop.

I ignored him, so he spoke again. "We can't have our first time here, Cricket," he explained. "*You* can't have your first time here."

Oh yes. My traitorous body took the reins and pretended it knew what to do. For a second there, I wasn't a virgin. I was brave Hallie. I nodded, not upset that he pointed out, but a little disappointed all the same.

I leaned back, putting space between us. Afraid of me slipping away, Dan held on to my legs, locking them around him. My torso floated, I looked up at the sky to the full moon, and my arms danced above the water.

"We do things for the first time all the time, Dan," I finally said.

He paused to consider. "Still, I have no condom and believe me, you wouldn't want your first time to be in water."

I guessed he was right. But still felt a little anticlimactic. My silence must have been the sign I agreed with him, because suddenly he let it go a little of my legs, just to bring it up to the middle of his chest. I lolled my head to the side to see what he was doing.

"I can still get you off, Cricket. That would be very much ok."

"You think so?" I let a small smile slip past my lips.

"I know so."

"What if I want to touch you, too?" I asked.

His eyes locked on mine. "You're going to wait for your turn."

When I was going to ask if he wanted to go some place else, I felt it. His hot mouth nipped the inside of my thigh, my both legs shook with reaction.

I felt the wet strands of his hair over my legs, and then a lick. "Is this ok?"

I was barely finished saying yes when his thumb brushed over my clit. I sat up immediately, splashing water like a dork. Water in my nose. I coughed, and he held me closer, nice enough not to laugh in my face. He held me as I coughed, and once I was finished, he nipped my jaw and ordered. "Lie back again."

I sucked in air, his order vibrating me head to toe. I was lowering myself back into the water when his lips took my nipple over my swimsuit. My legs trembled around him, I whimpered in shock as he took the other nipple, too, like it was jealous. Before I was even over it, his palm pressed over my chest, letting me lower once again. I floated back, my ears went underwater, blocking any noise. I took a breath, watched the moon as I felt his thumb swap over my clit again. My knee jerked a little. He held me still.

Slowly and daring, his forefinger and middle played little circles on me and my back arched. My own moaning sounded strange under the water, and then, quickly, I felt exposed when he hooked the bottom of my swimsuit to the side, showing my skin to the night air.

A second later, his mouth descended. His tongue was hot, swirling around, taking the breath out of me. My legs twitched, and he held me in place. The water made me feel like I was in space, weightless as he licked me relentlessly, building me up little by little.

And I was about to crash.

I was sure I moaned his name. The sound escaped my lips unbidden. I felt him growl between my legs, the sexiest thing that ever happened to me. I was dizzy, weak, delirious as the climax uncoiled in my stomach, my hands closed in a fist, grabbing water.

He opened me with his fingers, giving himself room, and in the back of my mind I remembered I should be a little shy and still, I wasn't. I was glad when his tongue swirled unobstructed, when he sucked just a little, and my eyes rolled to the back of my head.

His thumb played with my entrance, not really penetrating, but messing with my head. And I shook, clamping my legs on his face. I felt the scratch of his beard, and he pried my legs open once again, steadying my body.

My breathing came out choppy. I was a raft floating away and the waves of my orgasm wouldn't let me still.

When Daniel talked, his voice vibrated inside me, a command for me to let it go. And I obeyed without question.

Shock, I whimpered too loudly, weak, and I floated away as I rode the biggest orgasm of my life. I dove, then rose my body upright, above the water, brushing my wet hair from my face. I was on the other side of the hot springs when I opened my eyes.

Daniel looked feral, his hair wet and plastered over his forehead, his hazel eyes wild.

We watched each other from afar, my mouth dry, his curving in a smirk. He crooked a finger at me. "Come here, Cricket. I'm not done with you yet."

Hallie Delos Santos was a lot of things, but not dumb. So, I went to him.

18.

Life was good.

No, life was great. We were leaving Camp Nightfall. I was feeling happy and confident. And if I closed my eyes? I could still taste Hallie in my tongue and hear the delicious sounds she made back in the hot springs. Those four days changed everything.

"You changed, Delos Santos."

The accusation rang in my ear, cutting through my peace. In a minute I was outside with a clipboard in hands and talking to the kids, and in the next, I was jumping inside the bus, growling at Ryan.

He stretched comfortably in the driver's seat, a lazy smile so perfect I could imagine the handful he was as a teenager. As I stepped inside, Hallie's hand found my chest holding me in place.

I shook with anger.

His comment wasn't innocent. I could tell by the way he said her name, the slime quality of his tone of voice.

"Hey, Mr. M., is everything ready?" He blinked at me, unbothered.

I vibrated under Hallie's palm. I wanted to break free, to break Ryan's bones. I was done with patience, done with being the good guy.

But if I thought Hallie was going to accept Ryan's sudden change of subject, I was wrong. My girl tipped her chin up and with a challenge asked; "What do you mean by that, Ryan?"

His eyes flickered to her, surprised she talked back. In a flash, he recovered, his mouth opening in a smile once again.

"All grown up." He rolled his shoulders back. "Look at you."

Hallie's eyes narrowed. A beat passed and none of us moved, but then she nodded. "Well, you haven't changed at all."

She removed her hand from my chest, but I wasn't holding myself back anymore. Hallie was ready to be heard, proving once more she could handle herself.

It was the hottest thing I'd ever seen.

I moved away from Ryan and helped the kids with their luggage. Counted their heads twice, consumed by an irrational fear of forgetting someone at Camp Nightfall. Our hosts said their goodbyes, and soon we were on our way back to Bluehaven.

"Told you," We waited by the bus as the parents picked up the kids.

"What have you told me?"

"Hey, Mr. M! Be careful with my wings!" Carmen shouted, nodding toward the bag I was holding.

My lips twitched. "I'm being extra careful," I said to the student and turned to Hallie. "I said it was going to be ok. The kids love you."

"Do they?" she challenged.

Three girls got inside a car, but not before waving their goodbyes to the woman beside me. I arched my eyebrow at Hallie.

"I guess it went ok." She shrugged, but I heard her delight loud and clear.

Impatiently, I waited as one by one all the students left and the only thing I could think about was getting Hallie to come back home with me.

My mind was certain; my bed was where she belonged. I hooked my arm around her waist, flushing her side to my chest.

"I know how to cook two dishes. Are you hungry?"

She looked up at me. "Only two?"

"Yes. But *really* well."

Hallie giggled, turning her body toward mine, her hands laced behind my neck.

"Let me feed you, Hallie," I insisted.

She tilted her head, biting her bottom lip. I followed her movements as she smiled timidly and came for a small peck on my lips.

"I'm going home."

"I'm not opposed to cooking for you at your house, but I have to say, I'm a messy cook."

Hallie bit a smile back, shaking her head. "I have a lot to finish before the first try of the costumes. Those four days threw my schedule for a loop. I'll be locked in my sewing cave. Sorry, Dan."

I got almost distracted by how much I loved when she called me Dan. I buried my hand in her hair, messing up the ponytail.

"Can the kids just wear whatever they have at home?" I asked, knowing the answer.

Her face fell. "No." I had to chuckle at her vehemence.

"And Dad is collecting me. I texted him already."

"Cricket..." I groaned. I could at least bring her home. My truck was just a few feet from us, exactly where I left four days ago.

"I have pants to tailor, Dan." She told me with fake impatience. "Do you understand how hard it is to tailor them?"

"No," I deadpanned.

She bit her lip. Her hands fell to my chest, picking invisible lint.

"Well, dresses I can drape. I can pin them first and have in front of my eyes how they look before I stitch. But pants? That's pure math. I need to concentrate and we both know I won't be able to achieve that around you."

"We could buy pants," I said, just to tease. "What am I saying? You probably have a reason why the pants can't be bought?"

"A good reason," she confessed, a little sparkle in her eyes. "They will mimic a goat's leg. I really think it will work, but I might need stuffing in some parts. Sometimes I see things perfectly in my mind, but I need to test around to be sure. We'll see."

I loved how much she loved her work, and even though I'd liked to keep teasing her, I accepted the pants had to be done first. So I grabbed her waist, gripping tighter as I asked, "Saturday?"

"Saturday what?"

"Can I feed you Saturday?"

She chuckled a little. "Are you saying *feed* because you're scared to ask me for dinner?"

I tsked. "Remember the shy girl who barely talked?"

"I can give you the silent treatment if you like. I heard it's my A game."

"No, sassy it is." My hands spread and reached for her neck, thumbs over the delicate skin between her neck and the shell of her ear. She was soft all over.

"I love when you're like this. It's a side of you no one gets to see and I'm a greedy motherfucker, Cricket. I like to have it all."

Hallie trembled in my arms and that was all the invitation I needed. I teased her mouth with mine, angling her head up the way I wanted. The rough pads of my fingers glided over the smoothness of her. Hallie's tongue wrestled against mine. Her little sigh hit right in the middle of my chest.

A blatant horn threw us apart. I stepped away, looking down at my shoes, knowing the minute I looked up it was Preston's unhappy face I was going to see. Hallie brushed the hair out of her face, putting what I messed up back in place. With a little smile, she raised her hand. "Hey, Dad. I'm coming."

So then I asked, "And that's how I die?"

"You can stay as long as you want."

"Hm...." I replied, stretching myself on the couch. "And that's nothing to do with the fact that the fence at the back of your property needs repairs?"

Even through the screen I could spot Abby's incriminatory blush. "Don't be silly, Dan."

"Will I bring my toolbox, anyway?"

"Who the hell said the only reason I want you to come over is to repair things, Daniel Miller?"

I laughed, shaking my head. "You."

Her eyes bugged. "Did I?" she asked with a tiny wince.

"Yes, Abby, you said it the last time you were here. To Hallie's dad."

And that was enough. Just to have her name on my tongue was enough to make me lose all concentration. I glanced at my front door again, like Hallie managed to arrive without me noticing.

"How's Hallie, by the way?" Abby asked with a glint in her eye that made me roll mine.

I wasn't in sixth grade. I wasn't kissing a girl and coming home to tell my friends.

"She's good, Abs."

"Did she miss you over the days at camp?" Abby pouted in a joke.

Shit. I guess one thing was not telling her about how I was progressing with Hallie, but another was to lie. My hand went absently to the back of my neck, squeezing it. "She actually went with us. Helen's husband wasn't well."

I tried to deliver the news as carelessly as I could, but Abby's eyebrows shot up, anyway. "Did she? And you forgot to tell me?"

"I'm tired. It was a long week watching teenagers twenty-four-seven. Even at night." *Especially* then.

"I hope you didn't watch kids sleeping. That's creepy, Dan." Abby wiggled her nose. And right in that comment, Mark came along.

"Is Dan watching kids sleep?" My brother appeared on the screen and I groaned.

"No." I rubbed my face. "Abby is trying me."

"Hallie went to the camp with him." My sister-in-law elbowed her husband.

"It wasn't a trip that I invited her on," I explained, shifting in my seat. "Helen's husband wasn't well..."

The doorbell rang.

Breath that was a mix of apprehension and relief left my lungs. With a finger hovering over the off button, I told my family, "I have to go."

It was all they heard before I disconnected, and like a teen, I hopped the couch and ran for the front door. Things changed between Hallie and me in those four days, and I was ready to take it to the next level. All my reservations, all the reasons I shouldn't do it, were thrown out the window.

I swung the door open after composing myself a little and found her there, all dressed up, looking... different.

Different good. Refined, but still very Hallie. She was wearing a black dress that flared on her hips. Tiny silver spikes adorned each shoulder like the badass she was. Legs for days, black boots. It was getting pathetic how much I salivated over Hallie. She was so fucking beautiful and unexpected.

"Can I come in?"

Like a moron, I was standing there, gawking at her. But the request took me from my stupor. I grabbed her by the waist before she could even step in, taking her mouth in mine.

"Hi." I breathed her in.

"Hi," she replied with a little tint on her cheeks.

I closed the door quickly and released her. She took the first steps around my house, taking it in and, for some reason, I held my breath. The house had good bones, great, spacious rooms and plenty of windows. But when Kelly left, she took the personality with her. Everything pretty was hers, and once she moved all her belongings, I realized my house was nothing but a shell.

Now it was becoming a home once again. The garage was turned into a workshop for my projects and every piece of furniture in the house I made with my own hands.

I watched as Hallie's fingertips danced over the hall table. It looked rough, like tree bark itself, but soft to the touch.

"This is gorgeous," she whispered, reverent.

"Thank you."

She glanced back at me, and I could see the second she realized it wasn't just my good taste that brought the table here.

"Oh Dan..."

Hallie touched the hall table once more. It was almost erotic, the soft way she let her fingers wander. I chuckled, taking her elbow and stirring her away.

"There's plenty to see yet, Cricket, come on."

She looked one last time, then faced me with a little smile. Taking me by surprise, she rose on her tiptoes and kissed the side of my mouth. "I love your house."

"You only have seen the hall," I argued.

"It's the best hall I've ever seen."

I shook my head. "Come on. I'm supposed to feed you, right?"

I moved down to the kitchen, the place I was really proud of. I shamelessly watched her as we turned, the sturdy banister that opened to the kitchen, in which the central focus was my most beloved piece: a big mahogany table with six sturdy chairs around it.

I always wanted a table like that. Wood worked in a way to enhance its own design, but Kelly always preferred things with a modern touch. When I was alone in my empty house, I started to work on that table every second of my spare time.

At first it was just to fill up my days, before I even went to Helen and asked if she wanted help. But soon, I realized it was important for me to finish it. It was supposed to mean something. When I finished and put it in its place, I felt somewhat underwhelmed.

As Hallie's hand found her mouth and her eyes widened, I knew I meant to make that table for her. It was ridiculous to think that, and definitely far too romantic for me. But I couldn't shake the feeling that Hallie Delos Santos was the only one who really could appreciate what I had done.

Something clicked for me right there.

"This is incredible." She twirled around, eyeing the kitchen cabinets too. "Is it all you?"

I nodded as I leaned on the banister, arms crossed over my chest.

"Show me more." She demanded.

"I made lasagna. Don't you want to eat first?"

"No."

I held my smile, nodding towards the backdoor, "All right, Cricket. Let's go."

She went first, her eyes still devouring my house. My parents always told me I had talent. Mark and Abby begged for new furniture as Christmas and birthday gifts. But it was Hallie's silent appreciation that filled my chest with pride.

The workshop in my garage was simple. I installed shelves on the right side to hold tubs of stain and whatnots. Cabinets to the left for the tools, investing in glass doors so I knew where everything was always. My power tools were neatly displayed, and right in the middle was a simple workbench and a table saw.

"Is this you?" she asked with her back turned, examining my roll of power tools.

"You talk like you're just getting to know me."

She spun on her spot. "You are a reserved person. And that's coming from me."

I opened my mouth to argue, but she shook her head. "I'm not criticizing. I like to know how you deal with the world."

"Deal?"

She lifted a shoulder. "Yeah, I put everything into sewing. Everyone does a different thing. Sometimes it's a hobby, sometimes it's a way of life." She opened her arms. "This is you."

I dipped my chin. Hallie walked to my workbench, turning her back to me as she examined the details. I tried to hold myself back, let her do her thing, but as soon as she leaned on the table, her dress went up a little and my feet walked independently of my will.

Soon, I was plastered on her back. The little gasp she let out was good enough to eat.

My hands closed over her hips, bringing it back to me. She straightened up, and I took it as an invitation to get a bite of her neck. I hummed when the taste of her overwhelmed me. Her soft hair tickled my face. "Hallie..." I said just because her name was always on my mind.

She didn't reply but whimpered as my hands rubbed the front of her dress, from the narrow waist up, taking two handfuls of her tits.

"No bra?"

"It wouldn't look good with this dress," she replied, trying to keep her voice in check.

I chuckled, my right hand left her chest, wrapping around her, lifting her dress and trembling when I found she wasn't wearing underwear either.

"You're a liar, Hallie Delos Santos."

My rough palm was big enough to take one full cheek in my hand, my denim clad leg pried her legs apart.

"I'm trying this new thing," she told me, breathless. "Being brave."

I hummed with approval. "Don't move," I ordered.

She was leaning over the table, her dress hitched up, showing off her ass. I kept my left hand in place, but the other roamed in front, roughly to her thigh, as she sucked in a breath. I delved between her legs, my thumb circling her clit. Just to tease her a little.

"How is bravery going for you, Cricket?" I wanted to know.

"Honestly? Fantastic."

We both chuckled, but she was cut short when I dipped a finger inside. My moan mixed with hers when I found her wet and ready. I licked her neck and took a bite as Hallie held on to my worktable with white knuckles.

"Hold on there, Cricket. I'm going to make you come all over my workshop."

She didn't protest; she didn't argue. No, not Hallie. She bobbed her head, bracing herself, eager as she could be. Her ass tipped up, holding the table like a good girl as I worked her. One finger fucked her shallow, my thumb over her clit and my other hand gripped her ass and kept her in place.

Cricket moaned and pleaded. Louder than I thought she was capable, and right over her ecstasy, I slapped her ass; her whimper let loose, and she came apart so pretty for me.

My mouth hovered over her shoulder. A small nip and then a kiss. "I'm going to be addicted to seeing you come, Cricket."

She let out a breathless laugh. "I guess it's an addiction I'm happy to oblige."

I chuckled, groaning at how fucking enamored I'd become in the last weeks. Hallie always gave as much as she got. She matched me in every way, pressure and intensity. *She matched me.*

Her body sagged to mine, her back to my chest as I removed my hand from her and smoothed her dress over her ass. She chuckled at my care. One-eighty from the man who just made her orgasm in a workshop and slapped her ass right there, too. But there was fire, passion and everything Hallie brought on me, but also an intense need to care for her, to be better than everyone else in her life.

"So tell me, Dan," she breathed out, puffing away a strand of hair that fell over her eyes. "What does your bedroom look like?"

"Hallie..." I shook my head, tipping forward as I rested on her shoulder.

I wanted nothing but to fuck Hallie Delos Santos.

Since Camp Nightfall, I was almost certain that if I didn't fuck Hallie within the inch of her life, I was going to die of want. But I also knew she was a virgin. And more than that, her relationship with people was always stilted. She was difficult to trust, my Hallie, and I needed to take that into consideration.

"What's wrong?" she asked when I didn't promptly drag her to my bedroom.

I turned her in my arms, placing my hands over her soft cheeks, a thumb caressing her bottom lip. She had trust issues for a goddamn good reason, and I refused to be someone who abused her trust.

I wanted to prove to Hallie that good people existed in Bluehaven, but this wasn't the way. It didn't matter how deeply I felt about her; it didn't matter how much I thought we were perfect together.

Hallie deserved better.

And I gathered all my might to tell her so. To tell her all the words I carried around.

"Dan?" Her eyes traced my features, her hands clutched my shirt. "What's wrong?"

The edge in her voice was palpable. I opened my mouth to speak, but she was faster.

"We don't need..." she flinched. "We can just have dinner."

I laughed a humorless laugh. "Hallie... Being with you is everything I've ever wanted."

She licked her lips, encouraged by my words. "So be with me."

I groaned, kissing her gently.

"Is it because..." she cleared her throat. "Because you know... I never...?"

I shook my head. "Of course not. That means nothing."

"So... If you want to have me, you can have me." Her hold on me intensified. Literally and figuratively. Her little fingers held me in place; her eyes haunted me in dark wonder. Going on her tiptoes, she kissed my jaw. Nipped it and then my earlobe.

I wished to be stronger. I knew I could.

But I grabbed her and hoisted her up; her legs closed around my waist like she belonged on top of me. I suspected she did. I took her mouth; she grabbed the hair in the back of my neck, and I turned us around, going for the bedroom.

We kissed as I crossed the kitchen with the forgotten lasagna that I now planned to eat *after*. She was relentless, even when I warned her I was about to damn us both if she kept licking my skin that way as I climbed the stairs. But this was the best version of Hallie. She laughed carefree, teased me and kissed me with such freedom, I never wanted to stop her.

And it was her laugh that I used as an excuse. All I wanted was for her to be happy, and I told myself I made her happy.

I brought her to my room, and I dropped her onto my bed. I took her boots off and threw them somewhere in the corner, grabbed her feet and kissed her ankle. Her jet-black hair fanned across my white sheets. And then she raised her body on her knees, looked me directly in the eyes and took her dress off.

And I died a thousand deaths.

19.

His bedroom was simple. An enormous bed, an obscenely sexy dark wood headboard and soft white sheets.

It smelled like him; it felt like him.

I tossed my dress to the corner where my boots went. I knew Dan found me attractive. He said it before, and he acted like it. I could spot the proof straining his jeans right now, but I was still Hallie, and my fears were still mine. I always averted my gaze when I looked in the mirror, scared to find the same faults Katie pointed out all those years ago. And now, I was baring myself to him. To the one I wanted to like me the most.

He kneeled on the bed, his hand in my hair, on my cheek and then tipping my chin up. "You're going to kill me, Cricket." His voice was husky.

I shivered all over, my body going soft as his other hand took my waist, held me upright. I felt the scratch of his beard on my neck and then the hot, wet swirl of his tongue. It was always like that with Dan, like he was tasting his favorite meal. My heart thumped when I realized I was it. I was Daniel Miller's favorite meal.

We kissed, my hands hung over his shoulder, his palm chased my breast, and the calloused thumbs played with my nipple. I arched my back, a moan running free from my lips, and Dan devoured it. My whimpers, my tongue, my nipples. He wanted to eat me whole.

With that gentle touch of his, he lowered me into his bed, the rough material of his jeans stretching my naked legs as he came on top of me. I palmed his back under the shirt, and ran up my hands, urging him to remove it.

"You want this off?" He teased, but obliged straight away.

"It's just not fair," I argued. "I'm naked."

"I know," he said, taking a nipple between his teeth. Careful and taunting. I arched as he pulled just a little. "I like you naked."

"Is that right?" I rolled my eyes.

His shirt was gone. I groaned at the first feeling of his warm skin over mine. My hands danced over his perfect stomach, up his nipple and the hairs over his chest. I bit his shoulder. He hitched my leg, opening them, my feet lacing around his waist. He kissed my collarbone and pushed his hips down. It should've been painful. The zipper was right there, but all I felt was goosebumps over my body and the urge to plead for more.

He did it once more, a pressure over my clit. I was soaked since he made me come into his workshop, and I was ready to do it again. I wanted him. All of him. Over me, inside me. I feared my own hungry thoughts. It was like someone else took over. I let myself desire and feel desired.

I reached for his zipper; his elbow held his body up so as not to crush me. I worked the button, and then the zipper down. He helped me to tug his legs free and I sucked a breath when I saw him sitting on his heels, black underwear tenting.

I went up on my elbows and for just a second, we watched each other. And then he moved, pulling down the underwear with a grace I wouldn't expect of a man so big. Once the boxers were out of the way, one leg out of the bed and the other kneeled between mine, we watched each other again.

My eyes ate his skin, his perfect abs, his trail of hair down from his navel. I never saw a man naked, right in front of me, but I knew I was lucky Daniel was the first. He stood there like a marble statue, an explicit one, with something between his legs. I wondered if it would fit me.

His hands closed on the base of his dick, and my eyes followed as he tugged up, my cheeks warmed and I whipped my eyes to find his, a little smirk playing on the side of his full lips.

"Reach behind you and get the condom, Cricket," he asked, nodding to the bedside table with a single drawer on our left side.

I stretched my arm and turned just a little, opened the drawer as I felt his hand up my leg and over my hips. I turned with the foil package between my fingers as he made himself home between my thighs, holding my legs apart with his big hands sprayed to the side, his thumbs running circles across my skin.

Everything he did was perfect, like he had a map to my body.

Dan ripped the condom's package open and sheathed himself as I watched. Slowly, it was a show, and he was performing just for me. I held my breath, and he laid over my body, looking down to kiss my nose. My hands ran to embrace him, my legs opened, my knees hooked to his side, my foot over his ass. He leaned as one hand found my leg and held it up, like he couldn't stay a second without touching me.

"You tell me if it's too much," he asked.

I nodded quickly. For the first time, I felt the coil of fear in the bottom of my belly. Not afraid of being with him, but of all those things people say about virginity. I didn't believe it said anything about me, of course. I hadn't done many things yet. Throughout my life, I was going to do many and many things for the first time. I wasn't afraid of losing my virginity because I didn't think I was going to lose anything about myself.

I feared other things, though.

Of being bad at it, of being too shy for him. Of hurting and not enjoying it properly. Of him being bad and then my perfect man wasn't so perfect anymore. All the silly things ran through my mind, and it was forgotten when I felt his thumb playing those delicious circles on the inside of my legs.

"Don't go too far," he said with a smile, knowing well my thoughts ran amok.

I tipped my chin up and captured his lips, giving a slow kiss, full of intent and enough passion to feel his body move against mine. His hips pressed me down and when I moaned inside his mouth, I felt him bucking like I unleashed something inside of him.

His hand covered my waist, holding me there and nipping my jaw. He teased me with his tip. I felt it right on my oversensitive clit. A needy whimper surfaced, and Dan took over. Holding me still, aligning himself to my entrance as his eyes found mine. Those beautiful hazels in a silent request.

I nodded again, and in a flash, he pushed inside, just a little, but felt like an invasion. He lowered his head, biting my earlobe. "Breathe for me, Cricket," his voice strained.

I kind of did, a deep breath, but then he pushed himself again, circling my nipple with his thumb and then I was sucking air in and moaning right after.

"Are you with me?"

I nodded, but Daniel tsked. "I need your words, Hallie."

He hitched my leg at an angle and pushed again. I took more of him and held my breath. I knew it was going to be too much. But he kissed me and touched me, and I felt my legs turn liquid. My heart sped up.

"You have enough of me," I found it in me to say.

"I want more." He pushed, and I felt the exact moment he bottomed out. "I want all of you."

I held onto him like a lifeline. "Greedy."

He moved, bringing his hips back and forward. "When it comes to you, I am."

I threw my head back, and he took the opportunity to lick between my breasts. Over and over again, he pounded on me, careful and careless at the same time. I wiggled under him, heat curled down my spine every time he thrusted deep. He moved me like a raggedy doll, his hands biting into my thighs. He turned my hips the way it fitted him better. He bit me, I ached, and he soothed with his tongue.

He took my words, my moans, and my trust. I held on to his strong shoulder. I cried his name, and he drove his dick all the way to the hilt.

He swallowed my pleas; I shuddered under him and he thrusted with abandon. Once, twice, and then he was coming. Jaw set, muscles taut. Never in a thousand years would I forget the way he looked when he came on top of me.

"Jesus Christ, Cricket."

My laugh was hollow. It felt odd coming out of my throat. I never had overused my voice before. "So, I did well?"

He pulled from me, lying on my side but keeping a possessive hand over my stomach. "You're fantastic."

I turned to him, my beaming smile so big it was a little pathetic. But Dan didn't seem to think so. His smile matched mine. His hair plastered with sweat over his forehead, his breathing labored.

And suddenly, I was home.

My legs dangled on the edge of the most beautiful table I'd ever seen. It was sacrilege to sit on top of it, but it was Dan who hoisted me up and then put a plate of lasagna in my hands. I ate happily, dressed only in his signature plaid shirt, my hair tousled and cheeks rosy.

The man himself watched me eat, leaning over the counter in a low-hung pajama and a silly grin on his lips.

"You're looking at me like when you were trying to make me talk."

"I'll never stop trying."

I lifted a shoulder and took a bite. He watched me eating, which was a little unnerving, but soon I got lost in the flavor. The lasagna was amazing. I moaned when the flavors exploded in my tongue.

"Is this one of the two things you know how to cook?" I pointed to the plate with my fork.

Dan nodded slowly. "My mother's recipe. Abby is trying to get her clutches on it since high school."

I laughed. "Your mom won't share? Not even with her daughter-in-law?"

"I'm told it's a secret sauce from her Italian side. The risotto is also amazing."

"I gather is the other thing you know how to make?"

"You know what I am feeding you next." He winked.

"I don't mind the rotation. I could eat this forever." I took another forkful. "I wished I had recipes from my mother."

"Preston has nothing?" He wanted to know.

I shook my head. "Mom was Filipino. I remember she cooked a few traditional dishes when I was little, but my dad never knew how to make them. That part of me got lost."

Dan crossed his arms over his chest. "How about we collect a few recipes online? You can check for something you remember."

"Yeah…" I frowned, wondering why I never thought of it.

"You said it, Cricket. That's part of you. It doesn't need to be lost. It's hard for Preston to celebrate a culture that isn't his, but it's yours. We can make new traditions."

I smiled. "Can Dad be part of it?"

He walked toward me, shaking his head. I put my plate to the side. When he reached me, his palms covered my tights and up, leaving me exposed.

"Well, I had a different kind of dinner in mind. But I guess I can reschedule it for now if you insist," he told me. "Lean back, Hallie."

I did what I was told. Leaning back, he placed my knees apart, bringing my ass to the edge of the table. His breath fanned over my leg, nipped the inside of my knee. My head tipped back, taking a breath at the same time he licked me long and wet, giving a swirl when he reached my clit. My leg jerked, and he held me still.

"Quiet, Ms. Delos Santos. It's my dinner time, now."

Doorbell.

I heard it in the distance, a faraway dream. It rang again and my eyes flew open. A heavy hand weighed me down, right on my waist, keeping me close to his chest. A leg over mine. I felt his erection between my ass cheeks. I never slept with anyone, but I thought I was doing great. I fit so perfectly in his arms; I loved his house, his furniture, his taste. I couldn't wait to see what kind of meal he had planned for breakfast. I hoped it wasn't lasagna or risotto.

Doorbell.

I moaned, moving and making the man behind me move, too. "Dan," I called.

"Hmm," he replied.

"Dan, your doorbell."

Like it was rehearsed, it rang once again. "See? Someone is at your door."

"Tell them to leave."

"I'm not answering your door."

"Neither am I."

I giggled. He held me closer, his hand roaming from my stomach to between my legs. Last night he said we weren't going to do anything again since I was a little sore. After our little dinner date in the kitchen, we had a shower, and I might have used my hands on him. And then in the middle of the night he woke me up with kisses, and in a blink, he was inside of me again.

I was sore, sure. But it was a delicious kind of sore, throbbing in a way I didn't mind one bit.

I felt the pad of his finger circling over my clit. I gasped at the same time the doorbell rang again.

"Dan..." I shook my head when he dipped a finger. "Go answer the door and tell them to fuck off."

He chuckled behind me. "It's like I'm a bad influence."

"You are," I agreed. "Here I am, naked in a much older man's bed. What would the town of Bluehaven ever say to that?"

"The town of Bluehaven needs to go fuck themselves."

"Great. Start saying that to whoever is at your door." And the doorbell rang again, this time came accompanied by rushed knocks.

Dan stiffened, worried for the first time. Someone was too keen on talking to him. It was still early enough, and my senses flared. He removed his hand from me. I tried not to whine. With a quick movement, Dan checked his phone on the bedside, probably not finding anything as he tossed on the bed the next second. He fished his bottoms from the floor, and I watched, sitting up.

"I'll get rid of them," he guaranteed. "Don't you dare get dressed." As a warning, he kissed me quickly and then tweaked my nipple.

"Hey!" I slapped his hand away, but he laughed and left the room, jogging downstairs.

I let out a satisfied sigh. It was Sunday. We could stay naked for the rest of the day if I told Dad.

About not coming home, not the naked thing.

I left the bed, searching for my phone, when I heard Daniel's shout whisper. "What the hell are you doing here?"

It was something about the tone of his voice that made me stop. The way he whispered, clearly scared of me overhearing.

I knew how to keep quiet. I knew how not to meddle in people's business.

Still, I tip-toed to the door and opened just a little to let the voices invade the bedroom.

"Are you fucking serious?" A woman's voice called. "Who do you think you are?"

"Who do I think I am?" Daniel replied with more disdain than I've ever heard in his voice. "You need to get out of *my* house."

The way they argued had my hands closing on my dress. I put it over my head, and something in me stirred with awareness.

"I won't go anywhere before you give me answers," the stranger demanded.

But even as I thought of her as a stranger, I didn't believe it. It was something in her voice, the intonation. The way she pronounced each word. I knew that voice. My body shook, but my brain wouldn't catch up. Who?

Who?

I completely opened the door, my feet padding on the floor, my ears waiting for more.

"I don't owe you any explanation. You need to leave." Dan's harsh tone said.

"I told you I won't leave. This is ridiculous. I had fucking Ryan calling to tell me about this bullshit. What the hell, Dan?"

The hairs of my arms stood up. I took a step toward the stairs, enough to have a perfect view of the front door.

In front of Daniel, still in his pajamas, she stood.

A beautiful white dress, blond hair cascading down her shoulders like liquid gold. Perfect nose, professionally shaped eyebrows and a sneer on her lips.

The last time I saw her, she was in gym clothes holding a Polaroid.

She looked different, but I'd never forget Katie Campbell's face.

20.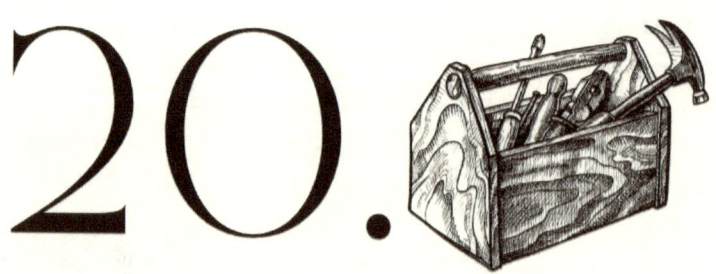

I KNEW BEFORE I swung the door open.

Before I trekked downstairs, before the doorbell even rang. The cold sweat ran down my spine, my knuckles white when they closed around the doorknob.

I knew it was coming. The world had its own way of righting a wrong, and I was wrong. I just wished it wasn't like this.

But I couldn't blame the stars, fate, or the universe. I was a grown man, and I knew what I was doing. I lied to get my way. Yeah, the words weren't pretty, but I couldn't keep excusing myself anymore. I had to face it the way Hallie was going to see it. And she would see deceit. Nothing more, nothing less.

I could have spoken up, I could have avoided it all. But I didn't, I shamelessly kept going and the past always—*always*—catches up.

My time was up, so it wasn't a surprise when I opened the door and the blond woman stared back at me. I knew in my bones it was time for the truth, but it didn't mean I would not fight it.

"Leave," I said at once.

Katie's eyes widened. She had so much of her sister, of her mother. I could see it now. Her mouth was closed in a thin line. I remember when she used to smile at me. Sassy, full of humor. A young, selfless nurse, I was told. My blood ran cold.

"What the hell is going on, Dan?" she spat once the force of my opening blow wore off.

"Nothing is going on," I replied, holding myself not to turn my face in the bedroom's direction. I didn't want to give her any sign of what was going on upstairs. I'd die before I let her put eyes on Hallie again. "What are you doing here?"

"Is that all you have to say to me?" She crossed her arms over her chest.

I shook my head, pinching the bridge of my nose. Once upon a time, I liked Katie's confidence. I always liked outspoken women, and she was one. She even reminded me a little of Kelly, which was weird at first. But I accepted I had a type. But Katie was nothing like my ex-wife. Kelly was a lot of things, but she was never cruel. She wouldn't dare to go over another person.

Katie's confidence was hungry. It needed to be fed over and over again, and her main meal was the naked girl in my bed.

Not anymore.

Awareness prickled my skin. I hated that Katie was breathing the same air as Hallie. I hated I was the reason for it.

"You're the one who came to my house Sunday morning without warning. Don't you think I should be the one asking, what do you want?" I knew what she wanted, of course, but I was going to keep pretending. "What the hell are you doing here?" The line was delivered with such force, even I winced. I was supposed to be keeping quiet and drive Katie away, but I couldn't help my voice to rise, the hairs on the back of my neck to stand still.

"Are you fucking serious? Who do you think you are?" She retorted.

I bit back a growl. I was done with this. Even if I wasn't desperately trying to protect Hallie, even if she wasn't waiting for me, I'd still want Katie out. I told her to leave once more, barely keeping the disdain out of my voice. It couldn't be helped. But she wanted an explanation, and I was tired of pretending I didn't know for what.

"I don't owe you any explanation. You need to leave."

There. Assertive. Firm. I was almost threatening to call the cops. I just wanted her out.

"I told you I won't leave." She pressed a hand up to her forehead. "This is ridiculous. I had fucking Ryan calling me about this bullshit. What the hell, Dan?"

I opened my mouth, but we were interrupted by a tumble upstairs. I closed my eyes in defeat, breathing through my nose, holding the door open even though all I wanted was to close it. But if I closed it, Katie would start a scene. I had no doubts about it.

"I need you to leave right now." I gritted over my teeth.

It took just a second for my desperation to give me away. Katie glanced upstairs. "She's here, isn't she?"

"I'll call the cops, Katie," I said, but it fell on deaf ears.

"Delos Santos?" It was a mix of hatred and mocking. "Are you fucking with me?"

Hallie's last name was the prayer unsaid. In the second that it was off Katie's lips, it floated through the house, bounced off the walls, and filled the gaps of our existence. Intertwined. Hallie, Katie and me. I was the fucking string that connected them. I was the thread that should be cut.

I opened my mouth to order Katie out once more. I said it so many times the words started to lose their meaning. But the last orders never left my lips. The heavy boots on the wooden floor announced my time was up. I tipped my head down, knowing well my fate.

The excuses ran through my mind. One worse than the next.

It's not what you're thinking.

I didn't know.

She's leaving now.

Fake. Premeditated. I knew this was something I had to face eventually, but my whole body screamed not to be now. Not like this. Not when it tasted so much like betrayal and my lips still tasted like hers. Katie raised her eyes beyond my head. I felt the tingle in the back of my neck, and, with a sigh, I turned to look at Hallie.

Completely dressed and still looking thoroughly fucked. My bite marks over her neck, her tousled hair messy from my hands. She was always regal, my Hallie. Chin up and grace that people couldn't grasp. I wanted her to look at me. I wanted her to see how sorry I was, to read between my frown, my apologetic gaze. But her eyes burned on the woman behind me. Unreadable.

Maybe that was why Katie was so bothered by Hallie. Katie tried to break her for years, and look at her now? Perfect, gorgeous and whole.

"Aren't you pathetic enough?" Katie's voice sliced through the silence, breaking the spell.

I whipped my head back to Katie, a growl growing in my throat like a caged animal. "Don't speak to her like that."

Katie huffed. "This is her petty revenge from high school. Can't you see?" And looking back at Hallie, she added. "Leave me alone!"

Of course, Katie thought Hallie was planning revenge. She was mean enough to do it, so she must have thought everyone lived like that. I shook my head, exasperated about how wrong she was, but Hallie called me.

"Dan?" My whole body warmed with her voice. I stepped away from the door, leaving it unattended. My biggest fear just happened in front of my eyes. Nothing mattered anymore. "What's happening?" Hallie asked.

I faced her, my head tipped up to look into her eyes. My hands shaking, proof of my cowardice. "Nothing is happening," I told her in sweet tones. "Katie is leaving." Not as sweet as when I spoke the other woman's name.

Hallie stilled on the steps, just three from the bottom. Her eyes darted between Katie and me, like it was a math problem she couldn't solve. It was my fault. I had all the answers, but I didn't want to have the conversation there in front of Katie. Not when she could twist things just to watch it burn. Not when she was calling Hallie names.

Katie roared behind me, but even that was muted when I looked at Hallie. She frowned, and her gaze found mine. Questioning in silence.

I could always hear her without words. I always gave her answers before she asked them, but there, when I should've given them, I remained quiet. Her lips quivered, something mean Katie said behind our backs. She was talking still, but I couldn't hear anymore. My hands closed in a fist, and Hallie followed the movement. She read the apologies in my eyes and the anger steaming off my body.

"I was going to tell you."

Even as I said it, it sounded lame. She needed the whole story, and I was giving her crumbs. I turned to the blond banshee, jaw set. "Go away."

Loud. Unflinching. I was done.

"Dan." Katie hiccupped, taken aback by my tone for the first time. "Don't you see what she's doing? She hates me, always has. This is a plot." She shook her head, looking back at Hallie over my shoulder. "Did it help? Did it make you feel better sleeping with my boyfriend?"

Time stood still. I was too old to be someone's boyfriend, and I certainly wasn't Katie's. I growled about the wrongness of the statement, but Hallie was on the move. Like lightning struck and set her free. She went down the stairs, passing Katie and me at the bottom. I called her name because it was my favorite prayer, with no plans of what to say if she actually let me speak.

She didn't, though. Hallie marched to the side, grabbing her bag and hurried to the door.

"Hallie, I swear, I broke up with Katie six months ago." I turned to Katie. "We broke up six months ago!"

"The whole town knows you are together. I knew it was a plot to get my attention..."

I left her talking because Hallie was moving across my lawn. Out of my property, out of my life. It was the first hours of the morning, a couple of neighbors were leaving for church, and another grabbing the newspaper. Normal Bluehaven stuff. And there I was, barefoot, with my pajama bottoms, running down the street after Hallie, leaving Katie's screeches behind.

By noon, the whole town would know what happened. I put Hallie in that position. They would talk and tear her apart and I was the responsible this time.

"Hallie! Hallie, please!"

She spun with force, a fierce expression, tears down her cheeks. I hated myself right there. I wanted to protect her so much and I couldn't. I was a coward, like the rest of the town.

"You dated Katie Campbell?"

I halted. My lack of response was enough for her. Her head shook. She took a step back, and I followed with one forward.

"Hallie I..."

"Your ex-girlfriend is Katie Campbell." An arrow without mercy. And then she turned and marched away. I was on the move the next second, jogged in front of her, stopping in her tracks.

"We broke up months ago, I promise you. I have no idea what she's doing here..."

"She's here because she thinks I'm plotting revenge!" Hallie yelled. "She's here because she knows the whole picture when I don't!"

"She doesn't, not if she thinks you would..."

"Yes. I wouldn't get with you to stick it to her because I'm not insane. But it's more than that. It's because I didn't know Katie was your ex." As she said it, she winced.

My hands raised, like I could prevent her from running. "Hallie, listen to me. Can we talk?"

"How long did you know?" She asked quickly, a tear running down her cheek. She wiped it with the back of her hand.

"Hallie..." I shook my head. Ashamed.

"How long did you know your ex-girlfriend was the same one who took those pictures of me?"

I closed my eyes. I opened them again, and Hallie was still there, watching.

"When I learned it was her, I liked you enough already. I didn't want you to think..."

What didn't I want her to think? That I was hiding it? That I was stupid enough to fall for Katie's charm?

"I liked the way you looked at me," I added lamely.

Now she looked at me like she looked to the rest of Bluehaven. Disloyalty. I liked to be the one exception, but now... Now I was one of them. One of Katie's.

I hated my skin for ever touching her. I hated my past self for never seeing the cruelty the easy smile hid. I was ashamed for ever thinking Katie was a good person. A nurse, a young girl full of friends and a loving family. God, we weren't even that serious. I never met her family, but she talked enough of them for me to think they were good people.

"When? The Ferris Wheel?" she pressed, and I nodded.

It was only when Hallie said the name of her tormentor that I put two and two together. And once I did, everything fell into place. I knew Sharon and Delilah were Katie's family, but when I asked Hallie if she knew why the Campbells hated her, she said no.

I could've pressed for a better answer, but I felt safe about the answer I had.

I rubbed my face, collecting my thoughts. "I broke an arm a while back. Mark was with me and insisted on driving me to the hospital, next town over. She works there as a nurse. I never knew... Hallie, it was our first date already when I found out she was from Bluehaven. I..."

"She got a date." She smiled between tears.

I flinched. I thought my stupid plan of making my mother's recipe was intimate enough for her. But maybe she wanted a date around town?

"Our date was special. I wanted to show you my house, my life."

Hallie nodded, stopping my explanations. "It doesn't matter. I don't think it matters."

Her tone made my blood turn cold. The finality of it, the slight rolls of her shoulders. She was already done with me, even when the words weren't hanging between us yet.

"Hallie. I'm so sorry. I was going to tell you. I didn't want you finding out like this. It was a coincidence. A horrible one."

"It was a coincidence," she agreed, and for a second, I almost thought I won. It was a freaky coincidence that the first woman I started to see after my divorce was the same person who drove Hallie out of town.

"I should've told you the second I realized," I offered.

"Yes. But you were right. I'd never get close to someone who..." she blinked out tears. I stepped in her direction, and she stepped away. A simple gesture that sliced me through.

"Hallie, I'm so sorry." It was the only thing I could say.

"I know." She nodded. "I'm sorry, too." I didn't like that one bit. Too raw, too final, too resolute. Hallie's pain was the loudest. I saw it in her eyes, her frown, the shake of her hands. It tasted like spoiled milk on my tongue. I felt over my shoulders and clogging my lungs.

"You don't need to be sorry."

Her eyes unfocused from me, looking over my shoulder. I knew she was watching Katie somewhere in the distance. I didn't turn around. I was done looking at Katie's face.

Her eyes fixed back on me, swirling in tears, making them look like bottomless black lakes. "I could get over many things. But this? Her? You were right. I'd never talk to you if I knew. I'd never be with you, I'd never..." she swallowed, looking down and then back at me with a frown. "I can't never."

She stepped back and then turned. I watched as she left, getting lost in the street. More neighbors were out of their houses now, curious about what was the commotion. I stood there like a statue, my Adam's apple bobbing, my eyes stinging with tears.

I fucking lost her forever.

I knew it in my bones. I slept with the devil and I could never take that back.

Like a riptide, Hallie went. Crushing, destroying, leaving me barefoot as she walked home without looking back.

21.

THE NEEDLE PRICKLED THE pads of my fingers, but I kept going.

One stitch after the other. The sewing machine stood unused at our shed, but today I was punishing myself. I brought my work to the living-room, face to face with my mother's picture right in the middle of the wall.

It was Monday. I called Marian with a fake cough and bailed work, then texted Mrs. Carr and lied, too. Sunday morning, when I arrived back home with tears still hanging off my lashes, Dad was at church. It gave me time to have a shower and clean Daniel's smell off my body and hope to wash off the humiliation as well.

Humiliation that was unwanted, not needed. I believed him. It was just a freaky coincidence. Even when the rage coiled in my stomach, like a cobra waiting to strike. Even then, I reminded myself he was right to hide it from me. Not right exactly, but he was right to assume I'd never have given him a time of day if I knew he was linked to Katie.

I wanted to ignore it. They broke up, he said. He was with me now. I wanted to roll my shoulder and accept that in a small town, sometimes things like that happened. I wanted to be stronger and forget my past for once and for all.

I was disappointed with myself. I thought I was stronger when I decided to come back to Bluehaven, ready to face them. It wasn't everyone in town who did me wrong, but it was the shadows who haunted me. I was for so long scared of moving, of buying the wrong clothes, eating the wrong things. For years, their snickers followed me around and I forgot it wasn't the entire town.

Daniel was a beacon of light. The biggest proof I wasn't the same Hallie anymore and Bluehaven wasn't that bad. And now... Now he was tainted.

I recoiled from my own assessment, stitching the fabric in my hands with fury, until I got a little too aggressive and prickled my finger again, drawing blood. I stopped, sucking the blood between my lips. I raised my head and looked at Mom.

She was beautiful. Smiling down at me, untouched by time. Eternally young.

"I wished you were here to tell me what to do," I whispered, too low to be heard, but loud enough to reach heaven.

I blinked tears away, resting my hands on my lap, tired of pretending to work. I was so lost in Mom, I almost missed Dad's heavy steps coming home for lunch. He stood by the door, a frown similar to mine, arms across his chest. I sniffed away, looking down, scared of being caught crying.

"What the hell happened, Hallie?"

"Nothing." It was quick, but he spoke over me. "Don't lie."

I sighed. Daddy wasn't dumb. Of course, something happened. I left for the night, something I never did before, and came back crushed. Even though he never witnessed how I looked when I arrived from Daniel's, my misery was palpable.

Dad stepped inside the room, a vein on his neck pulsed. That wasn't the Preston White I knew, the easygoing, loose laugh at the hardware store. He looked bigger, broader, commanding.

. "Bug..." He shook his head, daring me to lie once more.

"I can't now," I told him. "I can't talk right now."

A beat. Dad was so tall, so big in the eyes of his only daughter. He looked ready to murder, and I wiped a lonely tear away. He took his eyes from me and looked at Mom's portrait, like she was there, a mediator between us.

For a second, we both stared at her, silently begging she would barge at the front door, talking fast and a lot. To fill the house with her voice, with her mess, with her loud TV as she cooked. All those little fragments of memories. I gripped onto them and prayed she came alive from the picture and resumed activities sixteen years after her death.

She didn't. So eventually, we faced each other. The only ones still alive. The hole in our house never felt so big. I always needed a mother, but now? I screamed for one. I craved a lap to cry on, kind words and a caress in my hair.

"I'll wait, bug," Dad said. "I'll wait until you're ready."

The tiniest of smiles came over my lips. Grateful, if not for anything. I was grateful for Dad.

I DITCHED THE TRAY to the side and hurried to the kitchen. A busboy made a face when I almost bumped into him on my way in. Heart thumping fast in my chest, I let out a breath, combing my hair out of my face just to catch Torres at the grill watching me.

I opened my mouth to explain myself. But what explanation did I have?

I was supposed to be working when I couldn't feign illness anymore, and now I was hiding in the kitchen. But I couldn't go out there.

The whole of Bluehaven knew something happened between Daniel, Katie and me. The scene in front of his house wasn't left unnoticed and, of course, all kinds of gossip flew about. Things about Daniel being a predator and getting on with us when we were at Bluehaven High. Talks of a love triangle, a threesome and everything in between.

Every single night I waited for Dad to come talk to me, demand answers for whatever he heard around town. But like the last time, the stories didn't reach him, thank goodness. Maybe people had just a little sense.

It wasn't new to me. I could handle Bluehaven gossip. What I couldn't handle was to be in the same room as *him*. So I was holding on well, ignoring the whispers and just going about my business, but when I saw the flash of caramel hair, the plaid shirt, and forearms dotted with blond hairs...

I couldn't.

I ran.

Marian entered the kitchen, wagging a yellow pencil in my direction. "Why are you hiding in my kitchen?"

I lifted a shoulder.

"You're hiding, right?"

I twisted my lips, but eventually nodded fast. She dipped her chin. "I'll cover for you."

I breathed, relieved, and Torres offered me a can of soda with a smile. I took it and drank, thinking about what I was supposed to do if Daniel came to Torres' every day. How the hell was I supposed to work?

Ten minutes later, Marian was back. "You know, I was ready to talk you through a breakup when you were a teenager. This talk is overdue."

I hopped down from the counter I was sitting on and straightened up my apron. "You don't have to talk me through anything."

"You hear that?" she asked her husband, who flipped a burger while snickering. "She's hiding in my kitchen and tells me it's all good."

Torres chuckled, and I frowned at his back. "I said I don't need to talk through it. Not that it's ok."

Marian looked me up and down. "The man looks like a damn movie star and when he said your name, it was like he was slashing a part of his arm. What did he do so bad, Hallie?"

To this, even Torres stopped working to face me. I closed my eyes and I shook my head.

"Tell me you don't listen to gossip, Hals," Marian said. "That story about him and..."

"Not a story." I gulped.

Her eyebrows shot up. "I hope the part about the threesome is a lie."

"Gross, Marian." I made a face. "I mean, she's his ex. He and Katie." I took a breath. "Katie and Daniel," I said, just to drive the knife further to my chest.

"It's not something you can forgive, right?"

I didn't ask how she knew about my trauma with Katie, but gossip always comes to the diner first, so it wasn't a surprise.

"It's not about forgiveness," I told her truthfully. "I just can't. It's the only thing I can't."

Katie and Daniel were the two people who saw me naked, ironically. Of course, more people were there in the locker room, and much more saw the pictures. Nevertheless, it felt like that. Katie took and to Dan I gave willingly. And it didn't matter how much my heart hurt, I couldn't get over that. That connection, that... Lie.

He lied because he knew we were doomed. We were over before we started.

I TOLD DAD I was going to help organize the shelves with the new stock, and he accepted. It was Saturday, most of the costumes were already done and I spent a full hour looking at the dress I started making for myself so many weeks ago, but bailed again when I got distracted with other things.

Tired of my inner war, I grabbed my things and marched to White Hardware with a chicken pasta lunch for Dad and Cole. Dad helped a customer while Cole managed the till, and I worked around them. Cleaning what didn't need to be cleaned, fixing things that weren't broken.

I took a bunch of things from the first drawer behind the counter just to organize and put it back in again. I was so engrossed in my useless task

I barely noticed when the bell above the door chimed and the whole shop stopped.

My hands stilled on my task and I watched as my fingers shook. The surrounding air charged. His scent reached me like a brick wall. Drawing a calming breath, I looked up. He was barely at the door, those hazel eyes eating me alive.

"Hallie..." Daniel started.

"No," boomed Dad. "No."

He crossed the shop, and I was already shaking my head. "Dad..."

"I just need to talk to Hallie for a second, Preston."

"If she wanted to talk to you, she would have sought you."

Dad knew nothing about the ordeal, but his loyalty was heart-warming.

Dad and Daniel were locked in a stalemate, as Cole looked like the cat who got the milk. We all stood in silence, and then, one by one, the customers left. Only a few that time of day, but finally, when the bell above the door rang for the last time, I licked my lips and ordered. "Talk."

Daniel looked around. Dad and Cole were there. Not ideal, but I didn't care. He knew we were done, but still he came around Torres'. Still, he texted and called. He knew my reasons. He knew why this could never work. But I simply couldn't be alone with him. As it was, with the giant watchdog that was Dad, I barely could hold still.

He cleared his throat. Dad was wearing a scowl and his student had the biggest smirk yet.

"I had no idea you and Katie knew each other." It was his first sentence.

"Not at first." I pressed my fingers to the counter.

"No. Not at first." He swallowed. "I broke my arm last year, and she's a nurse at the hospital. We met and started dating."

I closed my eyes. I heard shuffling, and when I opened them, I realized it was Dad coming closer. Trying to get between me and Daniel.

"I know that already," I strangled out. "You should've told me on the Ferris Wheel. Right there when you realized it was the same person."

He raked his fingers through his hair, looking exhausted. "Right after you told me everything she did to you?" he pierced me with a look. "How could I tell you the monster who haunted your dreams was someone I dated?"

"She doesn't haunt my dreams." Not anymore. I stuck my chin up.

"I didn't want that connection."

"I get that."

"My choice was poor," he added.

"It was," I agreed.

"Hallie..."

"What about Sharon and Delilah?" I wanted to know.

He shrugged. "I knew it was her family because of the last name, but I never met them. We weren't serious."

"Serious enough for her to think I used you to get to her. For Ryan to be reporting to her. Have you ever met him?"

If he did... God, he was a good actor. The way he acted when I revealed Ryan was there that day... Not possible. That was a lie.

Daniel shook his head, a tick in his jaw. "I never met her friends. Cricket..." I stilled with the nickname. He sighed. "Hallie. I dated her for a few months. It wasn't serious. I was messed up after my divorce. When I saw it was going toward something I couldn't give, I broke it off. She was upset, sure, but nothing crazy. I'd never thought she was going to knock on my door like that."

My fingers closed around the cloth I was using to clean the drawers. I dared to look at my side. Cole was done smirking, his eyes cast down like he wanted to disappear. And then I made the mistake of looking at Dad.

His blue eyes devastated me. Confusion pained his features, shaking like he was holding by a thread. That was my fault. I knew it. I took such a wonderful dad and threw him in the dark. He was never going to win that battle. The obstacle wasn't parenthood; it was me.

I turned back to Daniel, the urgency to speak to my father rang in my ears. I looked right into Daniel's handsome face, his open expression. I wasn't going to shame him for having a rebound relationship with Katie. Suddenly everything weighed on my shoulders, and the tears threatened to drop.

"I told you everything," It came like a whisper. An accusatory whisper that shook the walls of my dad's hardware shop. "I told you about the most horrific thing that happened to me and... What do I know about you, Daniel?"

This ignited something in him. He poked the counter between us. "You know everything about me."

"Do I?" I frowned. "I don't think so. It was one-sided. You were so busy trying to take the words out of me you forgot you had to give something back. And honestly, I let that happen. I wanted to feel brave, and I wanted to share for the first time in my life, but what happened Sunday? When I was with you and my nightmare came knocking? Jesus, Dan ." I breathed it out. "You know me inside out. There's a disconnection here and... I will not pressure you. I know what it's like to be silent and keep people out of your business, but I won't be waiting around to figure out things about you by accidents knocking on our door."

"Hallie... This is not—"

"This is how it felt," I hammered down. "I might be quiet, Dan, but sometimes I make loud decisions."

We looked at each other for years, centuries. Probably just a second. He dipped his chin down, accepting.

"Goodbye, Dan," I said at last.

22.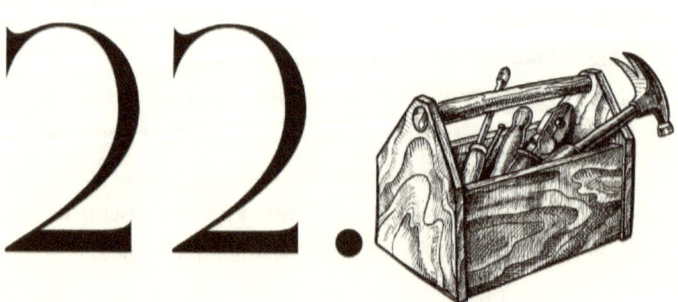

"Is it true?"

I narrowed my eyes and scanned the classroom, and yes, we were the only ones in an earshot. The next student was two benches to the left.

My classroom was quiet, everyone working on their piece as AC/DC played in the background. Nothing had changed in that area. The workshop was still a sanctuary where my troubled kids could rewind and create something solid.

Cole was working in an entertainment center, mask on as he stained the wood crouched on his bent knees. I looked at his work under furrowed eyebrows. Cole was a student, and he knew too much of my business. I wanted to tell him to pay better attention to the work in hand, but even though he was sneaking glances waiting for my reply, his stain work was impeccable. Son of a bitch.

"What are you talking about, Thompson?" I grumbled.

Leaving the paintbrush to the side, he went up to his full height, and he put his mask down.

"The things everyone is saying about Hallie and the Campbells."

"What's that to do with you?" I spat.

The fucking nerve. Cole looked from one side to the other, shaking his head. "You know that saying? It's a secret, so everyone knows?"

"Isn't that a line from *Harry Potter*?" I watched it recently with Rose and April.

For the first time, Cole's cheeks warmed, making him look like a kid besides his height.

"The point is that Katie is telling everyone Hallie tried to steal her boyfriend in revenge."

"I broke up with Katie months ago," I said automatically.

"Great, don't care." Cole shook his head. "Don't shoot the messenger. I know this Katie is obviously lying."

I rubbed my face. "Goddamn Campbells." Cole hummed, more of a surprised sound that made my ears twitch. "What?"

He rolled his shoulders. "Nothing. I just... That's not very Delilah, you know?"

My eyebrows soared. The Delilah I knew? She was as much as a bully as her older sister.

"Don't get me wrong, she's a piece of work. We were in the same class together since kindergarten. She's dramatic, over the top and an overachiever."

The word *actor* rang in my head.

"But she was never a bully. Never stood to this kind of behavior, quite loudly, actually. She's... She's a loner. Never really close to anyone." He shrugged. "I don't know... For what I heard about her sister, they sound like the polar opposites."

To me, she never showed to be anything but a horrible bully, a spoiled brat. But Hallie had been saying she was just a kid. Saying we don't know if Katie poisoned her mind. Whatever it was, I didn't care about Delilah Campbell. I wasn't interested at all in her sad little story about being a loner because she was horrible to Hallie and that was enough of a sin to me.

"Don't listen to gossip and go back to work," I barked.

Cole chuckled, proving I had no authority. "I don't listen to gossip, Mr. M. But I am saying people are making it impossible for Hallie to live her life. She bailed once... Why wouldn't she bail twice?"

The answer was on the tip of my tongue. Because she was older and stronger. Because she deserved to live in peace as much as the next citizen of Bluehaven. Because she survived when her mother passed, when kids bullied her, when people called her names. She survived that horrible day in the locker room.

Hallie Delos Santos was a survivor. And she wasn't going to bow down now.

I opened my mouth, but closed it when I heard the commotion. A smack at the front gate, rushed steps down the corridor and then a thunder in the middle of the school.

"Anderson!"

Unmistakably Preston White.

I jumped into action at once, holding a hand high to the class. "Stay where you are."

When I opened the door, the blurred shape of Preston was stalking the corridors, calling the principal's name once more. From everywhere across the hall, doors were opened. Students stuck their heads out while some just watched from the small glass window at each classroom's door. Staff stopped in their tracks with hands over their mouths. My own students piled behind me, ignoring my wishes.

"I said stay back!" I growled, but didn't grace them with a look.

Anderson finally left his office, raking his hand over his head, shocked to say at least. "What's the meaning of this, Preston? You can't come in during school hours-"

He never got to finish that sentence. The man clocked the principal with a furious hit straight to the jawline. Anderson was smaller. He stumbled back, his secretary muffled a scream. I ran, putting myself between them, my hand on Preston's chest, keeping him back.

Anderson shouted about how Preston dared to do such a thing, urging the teachers to call the police.

I shook my head. "I wouldn't do this if I—"

Preston laughed. The ice quality of it made my blood run cold. "You better call the police, Anderson, otherwise I'll finish you up. Hurry, the clock is ticking."

Preston advanced again, and I held him back. His eyes flashed to my face like it was the first time he noticed I was between them.

"Do you know?" He asked. "Everything?"

I gave him the smallest nod.

"And you let him walk? Let him care for the children?"

Shame washed over me. Yes, I felt all those things Preston was feeling. I was done with the way Anderson managed things way before I knew what happened to Hallie, but I never thought about the other kids. The other Hallies under his thumb.

"Your job is to protect kids," Preston was shouting, "You should protect *all* kids!"

"Get this man out of my school!"

"You better not call the cops, Anderson," I gritted over my shoulder.

"And why is that?" Anderson scoffed.

"Do you still have her pictures?" Preston cut in.

I breathed in as everyone else stopped breathing. The bell rang, but no one moved a muscle. The kids were watching over the teachers' shoulders anyway, some even filming the fight. Anderson's bravado faltered as he looked left to right, shaking his head, negating anything before it was out there. Nothing smelled more like guilt.

"I don't know what you are talking about."

"When a member of your staff took pictures of my naked underage daughter and distributed it to the class, did you keep the pictures or not? I know you had them when you accused my seventeen-year-old to be the one sharing them. Do you still have the damn pictures?"

I could've heard a pin drop. Anderson's secretary stepped back like her boss was infected. Teachers held onto the children. I heard Mrs. Garibaldi say, "We should call the police." But I knew she meant on Anderson and not Preston.

Something didn't click, though. "Member of the staff?"

Hallie's father only spared me a glance, and then his eyes were glued back on the disgraced principal. "Katie Campbell is a year older than Hallie. She was hired as a coach assistant at the time."

I let Preston go and turned in a growl, prowling toward Anderson. "Is that why you wanted to bury this? To protect yourself and the Campbells?"

"I did nothing!"

My gaze snapped to the other teachers, watching one by one, assessing who knew. My gaze stopped for a second on Helen, her mouth set in a straight line. Her hands shook as she stood beside the teacher's lounge door.

"You had pictures of a minor on your desk." My jaw ticked. "Not just you blamed her, but you failed to contact her father?"

Giving up on the pretense, Anderson's arms shot up. "Everyone said she was giving the pictures to the swim team!"

"Who told you that? Ryan? Who is now your school bus driver?" I shook my head. "The one who was laughing and holding the door so she wouldn't escape?"

My words fell on the floor between the principal and me. Preston shuffled behind me. I could almost feel the energy oozing off him. Dark menace. It matched mine. The school remained quiet. I felt the ground shake beneath my feet, but I knew it was just my rage.

"It wasn't what the other—"

Anderson started, but Preston was losing his grip. "And you believed them? You heard all the students who were guilty, decided it was my daughter who was the one to blame and not just cornered her, but put this under wraps? What's your excuse for not telling me?" Preston asked without really asking. "I know why. You knew I'd never believe that. I'd dig until the ends of the earth and find the people responsible for this assault. Your top two from the swim team, and a member of the staff whose parents donated thousands and thousands of dollars to the school. You chose money and trophies over my daughter. You let people talk behind her back, you let her go feeling alone."

I swallowed dry as I listened to Preston's speech. Anderson was a danger to the school. Preston was right; teachers were supposed to protect the students. All students. And Anderson was a man of vanities.

Preston stepped forward again, hands balled in a fist. I knew he wanted to make justice with his own hands. With one hand on his arm, I stopped him. He looked like he was going to jump me instead.

"Call the cops, Preston," I told him. "He's done. We'll make sure of it."

The man didn't move for a second, his vibrant blue eyes watching me, edging in red like his rage was so much, he couldn't help but to show it everywhere. A curt nod sealed Anderson's fate.

I wasn't naïve enough to think people would drag him to prison, but I was sure it was enough to have him fired. And if any other teachers knew about the incident and helped Anderson cover up, I was sure it was all going to come to the surface. Anderson wasn't exactly the loyal type.

With a sneer curling Preston's top lip, he gave one last look at the principal. The man was pale, eyes bloodshot in fear. Then Preston turned and walked away, his steps echoing in the hall until he was gone. Even in his absence, no one moved. No one dared to look at Anderson. It was Helen who finally spoke up. "Everyone, let's go. To the cafeteria."

It was the break, and for the first time, the kids weren't stumbling over themselves to get to the best table. The other teachers ushered the kids too, following Helen's initiative. When everyone moved along, I sprang into action, running after Preston.

I caught up with him by his car in the parking lot, his hands over the hood and his head down.

"Preston!" I called in a half walk, half jog toward him.

His blond head turned to the side, watching me come over without moving a muscle. Once I reached him, the words died on my lips.

"She told me after you left. Told me everything." His voice like gravel, gone was all that power he showed during the confrontation with the principal. "Was I that blind, Miller? So blind with grief I missed how much she was suffering?"

I called Preston blind before. Even resented him for not seeing and taking action. But the man in front of me wasn't someone to blame.

He was a husband who lost his wife in a tragedy so young, a man who raised his daughter the best he could. He was human. He couldn't be everywhere and see everything.

His hands left the hood, turning to me as his eyes scanned the building behind my back. "She was always such an easy child. Intelligent, independent. I thought I was lucky, I thought..." He shook his head.

"Hallie knows how to keep a secret," I offered.

His eyes focused on me. "Because she couldn't trust me enough. She had to keep the secret."

"It doesn't matter anymore. She's ok now."

"And the whole town is talking again." Preston's growl told me he was not even close to peace. A pointed look in my direction let me know he blamed me.

I suck in a breath, dipping my head down. "I know. I didn't know I..."

"Hallie said to me," he waved me off. "It was a freaky coincidence, she said. An incident."

The word incident was thrown there deliberately. So, he knew what Hallie called, what happened in the locker room. The tiredness caught me unaware. My shoulders slumped. I dragged my hand over my face.

"I can't change the past, Preston. I thought I was going to ask for forgiveness because I didn't tell her straight away, but I think it's more than that. She can't look at me without thinking of Katie." I confessed. "I..."

"You're scared she never will," her father finished for me.

I nodded. I was terrified to be forever Katie Campbell's ex-boyfriend. A crime she wasn't going to punish me for, but something she could never get over. The fragility of the situation was staggering. I never thought I'd see myself in a situation I couldn't fix.

When Kelly left me, I thought I felt powerless. I thought I cared a lot, and she was accusing me of something I couldn't convince her otherwise. I thought that was despair.

But as I stood there with Preston, I realized how wrong I was. Between Kelly and I lived resentment and the built-up frustration of two people who grew apart. But between Hallie and I, there was only love.

I saw my love for her so bright, so clear, but doomed. I couldn't change her past or mine. I couldn't do anything, and that nagging feeling that sometimes love isn't enough poked me in the ribs.

I wanted love to be enough. And if it wasn't, I was truly lost.

"Give her time," Preston spoke up.

"You think that's what she needs?"

He shrugged. "I don't know, but time helps with wounds. And in the meantime, have Katie Campbell shut up about my daughter, or her house is the next I visit."

And with that, he finally got into his car.

THREE DAYS AFTER MY talk with Preston, she waited for me in front of my house. Flowery dress flowing in the wind, blond hair in waves. I parked my truck in front and couldn't dare to take my hands off the wheels. She waited patiently, like the perfect lady she ought to be. Knuckles white, I glanced out front and our eyes caught. I wanted her away from me, but Preston's words rang in my ear.

She needed to stop saying things about Hallie. She needed to stop altogether and there wasn't much I could do to help, but I could do this.

With a last breath, I opened the truck's door and went outside. Her eyes perked up, and she smiled at me.

I hated her.

I hated myself.

"You have ten minutes," was my greeting, unlocking the door and throwing the keys on the hall table. I winced. Even my furniture had the memory of Hallie's fingers dancing over it.

I heard the door close behind her, but didn't look back to see if she was following me to the kitchen. When I turned around with my arms crossed over my chest, she was there. Waiting.

"You have to stop talking about Hallie," I started, directly to the point.

Her hopeful look turned ugly. "It's her that—"

My palm went up. I didn't even give her a chance to spin more lies. "Hallie isn't saying anything about you. I didn't even know your name for a long time."

"She got with you to attack me..."

I rolled my eyes. "Stop. She didn't even know I dated you until you barged in. I dated you for a few months ages ago, Katie. Why are you doing this?"

"Because I was waiting for you!" She yelled.

I frowned. "What do you mean, you waited for me?"

"I had a crush on you when you started at Bluehaven High. I wasn't a student anymore. I got a job as the assistant coach until I got things sorted for college."

"So, it wasn't only to torture Hallie?"

That was another detail I couldn't swallow. From what Hallie told me, it made it seem like they were the same age. That wouldn't make bullying better, but the fact was that Katie was over eighteen and one of the staff made it illegal.

"I'm not this horrible person she told you about," Katie defended herself.

"I already said she told me nothing about you," I gritted. "Keep going."

She nodded, looking all innocent. It made me angrier.

"I met you and you don't even remember. You were still married at the time, but I..."

"But you came on to me?" I asked.

"No..."

The way she said it sounded like a yes.

"And then I left... I thought it was it, but you came to the hospital. Single. Hitting on me. It was my chance."

I pinched the bridge of my nose. "And what does that have to do with Hallie?"

She reeled back, like I slapped right across her face.

"Nothing! This is between us."

"There's no us, Katie. There barely had been anything before. We were casual. I was just getting over my divorce, and it ran its course."

"Not to me!"

"I never gave you hope it was more serious than that. Never."

"I thought you could grow to..."

I sighed. "What does that have to do with Hallie?"

"You keep talking like it's all about her."

"It is!" My roar echoed. Katie took a step back. "You came to my house months after I gave you no hopes to be back together. You accused her of revenge when—"

"I was angry." She cut me off. "Ryan called and told me you were together. Other people around town too and I..." She stopped herself with a sigh.

"You had no right to come over here and speak to Hallie like that. You have no right to interfere with my life. I don't want to ever see you again now that I really know you."

"Dan, I don't know what she told you..."

"Katie." My tone was so sharp it could cut glass. "What you have done..." I held myself, sucking in a deep breath so the anger didn't consume me. "Each time I look at your face, my blood boils. Every time you say the name Ryan, I remember what you have done to her. There's no excuse, there's no reason." And I stopped her right before she uttered another word. "You did it because you're rotten and you wanted Hallie to be rotten with you. You wanted to poison her and make her as ugly as you, and guess what? It never happened. Not even at your worse, she kept being herself."

Katie shook right there in my kitchen, her expression turning monstrous.

"We were kids, Daniel."

"I think the fact you were over eighteen might change that narrative."

"She's not a victim, a damsel in distress you need to save. That's the kink, isn't it? She looks so lost and all traumatized. I'm the big villain because I never fell for it?"

Rage. I wanted to tell her Hallie never tried to convince anyone of anything. All she wanted was to be left alone. But the point was moot.

Katie wasn't going to understand how disgusting it was what she had done. I shook my head.

"I'd pray if I were you, Katie. The last word I had at school is that Anderson is being investigated because of what happened. Right now, everyone in Bluehaven knows." To this, she paled. I licked my lips. "You better pray it doesn't splash on you. On Ryan. And whoever else was there. You better pray like you never prayed before. Hold on to the pearls, you and your family, because the truth is in the open now, and everyone who was in that locker room, every teacher who turned their back, will be punished." Her jaw ticked. It was the only sign she hadn't turned into a statue. "Leave now."

My command left no room for arguments. Before the words were out of my lips, my hand was pointing to the door. I never wanted someone so far away from my home as I wanted Katie out of my life.

At the door, hand on the knob, she turned, a little smile on her lips like the cruel viper she always been. It was finally out for me to see.

"Do you think you're above it? You were there that day."

"Excuse me?" I stepped forward, my teeth grinding.

"I let her go. She darted out of the locker room, looking down, and I followed to see if she was going to Anderson. And she bumped into you, but you barely looked at her face. She was crying. Your hands were on her shoulder and you put her to the side. You're not a hero, Daniel. You don't care, just like the rest of them."

"Out!" I bellowed.

But the bitter taste never left my mouth.

23.

In Bluehaven, I could see a glimpse of water everywhere I went. The ground was flat, its geography narrowed, stretching along the coast. Everywhere I looked it was water and blue skies. Dad said it was what Mom always loved about it, a town so close to the water that salt stained the windows during a storm.

The beach was part of everyone's day-to-day life. Everyone but me, the girl who wouldn't go to the beach.

When Dad came home with a guilty look, I knew what he had done. Our conversation about the events of that day was a hard one. I hated reliving it, but telling Dad...

His eyes watered, his fist clenched. I hated them even more for hurting him. Dad believed he failed me. And when I finished telling him, when I finished painting the picture of Bluehaven through my eyes, I knew I had carved a knife into his heart.

Dad was all smiles and lifelong friends. He was fishing and sunny days. Church and reliable prices. I turned that good man into rage. He was a phantom of the person he had always been, and I wept at the loss of his innocence. I knew the roles were reversed, but in a house like ours, where the most important member left a gigantic hole, we needed to improvise. I had to protect him as much as he protected me. And I thought I did. For years, I was certain that protecting my dad was leaving him in the dark about what was happening at school. But now, when the past came back abruptly, and I left him looking so broken, I realized I did neither of us any good.

Everything was left in the open. No more secrets. Dad knew and confronted Anderson. I only needed a little probing for him to confess. The whole town knew if they believed mine or Katie's versions of the events, that was another thing.

I sat on that knowledge for a couple of days. Avoiding Torres' and my responsibilities, locking myself in the shed and working on that dress for me, the one I kept neglecting. And it was looking down at the dress, the colors I chose, the things I sewed into it, that my mind stopped racing.

It stopped. Needle between my fingers as I applied shells to the bottom of the skirt.

Shells.

I stood up at once and walked. I was alone, Dad at work, so I said nothing to no one. Just walked out the front door, walked across our street that poured into Main Street. Never stopped when people unashamedly gawked at me.

It took me exactly five minutes to reach the beach. A half wall of stone separated the sand from the promenade. I crossed it with one destination in mind.

The beach was the personification of my fears. Something so vital to anyone who lived in Bluehaven, and yet unattainable to me. It was the first warning that I was a rejected organ in this system. The sign that made me singular and them plural. It hurt, and I hurt Dad when I refused to fish with him without explanation.

But now what?

They were my past, and I proved over and over again I wasn't the same Hallie anymore. So I went to the beach.

The waves called to me, crashing into the white, warm sand. Perfect greenish blue into golden white. I breathed the salty air, so many years since last time. Down the half-moon steps from the promenade was where I sat. Took my sneakers off and buried my toes into the sand.

My little revolution.

I was done with being scared, done with giving in. It never helped. Being compliant never made them not bully me. Lying and covering up their mistakes did not protect Dad.

I was back at Bluehaven and, even though it wasn't my intention, I seemed to uncover every crease, putting light into every corner. I faced ahead with my chin up, breathing through my nose and letting the ghosts pass me by.

The steps behind called to my attention. Strong pounds on the pavement and a stop. I didn't turn my head to check who it was, but as every hair on my arm rose, I took a guess.

He descended the steps and only when he reached me, taking a seat to my side, I dared to look to my left.

I loved Daniel Miller.

It was obvious, crystal clear. I knew it when he could read me like a book, when our banter turned into easy friendship. When I saw myself being unapologetically me. I knew it when we kissed for the first time, and I lost myself in the kiss even with Ryan- of all people - a few feet away from us.

It took form when we had sex for the first time, when *I* had sex for the first time. Made unmeasured sense, all those things people talk about, planets aligning, stars shining, souls bonding. It was all true while we were together.

But loving him wasn't enough, so I prayed it wasn't forever.

"Are you taking it back?" He asked, his body turned to me.

He was wearing a soft gray tee drenched in sweat and basketball shorts, obviously exercising.

"I realized it wasn't no one's to take. Not even mine."

"Still, it took a lot of guts to finally come."

"It did," I agreed.

I loved he knew so much about me with the same intensity I hated. Silence took us for a few minutes. People walked by and played on the beach. Their laughter mixing with the soothing sound of the waves.

"What happened at the school, exactly?" I asked.

"You know about that?" His eyebrows soared.

I lifted a shoulder. "Dad came home looking guilty. He confessed."

Daniel nodded, looking at front and taking a long breath. "He was right to be angry. Right to ask for a principal to protect the students."

"I know," I said with a small voice. At the time, I waited days for the call. I thought Anderson was going to call my dad and tell him I was giving boys my naked pictures. I waited with the explanation on the tip of my tongue, embarrassed for Dad and me. Praying he'd believe me, wondering what version was worse. But the call never came, and by a week after the incident, I'd realized Anderson was covering up.

I should have been enraged. I should've come to Dad myself and told him what was happening. Instead, I was relieved. Happy for never having to tell him. With my head down, I was left alone for the rest of the term. I got into a good college and told myself never to look back.

"People are looking into it," he said. "I want you to be ready, if someone comes asking questions..."

"Someone who?" I turned and looked straight into his hazel eyes.

He didn't falter when he told me. "The school board. The police."

I winced.

"It's not just because of what happened to you. He's the principal in charge of the only school in town. They need to be sure that he wasn't..."

I nodded. They needed to dig to see if there were any more skeletons in the closet. Things he covered, pictures he kept. My own pictures I never knew if he threw away after it was all said and done. That was another thing I'd tried not thinking about too hard.

We fell into a silence, leaving me with goosebumps at how familiar it was. I could sit for hours beside Daniel, not saying a word, and never feel alone. My eyes stung with unshed tears, but I refused to move.

"It's a mess, isn't it?" He said after minutes in silence.

"What is it?" I asked, but I knew the answer before his reply.

"Everything." He rolled his shoulders back. "Us."

"It's me and this town, Dan," I told him sincerely. "My relationship with the place I was born is damaged, and I can't seem to untangle it. I can't..." I turned to him as a tear fell free.

"It's not just you." He swallowed. "I'm in the mess, too. I *am* the mess, Hallie."

I missed hearing him call me Cricket. In one second, I hated him for hiding so many things from me, in the next I wanted him to fight for me. I wanted to snap my fingers and forget about Katie and her posse, because each time I couldn't? I felt small.

Fizzing in my throat like the sea foam were all the things I wished to tell him. The recipe to our forever. But the words never surfaced, as they didn't exist. It wasn't a straight line.

"I just want you to know I'd change things if I could." He squeezed his eyes shut. "Many things. But I was learning too, I am learning. When your dad marched to the school, I'd realized I should have done that ages ago. I should have told you I knew Katie the second you said her name. I should've pressured Anderson right away and contacted the school board."

I nodded, looking away, since the intensity of his stare burned into me.

"Why didn't you?" I asked. "Done all those things you regret?"

I felt his eyes burning the side of my face, but I kept my eyes on the sea.

"Because I was scared. I said it before and it's true. I never wanted you to see me like I was one of them. I wanted to be the one for you, the one by your side. The one to protect you. I tried so hard to listen to the words you didn't say, follow the cues of your body language. And then, I found out it wasn't me."

"It wasn't you?" I turned to him.

"The one who was going to do all those things. I made a mistake I couldn't take back."

I frowned. "I don't want to punish you for your past. You didn't know."

I wanted to punish him for his present, for never telling me, but even I knew it wasn't really the issue. I hated he kept that for himself, but what I couldn't get over was his involvement with Katie. What I thought about late at night in my bed was her shrieks and ownership over him.

"It's a trigger, Hallie," he spoke with a resignation that cut me in half. "You can't stop yourself from feeling it, from reacting and I get it."

My hands shook. I gripped my knees, feeling so desperate. My mind told me I could never be with Katie's ex-boyfriend. I couldn't live with that shadow over my head, with her accusations that I stole her boyfriend for revenge. I wanted to live in peace and away from all of that, and being with Daniel seemed like a fight.

On the other hand, in my heart... I knew I loved him and only him. It reminded me of how stronger I was now and counted all the things I survived before. It whispered to me that he, Daniel Miller, was worth it.

And still my head paralyzed me. I wanted to break free, but I had no idea how.

I shot to my feet; Daniel followed my movements. "Watch my things?" I asked as I piled the house keys and phone with my sneakers and socks. I only gave him time to nod slowly, and I sprinted to the water.

Running.

Running until my legs felt numb. Until the hot sand became damp until the water embraced me. And then I dived, meeting the wave, my arms moving with my legs. Against the tide, a salt taste in my lips. I swam until my chest burned and I needed to bring my head up. My tee glued to my body, my jeans heavy and wet.

I rubbed my eyes and brushed my hair back. I fell and floated, taking the sun above my head, burning hot, showing red under my eyelids.

When I walked back, Daniel was up. Waiting, hands on his waist, watching me walk toward him.

We were only a few feet apart when he took something from his pocket. Looked like a note, a paper of some sort. He raised it to me and then deposited with my things.

"Read when you're ready."

I nodded, stopped in place as he cast me one last look, climbed the stone steps, and left the beach.

"Say the word and I'll kick them out."

I was shuffling through the latest orders I took and for a second, I barely understood that Marian was talking to me. I pinged them on the spinning wheel by the kitchen's window when I turned to Marian with a frown.

She jerked her head toward the main floor. I followed with my eyes and then I saw it, just beside the big windows, the Campbell family. Sharon and the husband I'd never seen, Delilah and Katie. All sitting at the table, talking to each other like it wasn't a crime to smile that much.

Months ago, I'd have hidden in the kitchen. Or if I was feeling bold, actually take on Marian's suggestion. But that was before. Before jumping into the sea, before getting Daniel's letter that still burned unread in my pocket. Before getting a call from the school board asking to see me for a meeting.

It was before I dared to come back and stand tall. I shook my head at Marian, with a coy smile that honestly wasn't mine. "I'll handle this."

I marched with my head high, as every pair of eyes followed my steps. I slid beside their table with agility, my pencil right on paper and a smile. "Welcome to Torres'. What can I do for you today?"

Their conversation stopped the minute my voice was heard. Not just the Campbells, but the whole diner waited to watch the interaction. I refused to let myself cower, standing my ground. My smile did not falter.

"We would like a different waitress," Sharon requested.

"It's only me available," I told her quickly.

I wasn't there to pick a fight, no. But they came to my place of work, so they needed to deal with me. Look at my face. Right now, none of them did. Sharon talked to me while looking everywhere else. The dad had his eyes down to his phone, not paying attention to anyone. Katie watched her mother, a little smirk of satisfaction tugging to the sides. Delilah had her head down. Looking at the table, like she wanted to be anywhere but here.

I tried again. "Do you know what you want?"

"You heard me," Sharon said again. "We'd like a different waitress."

I opened my mouth to say they could only have me, but the dad interrupted. His eyes snapping away from the phone, he pinned Sharon with a look. "What's wrong with this one?"

Sharon licked her lips, challenging her husband.

"She's obsessed about me, daddy," Katie replied. Her voice was high to be sure to be overheard. "Maybe she's in love or something."

I snickered the same time Delilah whipped her head from the table to her sister, glaring at her. I watched for a second, but then the dad was talking to me.

"If you have a problem with my daughter, it's better if we have another waitress."

"It's Hallie, or you can leave," Marian called a few feet away.

Of course, she couldn't help being in the loop.

Mr. Campbell shifted in his seat, his eyes darting around the diner. All the eyes were still on us. "Marian, you know me," he tried.

"I do. I have a great memory. I don't know what that has to do with anything."

"Coffee?" I blinked at Mr. Campbell.

But he was barely paying attention. He was back, staring at Sharon, shaking his head. "Let's go."

Mr. Campbell and Delilah stood up. The other two held their ground.

"Sharon..." He whispered to his wife.

Sharon planted her hand on the table. "She's telling things about Katie. She's spreading lies."

I shook my head and took a breath. "I wouldn't worry much about that. After all, the school board started an investigation. If I'm telling lies, I'll be punished."

"Get over the past!" Katie demanded.

I tipped my chin up. "I did. All these years, all I wanted was to leave it behind. If I never saw your face again, it was too soon. But you, Katie, you lived in fear. You know what you have done, so you lived five years thinking I was what? Plotting revenge?"

"You stole my boyfriend." She said with a roll of her eyes, more to the watching crowd than to me, like she wanted to remind them of my crimes.

"Not true." I shook with bravery, measuring my words. "I was a minor, and you were an assistant coach."

"That's enough now!" Mr. Campbell said, and this time Sharon agreed, since she stood up ready to leave.

My words got caught in my throat, but something moved behind me. A big, warm, protective body.

"Y'all talk too much. Sit down, it's Hallie's turn to speak."

Torres. I glanced over at him, his expression unforgiven as he watched the Campbells. I nodded in his direction with a thank you.

My eyes pinned on Katie once more. Goosebumps told me I was never going to talk to her again. It was the last time.

"You bullied me my whole life. You kept me off the beach, bullied people not to befriend me. You were the one with a sick fascination." I sneered, poking my own chest. "You took me as a target and fired and fired our whole lives. But that day you crossed the line, Katie. That day in that locker room with your cronies, you crossed a line that followed you around everywhere you went. And now you are shaking, scared of revenge. But why would you think I'd plan for one? You're not important. I don't care about you and your nastiness. I never planned to expose you to what you have done. I never wanted the town to know or the school board. But look around us." I raised my arms, gesticulating to the people watching us. "You did it. You exposed yourself and now they all know who you really are. So, tell me, Katie. Was it worth it?"

Seconds ticked by. Everyone waited, but I knew she wasn't going to answer me. If she did, it wasn't going to be the satisfying confession I deserved. With shaking legs, I stepped back. Torres' hand closed on my shoulder in quiet strength. I smiled a little at him and then Marian, the woman, was beaming in pride.

I passed her as she whispered, "Never saw you speaking that many words, kid. Thought for a second it was your mama." My lips quivered, and she opened a huge smile. "Fearless."

I left the diner, still shaky and not sure where to go. But before my brain caught up, my hands were fishing the letter from my pocket.

Dear Cricket,

My secrets aren't guarded because I like it like that. I never considered myself someone to have them until you pointed it out. And you were right. I took your words without ever giving mine in return, and that was wrong. We needed to heal together, like partners, but that wasn't the way I acted. I was so determined to be your champion, I didn't realize you never asked for one.

You asked for a friend.

I know you might always look at me like one of them. And I swear I understand. I won't push Hallie. All I wanted was to see you thrive and if away from me is the only way you can, I can accept that.

But I still owe you my words.

My closest friend—as sad as it sounds—is Mark, who was the third person to hold me when Mom brought me back from the hospital. He always knew me better than I knew myself. My second best would be Abby, who is dating Mark since forever. Abby is my older sister, my best friend and the reason we aren't all crumbling.

My ex-wife Kelly used to be the third person on this list. We went to school together for our whole lives. I thought she knew me, and maybe she did. But we grew apart. I became a different person who she wasn't happy about. And I get it. I was unhappy, too.

I never thought I hid that part of my story from you. I married Kelly young. My closest friends are members of my family. I never needed to show myself to anyone. Everyone in my life knows about everything. My journey from school to college, my wins and losses at football. My decision to get a degree in education was simply because I had to declare a major. They were there when I proposed, and they were there when Kelly and I called quits.

My divorce messed with my head more than I cared to admit. I was alone in Bluehaven, away from my family. I was stuck in a limbo. I dragged myself for months. I was in that pit when I met Katie.

I was a mess. I couldn't give myself into a relationship because I didn't know who I was. I thought I never led her on. I thought she understood where I stood. The day I broke it off, she was sad, but we never ended on a bad note. At least it was what I thought at the time, but let's be honest, my head was right up my ass.

And then I met you, and it was like sunlight. You shook everything in me, you made me want more even when you refuse to speak to me.

And I was greedy. I was confused, and a little fucked up.

All from there, it was stumbling to get close to you. I made many mistakes along the way. I was selfish at times, but I tried to be better, too.

I'm not writing this to win you back. Not because I don't want you back, but I think I must earn your words now. The only way to earn your trust back is opening myself up.

And if, after all, you still want nothing with me... That's ok. I want you to know me, anyway.

Love, Dan.

24.

HE ALWAYS MENTIONED LOVE at the end of his notes. They kept coming, little folded notes delivered by everyone in my life. Sometimes they were long, like the time he wrote about his childhood and his parents, and sometimes they were small. Just a note of something he thought was funny.

I looked forward to them all. I loved the little pieces of his soul he gave to me when he wrote about college, or his reluctance to accept that working with wood was the only thing that made him happy. I started to understand why he was so ravenous for me at the beginning. Getting someone's words piece by piece was addicting.

I was thinking about them, my eyes darting from one side to the other, wondering if I was going to get anything today.

Mrs. Carr was checking the costumes. They were ready and she wouldn't stop gushing about every detail.

"Perfect, Hallie." She clapped. "Just perfect."

I smiled, proud when she reached for her bag and handed me a small note. My heart soared at the sight. I couldn't hold back my happiness when my fingers closed around the paper.

"You know I'm a sucker for grand gestures." Mrs. Carr sighed. "I didn't expect Daniel to be a romantic."

I tilted my head left. "Why not?"

"He didn't look the type. But that doesn't matter, does it? Every man is a romantic for the right woman."

I chewed on my cheek, afraid to open a bigger smile. Mrs. Carr tapped my hand, her fingers lingering a little. After everything came to the surface, she hugged me for a long time. Patting my back, whispering she did not know. I tried to calm her, explaining I was fine now. But that hug was for her more than for me, so I let her be.

When I left the school, I stopped by the parking lot, unable to hold myself for a second more. I unfolded the note and read Daniel's chicken scrawl:

I forgot to tell you. They called me Jell-O for a whole year at college after a party where I had so many Jell-O shots my tongue turned blue. I used to live with these two guys, Anthony and Darryl, both jocks too, don't judge too hard, Cricket. I still talk to them. We try our best to see each other every couple of months for a beer. They are stupid as fuck. Can't wait for you to meet them.

Love, Dan

The days went by, and the notes kept coming. I found an old hatbox, beautiful and vintage, and used to keep all my letters.

"We can stuff them all in the wall," Nova said once. Her fingers danced over the lid of my box.

She never asked to read them, but like Mrs. Carr, she thought they were terribly romantic.

"Stuff them in the wall?" I asked as I took the box and put it back in my wardrobe, turning after to sit in bed beside her.

"Like letters to Juliet? They do that in Verona. People bring love letters just like those and leave there."

"I think he wants me to read them."

"I think he wants you back." She arched an eyebrow.

"He said it isn't about that." My cheeks got warm as I said it. "It's about me getting to know him better."

Nova rolled her eyes and dropped dramatically on my bed. "And why would he want you to get to know him? And *I'm* the high school kid."

Besides my wait and love for Dan's letters, things around town changed too.

Not everyone believed my version of things. After all, I was the strange kid who barely talked, and Katie was the town's sweetheart. But more murmurs came to light when the school board closed around Anderson. After talking to me, they took all names I provided and asked me point-blank if Anderson knew what had happened. I told them the truth. I had nothing to hide anymore. After that, Ryan was fired, and Anderson, too.

In the days after Anderson was officially out of the school, validating my version of the events, the gossip picked up a bit.

Little by little, all kinds of kids started to come to me while I was working at Torres', telling me their own bullying stories. It bothered me at first. I wasn't a therapist or a people's person, but like Marian pointed out, "Sometimes people just want to say it out loud."

I nodded, still waving to the woman who just told me her horribly specific and traumatic story.

"It feels too intimate of a conversation to have with a stranger."

"Probably." Marian shrugged. "But you're their hero now."

She turned to the kitchen, and I followed her steps. "I don't want to be anyone's hero."

"The Unseen Queen," Marian mocked. "The Master of the Silent."

"The Misfit Rebel," Torres quipped.

I groaned. "Stop you two."

"Bluehaven is a town that thrives on status, Hallie," Marian interjected, serious for the first time. "It has always been. It's small, and prides itself in the beauty of the damn beach and the big houses... you know how it is. That was before you were even born. Cecilia and I used to laugh at how we were the zit in Bluehaven's perfect skin."

I frowned, hugging myself.

"This is the other side of Bluehaven you haven't met yet. But it was always there. You were the first to scream, but you won't be the last."

Maybe my name should be the *Reluctant* Rebel. Then Marian fished a note from her apron and extended her hand to me. I perked up straight away, my eyes with a shine that was impossible to hide.

"Man's got it bad, Hallie."

I think I enjoy teaching. I never thought about it because the job landed on my lap, but I think that's part of me.

I still want to do furniture, and the other day I started to work on something else. I don't know what it is yet, but I know it isn't furniture. I never let myself build something without a reason. I usually make a chair when a chair is needed.

Letting it go like that comes from you. I watched your face many days while you were sewing, so engrossed in your work. There's a passion there, a need that comes from who you are. It's primal to you and becomes clear to anyone who's watching. I want to be like that. I want to hold in my hands a piece of my soul.

Love, Dan

"WHAT DO YOU THINK?" Nova's voice interrupted my thoughts.

I looked at her over her shoulder, to the mirror in front of us. It was their last rehearsal, and the last try of the clothes. I stationed myself in front of the large mirror, tying the corsets and helping as much as I could.

Nova looked incredible. The dress fitted her perfectly, from the small cinch of her waist to the flowy gathering at the back. She held still while I fixed a small hair band of golden flowers and leaves intertwined with her curls.

"You look amazing, Nova."

"I can't believe you made this..." she whispered, looking down the white skirt. "If I didn't watch you sewing it, I wouldn't believe it."

"You wear it just right."

"I never looked this pretty. You'll have to make all my clothes."

"Deal."

Nova laughed and extended a note between us. I looked down at the paper to Nova's smile.

"Come on, take it. I had to play nice with Cole Thompson to be the one who delivered."

I laughed and took it from her hands. Looking down at another note from him, I bit my lip as the tears welled up a little.

"Ok, totally worth it just to see the look on your face."

"Stop it." I shook myself out of it.

"It's a good thing, Hallie, to be able to feel so much."

"You think?"

Nova lifted one shoulder. "I read a lot, I guess. And the emotional scenes always get me. But it's different from actually living something so powerful. It's a gift to love that much."

We looked at each other's eyes through the mirror and I gave her a small nod, agreeing. She was right. It was a gift. Every day I woke up thinking about Daniel, every day I craved for a little of him.

With each note, he became less and less hers. I wasn't sure if it was his plan all along, but with each letter, each story, each word, it felt more like he was... *Mine.*

Someone cleared their throat behind us, our eyes zooming to the blond who waited by our side.

"Can you help me with the corset, Hallie?"

I blinked at the figure of Delilah, her tone of voice, the way she held herself. It was a completely different person. I nodded as Nova shuffled along, leaving space for Delilah to position herself in front of me, presenting me with the ribbons of her corset.

I worked on them like shoelace, my eyes trained on the task in hands, too afraid to glance anywhere else.

"Tell me if I'm pulling too hard," I told her.

She said nothing for a second. I kept pulling the ribbons and adjusting until she spoke.

"I never knew."

My eyes flashed to her reflection. My tongue got caught, Delilah kept talking.

"Katie told me you were horrible. That you only pretended to be all nice to get things. I was young, and I believed her."

I nodded quickly, looking down at my hands instead of Delilah.

"When you came back to town, I already hated you. And Mom, too. She acted like giving in to the drama department was making your dreams come true."

That time I whipped my head up, looking into her blue eyes. "What about yours?"

Delilah shrugged. Helping with the drama department was going to make *her* dreams come true, but Sharon never cared about that.

"Then, every time I saw you was with Mr. Miller, I…" She shook her head. "It was easy to believe in her version of things. But it wasn't me who told her."

"It was Ryan." I agreed.

"I'm not really good with people." Delilah licked her lips. "She's my sister. I—I believed."

"It's ok," I said.

It was. It was more than all right. Delilah was a kid, of course she was going to believe whatever her big sister told her. She must have been eleven years old when I was in my senior year, hearing her big hero of a sister tell horrible tales about a girl at school? I got it. Even in her worst, Delilah was never as cruel as Katie.

I finished the corset in silence, only stepping back when it was done. Delilah's hand smoothed over the fabric, a small smile bright on her lips.

"You did amazing."

I dipped my chin and took a breath before asking. "What didn't you tell her?"

"What?"

"After the camp. It wasn't you who told Katie about me and Daniel. Why?"

Delilah smiled a little. "Because you helped me with Pandora. Even in the middle of this mess, Mrs. Carr told me you reported everything to her. Including how Pandora was impressed with me. They called my mother and all." Her face fell a little.

"Did it help? Are they letting you go to theater school?"

Delilah swallowed. "No. But I have a plan. A good one."

"Do I want to know?"

"Oh no, Ms. Delos Santos. You're an authority figure. You definitely shouldn't know."

And right there, against all odds, Delilah and I started to laugh.

Dear Cricket,

I tried to come up with something funny, but I couldn't. I'm sure you can call up Mark and ask for a top ten dumb shit I've done through the years, and he will have a field day to fill you in.

Today I can't do much, because I can't stop missing you.

I know... I know! I promised these letters weren't about that, but today, Cricket. Today is hard.

There's nothing specific about it, but I woke up missing everything about you.

Mostly your eyes, when you refuse to speak like it's not written all over your face. I miss when you joke around with me and how stubborn you are. I miss the things we were going to live. Things I imagined we were going to do together, like that weekend at Spring's Harbor. Or a trip to Mark and Abby's.

Today I miss lots of things that never happened.

I'm not perfect, and even in my fantasies, I'd do something wrong down the line. Days where I messed up. But I crave for those too, the days when we fight, learn something about each other and move on, stronger for it.

I always imagined something real with you. Not perfect. I wished for growing old, telling stupid jokes. Fights and reconciliation.

Boring days, tiring ones where I get to sleep with you curled around my chest. Days when you barely say a couple of words, but I can read your needs just by the way you arch your eyebrow.

I was always going to mess up from time to time, Cricket. I think we all will. It's only human. But it's the want that changes things. The want of making it perfect even if it's not possible.

Wanting to make you smile, to change the world so it caters to you and only you.

I want it. I want more than anything.

I will never stop writing to you, Cricket. But I think I'm running out of pieces of my heart to give.

I think you have them all.

Love, Dan.

25.

Wings, horns, flowers and flowy dresses.

The woods took form as the lights were tested upon them, my flowers shining, making my knees wobble in awe. We did a good job. An excellent job, actually. I blinked away from the stage, the hairs on the back of my neck rising, my whole body knowing Daniel was around somewhere. I came back to myself with a loud clap coming from Mrs. Carr.

"Everyone ready?"

"Where are the boys?" I asked, fixing Carmen's flowers by the hem of her dress. Another girl that looked more like a vision than a high schooler.

"With Mr. Miller on the other side of the stage."

My fingers stopped mid-action. Carmen snickered, watching me intently as I raised up again and pretended I didn't care. I cleared my throat and stepped away from Carmen, checking everyone's costume, keeping my hands and mind occupied, even as my heart thumped, demanding to see Daniel.

"You think we can win, Mrs. Carr?" Asked one of the girls.

I almost forgot they were still in a competition. In the theater's front row, sat the same committee who came to evaluate them all those weeks ago.

All around me, I could spot the signs of their anxiety. Biting lips, hands wriggling over their laps, frowns in place, making my fairies a little bit human.

Mrs. Carr picked up on that too, as she made a sign of a circle with her hands. "All right, everyone over here. Come on, come on, real quick. You too, Hallie." She urged when I was left outside the circle.

I squeezed myself between Nova and Carmen, and we all waited for whatever Mrs. Carr was about to say. I hoped to God it was inspiring because we could cut the tension with a knife.

"No one cares." Said Mrs. Carr finally.

Stillness followed that statement. It was Nova who broke the spell. "Hmm, Mrs. Carr, we care."

"You shouldn't," my old teacher told them. "I wasn't a fan of this whole competition idea to begin with... But we needed it for the funding. Our fight was always to get here, right now. Look at the dresses you are wearing, the magic of that stage right there. This is the win, girls. I couldn't ask for anything else. If we win, great. If we lose... I don't see how we could ever lose. Not when you all look the way you do. Not when everyone has their lines on the tip of their tongues. I know it's scary to give that much of yourself to something," she firmly said, almost making eye contact with them all. "But that's art. It's giving something and expecting nothing in return. It's being real, raw and unfiltered. I know for many of you this will be your first and last time on stage, so give it all. Leave nothing inside. Come back home empty."

The silence defined the fact we were in a school theater and those were teenage girls. They listened to Mrs. Carr like I once did, as she was the only adult that really saw them for who they were. I felt her words in my core; I wanted to leave it all behind. *Come home empty.*

She changed gears quickly, with a smile on her lips and a flourish of her wrist. "Are you ready?"

A song of yeses rang through the backstage, at the same time the boys started to come through the other side. Horns, leather cuff and the occasional horse mask. They looked perfect, too. My chest swelled with pride.

The lights dimmed, everyone scattered to their positions, and I held my ground, excitement coming to life and curling on the bottom of my stomach. Heavy red curtains were drawn as the audience clapped with enthusiasm.

And it started.

"Now, fair Hippolyta, our *nuptial hour draws on apace; four happy days bring in another moon; but O, methinks how slow this old moon wanes. She lingers my desires, like a stepdame, or a dowager, long withering out a young man's revenue,"* a mouthful from Adam, his voice carrying across the theater.

I followed Mrs. Carr's steps to offstage right, holding my breath like it was going to disturb the kids at the stage. Their first lines were delivered flawless, their beautiful faces perfect against the background.

Mrs. Carr moved around without being seen, holding an old script in her hands. She should've sat in the front seat, but Mrs. Carr wasn't just a director. She was a stage manager, coordinator, anything and everything.

I let myself be in the moment, watching the kids with a smile on my face. Mrs. Carr was right, the victory was tonight. All that we accomplished together.

"*The course of true love never did run smooth.*"

The line came like a punch in the stomach. Tommy's voice was firm and smooth as the perfect Lysander.

My insides turned to liquid, my hands shook, and the hairs on my arm rose. My eyes went up, to beyond the stage, beyond the kids, beyond lines and into the theater. Across the stage, his hazel eyes found me. They called me. In his full height, even from afar, he looked too tall, towering over everyone else. The beard looked longer than the stubble I was used to, his hair a little unkept.

We moved together, him from there and I here. My hands running on the heavy, red curtains dividing the offstage, his steps full of meaning. He was following me, hunting me. I couldn't take my eyes off him. The words he wrote in his letters came to mind, every little detail repeating in a loop. Heartfelt, silly. All the times he gave himself to me.

The man across the stage wasn't anyone's but mine.

We reached the end of the stage, where the trees he built were the thickest, where the light shone bright green. He stepped forward first. I frowned. Wasn't he afraid to be seen? Could the trees completely hide upstage? But Dan didn't even glance in the audience's direction. His eyes were glued to me. His certainty made my feet move. Copying him, I got through the fake trees behind the big ones, avoiding the light.

In a minute, we were in front of each other. I craned my neck to look at him, shooting an inquiring look.

He shook his head. "No one can see it. I created this so they could walk from left and right offstage."

"A secret tunnel?" I whispered.

"In the woods." He smiled.

Out there, I heard Delilah, her voice all melody and fierceness. My hands trembled and Daniel took them between his.

"I got your letters," I said.

"I meant it."

"That you were called Jell-O in college?"

His mouth opened in that delicious boyish smile I loved so much. "And other things too." He sobered up a little. "Can I keep writing to you?"

I licked my lips, my head bobbing in acceptance before the word yes even formed in my tongue. His thumb played circles over my wrists, his eyes down, watching our hands joined. A labored breath left his lungs, and it squeezed my heart.

"Dan?"

"Yes, Cricket?"

"When you sent me the notes, you said they were pieces of your heart."

He nodded. I gulped. "You said there wasn't much left now."

"Hallie..." he breathed, coming closer and taking my face between his palms. I fought the tears on the corners of my eyes as he darted his gaze along my face like he wanted to remember my features forever.

"Everything is yours. I gave everything to you. There's nothing left."

This time the tears shed unbidden. Dan wiped them with his thumbs, so delicate it took my breath away.

"Tell me what you're thinking," he rasped. "I can't read you this time."

I opened a watery smile. "I'm thinking you're mine. Just mine and never anyone else's."

He chuckled, shaking his head. "Cricket, in a room full of people, it's you who I hear the loudest."

And he took my mouth. Slashing with a force and passion I craved, his hands grabbing my hair and keeping me in place like he was scared I'd disappear through his fingers. I ate his desperation because it matched mine. I missed his cedar scent, his rough fingers roaming my skin, the bites he chased away with kisses. Tongues fighting, my breathing caught in my throat as somewhere out there on the main stage, I heard the line about lovers in the woods.

Epilogue

A BLOB OF WARM, wet sand flew to my leg, splashing right on top of my knee. I raised on my elbows arching an eyebrow at the pair who were trying hard to hide their grins.

"It was Cece," my husband told me, pointing to my two-year-old.

"Are you telling me that my toddler is attacking her mama?"

Dan shrugged, but Cece didn't look guilty at all. No, she was all smiles, sand everywhere, from her little chubby legs to her rosy cheeks and on top of her thick black hair. That girl needed a bath ASAP. I sat up, extending my hands to her. "Come here, you're going to get sand in your eyes."

Cece agreed, telling me a long, toddler version story of the castle she was making with her daddy, and I ate it all up. Moments like these were the ones I looked forward to the most. Like Daniel promised once, our lives were full of normalcy.

Messy babies, improvised dinners, bad movies he convinced me to watch. I loved the sleepless nights right after Cece was born, the bad diapers when she started teething.

Dan working away in his workshop—these days it was more of an art studio since he became quite the sculptor. My afternoons on top of the sewing machine, peddling as quietly as I dared, orders upon orders from my website that I desperately tried to fulfill between Cece's naps.

Those days weren't full of glamor. We weren't a getting dressed up to go around town kind of family, but I needed none of that. I always only wanted *the life*.

I cleaned Cece as much as I could, grabbing a wet wipe from my bag to be mindful of her eyes. When I was finished, she was smiling big. Cece was such a good baby, a happy one. Even during her worst colic nights, she was full of life. Just like the lady who she was named after.

Dan said it on our wedding day, "I promise you a life full of boring days, quiet nights and uneventful evenings."

Our guests didn't get it. The man was promising boring days right from the start? But we shared a smile because I knew what we were promising each other: a life together. Not like the flashy wedding we had. He dressed in the perfect tux and me with that dress I started designing when we first met.

No, what he promised me at the altar was a long, *imperfect* life together, and I couldn't wait to start.

Cece was done with me fussing over her, disentangling from me, she ran. My heart would've lunged with her if she wasn't going straight to her number two man.

"Dad!" I called and as he turned, I nodded, showing the toddler going his way.

Dad spun, leaving his fishing rod stuck into the sand. He took my baby with one arm, kissing the top of her head. I stood up as I cleaned the sand off my legs and extended a hand to my husband.

"Come on. You got me dirty, you have to clean me up."

I never saw someone stand up so quickly. I was giggling when he came for me, swinging me over his shoulder like I weighed nothing. I let go a girlish yelp. It must have called Dad's attention because he called from the shallow waters, "Don't drop my daughter, Miller."

"Never," Dan hollered back.

I let a *humph* out when he jogged to the water. I slapped his ass, and he chuckled without a care. We got in, and he still wouldn't let me go. I kicked my feet, but he kept me in place with one arm and spanked me with the other.

"Don't you dare, Dan!" I said when the water was on his waist level.

But he never replied, just swung me from his shoulders in one splash. I went underwater, my ass scraping the sand and right when I tried to get up, a wave came over my head, brushing all the hair to my face. I finally got some balance. Standing up, I brushed my hair back.

"You're out of control, Miller!" I told him.

He was wearing his best smile, not a bother in the world. "I heard you wanted to be clean."

My mouth opened in a perfect O, and soon he draped his arm around my waist, bringing us together with a quick move. His beard scratched my jaw when he nipped it, and I was putty in his hands.

"Tell me, you think Preston is up for babysitting tonight?"

I held him by his delicious shoulders, and his mouth tasted me right in the sensitive skin between my neck and earlobe.

"If you keep manhandling me, he'll know exactly why we are asking."

"We can do it just fine with Cece in the next room. But today, Cricket." And he licked me. A lazy, delicious swipe of his tongue. "Today I want to make my silent woman scream."

The goosebumps raised in my skin, and I shivered in his arms. "Let's go home then, because I'm ready to get dirty again."

Dan chuckled, letting me go just to drag me by the hand a second later. And I followed him, a silly smile right on my lips.

For a long time, I only had four people to love.

Mom, Dad, Marian and Torres.

I counted them like children counted shells on the beach. But then came the others. Mrs. Carr, who paved my way to the theater, and accepted who I was. Ms. Handall, who was like an older sister, caring for me when no one did.

Nova and the other girls, finally the group of girlfriends I craved so much. Abby, Mark, Rose and April. More and more, they broke down my walls.

But it was this man who gave the final blow. The man with the smiles, the calm and devotion. The man who wanted all my words and ended up getting much more than that.

It was Daniel Miller who brought me back to life.

Author's note

OH, HERE WE GO!

I hope you all loved Hallie and Dan as much as I did.

Writing this book was a rollercoaster, first because Hallie is so quiet and I needed to get in that mindset, but also because I have my problems with my hometown, too.

I needed to dig deep for this one, and in many ways I described Hallie's feelings like they were my own.

I wanted Hallie to be this quiet force of nature and thank god once I started to write, that side of her came alive.

For Dan, that was the easiest part. He's easy-going, lovable, but also hurt and a little lost. I knew his background, but it was only when they interacted for the first time I truly understood where this pairing was going.

I'm definitely not done with Bluehaven just yet, but I don't have an exact date when I'm going to tackle the next book in this series.

The biggest thank you to Marcela, who actually held my hand toward the end. I don't know how I managed to birth this baby during this time, but man, you were the doula.

And to Katleen, who really is the heart of Hallie, and took the time to explain fashion design to me like I was five years old.

Thanks to you, always, and every day. Romance readers are the absolute best.

-Amy